PRAISE FOR
The Third Life of Grange Copeland

"Alice Walker is a lavishly gifted writer."
—*The New York Times Book Review*

"A writer with a refreshingly original approach . . . Walker presents the family objectively, leaving it to the reader to decide how much it has been influenced by a heritage of bondage and by a knowledge of being surrounded by prejudice and hatred." —*The Washington Post*

"Almost no one has tried to tell us about the early lives, the inner early lives of black people. . . . Alice Walker is a storyteller." —*The New Yorker*

"Alice Walker is a vastly gifted, almost preternaturally perceptive novelist." —*The American Scholar*

"There's a stark, elemental drama to the family struggles Walker depicts in *The Third Life of Grange Copeland*." —*Salon*

"Alice Walker moves us by emphasizing the humanity we share with her characters. . . . A solid, honest, sensitive tale . . . leavened by those moments of humor and warmth that have enabled men and women to endure so much tragedy. . . . Walker seems confident to let narrative and characterization and event, the soul of a novel, speak for themselves."

—*Chicago Daily News*

"Graphic and authentic . . . moving, tender and all too tragic. . . . [Alice Walker] writes with power, sensitivity, and all-pervading humanity."   —*Publishers Weekly*

The Third Life of Grange Copeland

ALSO BY ALICE WALKER

FICTION

The Way Forward Is With a Broken Heart
You Can't Keep a Good Woman Down
Meridian
In Love & Trouble
The Color Purple
The Temple of My Familiar
Possessing the Secret of Joy
By the Light of My Father's Smile

NONFICTION

Anything We Love Can Be Saved
In Search of Our Mothers' Gardens
Living by the Word
Warrior Marks (with Pratibha Parmar)
The Same River Twice: Honoring the Difficult

POETRY

Absolute Trust in the Goodness of the Earth
Horses Make a Landscape Look More Beautiful
Revolutionary Petunias
Once
Good Night Willie Lee, I'll See You in the Morning
Her Blue Body Everything We Know

BOOKS FOR CHILDREN

To Hell with Dying
Langston Hughes, American Poet
Finding the Green Stone

EDITED BY ALICE WALKER

I Love Myself When I Am Laughing: A Zora Neale Hurston Reader

Alice Walker

The Third Life of Grange Copeland

MARINER
BOOKS

An Imprint of HarperCollins*Publishers*

Boston   New York

Mariner Books
An Imprint of HarperCollins Publishers, registered in the United States
of America and/or other jurisdictions.

www.marinerbooks.com

First published by Harcourt Brace Jovanovich, 1970

Library of Congress Cataloging-in-Publication Data
Walker, Alice, 1944–
The third life of Grange Copeland/Alice Walker.—1st Harvest ed.
p.   cm.
ISBN 0-15-602836-0
ISBN 978-0-15-602836-3
1. African American men—Fiction. 2. Grandparent and child—Fiction.
3. Children of prisoners—Fiction. 4. Custody of children—Fiction.
5. Granddaughters—Fiction. 6. Grandfathers—Fiction.
7. Uxoricide—Fiction. 8. Georgia—Fiction.   I. Title.
PS3573.A425T47 2003
813'.54—dc21   2003005923

Text set in Minion
Designed by Linda Lockowitz

First Harvest edition 2003

ScoutAutomatedPrintCode

For my mother,
who made a way out of no way

And for Mel, my husband

Sometimes I had an intense desire to cry because of something my father said, but instead, because life, cynicism, had taught me to put on a mask, I laughed. For him, I did not suffer, I felt nothing, I was a shameless cynic, I had no soul . . . because of the mask I showed. But inside, I felt every word he said.

—MANUEL, IN *The Children of Sanchez*
BY OSCAR LEWIS

O, my clansmen
Let us all cry together!
Come,
Let us mourn the death of my husband,
The death of a Prince
The Ash that was produced
By a great Fire!
O this homestead is utterly dead,
Close the gates
With lacari thorns,
For the Prince
The heir to the Stool is lost!
And all the young men
Have perished in the wilderness!

—"SONG OF LAWINO,"
A LAMENT BY OKOT P'BITEK

"The great danger," Richard told Sartre, "in the world today is that the very feeling and conception of what is a human being might well be lost."

—RICHARD WRIGHT TO JEAN-PAUL SARTRE,
IN *Richard Wright* BY CONSTANCE WEBB

Part I

Part I

1

BROWNFIELD STOOD CLOSE to his mother in the yard, not taking his eyes off the back of the receding automobile. His Uncle Silas slowed the car as it got to a place where a pointed rock jutted up out of the road: a week before he had busted an oil pan there. Once past this spot, which he had cursed as he passed to and fro over it during the week, he stuck out his arm and waved jauntily back at them. Brownfield waved sadly, his eyes blurred with tears. His Aunt Marilyn, not visible through the rear window of the car, waved a dainty blue handkerchief from her front window. It fluttered merrily like a pennant. Brownfield's cousins had their faces pressed to the rear window, and their delicate, hard-to-see hands flopped monotonously up and down. They were tired of waving, for they had been waving good-bye since they finished breakfast.

The automobile was a new 1920 Buick, long and high and shiny green with great popping headlights like the eyes of a frog. Inside the car it was all blue, with seats that were fuzzy and soft. Slender silver handles opened the doors and rolled the astonishingly clear windows up and down. As it bumped over the road its canvas top was scratched by low elm branches. Brownfield felt embarrassed about the bad road and the damage it did to his uncle's car. Uncle Silas loved his car and had spent all morning washing it, polishing the wheel spokes and dusting off the running board. Now it bounced over gullies and potholes in the road, tossing Uncle Silas and his wife and children up in the air and slamming them down again. Brownfield sighed as the sound of metal against rock reached his ears. The road was for mules, wagons and bare feet only.

"A wagon'd be easier," said his father.

"But not nearly 'bout as grand as that." His mother looked after the car without envy, but wistfully.

Brownfield watched the automobile as it turned a curve and was finally out of sight. Then he watched the last of the dust settle. Already he missed his cousins, although they made him feel dumb for never having seen a picture show and for never having seen houses stacked one on top of the other until they nearly reached the sky. They had stayed a week and got over being impressed by his small knowledge of farming the first day. He showed them how to milk the cow, how to feed the pigs, how to find chickens' eggs; but the next day they had bombarded him with talk about automobiles and street lights and paved walks and trash collectors and about something they had ridden in once in a department store that went up, up, up from one floor to the next without anybody walking a step. He had been dazzled by this information and at last overwhelmed. They taunted him because he lived in the country and never saw anything or went anywhere. They told him that his father worked for a cracker and that the cracker owned him. They told him that their own daddy, his Uncle Silas, had gone to Philadelphia to be his own boss. They told him that his mother wanted to leave his father and go North to Philadelphia with them. They said that his mother wanted him, Brownfield, to go to school, and that she was tired of his father and wanted to leave him anyway. His cousins told Brownfield this and much more. They bewildered, excited and hurt him. Still, he missed them; they were from a world he had never seen. Now that they were gone he felt the way he usually felt only in winter, never in June; as if he were waiting for something to happen that would take a very long time to come.

"I wish we lived in Philydelphia," he said.

"Well, we don't." That was his father.

Brownfield looked at Grange with surprise. His father almost never spoke to him unless they had company. Even then he acted as if talking to his son was a strain, a burdensome requirement.

"Uncle Silas like to talk about his automobile," said Brownfield, his lips bumbling over the word. It was his uncle's word, a city word. In the country they always said car. Some people still called them buggies, as if they could not get used to a conveyance that did not use horses.

"I wish we had a automobile like that!"

"Well, we don't."

"No, we don't," said Margaret.

Brownfield frowned. His mother agreed with his father whenever possible. And though he was only ten Brownfield wondered about this. He thought his mother was like their dog in some ways. She didn't have a thing to say that did not in some way show her submission to his father.

"We ought to be thankful we got a roof over our heads and three meals a day."

It was actually more like one meal a day. His mother smiled at Brownfield, one of her rare sudden smiles that lit up her smooth, heart-shaped face. Her skin was rich brown with a creamy reddish sheen. Her teeth were small and regular and her breath was always sweet with a milky cleanness. Brownfield had hands like hers, long, thin aristocratic hands, with fingers meant for jewels. His mother had no wedding ring, however.

Brownfield listened to the familiar silence around him. Their house was at the end of the long rugged road that gave his uncle's car so much trouble. This road looked to be no more than a track where it branched off from the main road, which was of smoothly scraped dirt. The road scraper, a man on a big yellow machine like a tank, never scraped their road, which was why it was so rough and pitted with mud holes when it rained. The house was in a clearing and at the edge of the clearing was forest. Forest full of animals and birds. But they were not large animals or noisy birds and days passed sometimes without a sound and the sky seemed a round blue muffler made of wool.

Brownfield had been born here, in the vast cotton flats of southern Georgia, and had been conscious first of the stifling heat in summer, and then of the long periods of uninterrupted quiet. As a very small child he had scrambled around the clearing alone, chasing lizards and snakes, bearing his cuts and bruises with solemnity until his mother came home at night.

His mother left him each morning with a hasty hug and a sugartit, on which he sucked through wet weather and dry, across the dusty clearing or miry, until she returned. She worked all day pulling baits for ready money. Her legs were always clean when she left home and always coated with mud and slime of baits when she came back. The baits she "pulled" were packed in cans and sold in town to gentlemen who went fishing for the sport of it. His mother had taken Brownfield with her to the bait factory when he was a baby, but he was in the way, and the piles of squirming baits, which were dumped first for sorting on a long table, terrified him. They had looked like a part of the table until one day his mother sat him down near them and he rolled over and became entangled in them. It seemed to him the baits moved with a perfectly horrifying blind wriggling. He had screamed and screamed. His mother was ordered to take him out of there at once and never to bring him back.

At first she left him home in a basket, with his sugartit pressed against his face. He sucked on it all day until it was nothing but a tasteless rag. Then, when he could walk, she left him on the porch steps. In moments of idle sitting he shared the steps with their lean mangy dog. And as the flies buzzed around the whiskered snout of the dog they buzzed around his face. No one was there to shoo them away, or to change the sodden rag that attracted them, and which he wore brownish and damp around his distended waist. For hours he was lost in a dull, weak stupor. His hunger made him move in a daze, his heavy eyes unnaturally bright.

When he was four he was covered with sores. Tetter sores covered his head, eating out his hair in patches the size of quarters. Tomato sores covered his legs up to the knee—when the tomatoes in his mother's garden were ripe he ate nothing but tomatoes all day long—and pus ran from boils that burst under his armpits. His mother washed the sores in bluestone water. Suddenly, out of his days of sitting and of picking the scabs from his sores, there evolved a languid slow order of jobs he had to do. He fed the pigs, brought in wood and led the cow all over the clearing looking for fresh grass.

When he was six his mother taught him how to feed and milk the cow. Then he became fond of the calm, slow patience of the cow and loved to catch her rich milk in a tin syrup pail and drink it warm and dribbling down his chin.

His father worked: planting, chopping, poisoning and picking in the cotton field, which ran for half a mile along the main road. Brownfield had worked there too now, for four years, since he was six, in the company of other child workers. His father worked with men and women in another part of the field. The cotton field too was generally silent. The children were too tired to play and were encouraged not to play because of the cotton. The grownups talked softly, intermittently, like the sporadic humming of wasps. The buzz of their conversations became part of the silence, for nothing they said came clearly across the field to where the children worked.

At the end of the day all the workers stopped. There were close to twenty grownups, and each had several children who worked in the children's section of the field. The children's job was to go over the rows their parents had gone over the week before—"scrapping cotton" it was called. When the children saw their parents put down their sacks they came and stood beside them at the edge of the field as all of them waited for the truck to come. Brownfield waited for the truck along with his father. His father never looked at him or acknowledged him in any way, except to lift his sack of cotton to the back of the truck when it arrived. Brownfield was afraid of his father's silence, and his fear reached its peak when the truck came. For when the truck came his father's face froze into an unnaturally bland mask, curious and unsettling to see. It was as if his father became a stone or a robot. A grim stillness settled over his eyes and he became an object, a cipher, something that moved in tense jerks if it moved at all. While the truck stood backed up in the field the workers held their breath. A family of five or six workers would wonder uneasily if they would take home, together, a whole dollar. Some of the workers laughed and joked with the man who drove the truck, but they looked at his shoes and at his pants legs or at his hands, never into his eyes, and their looks were a combination of small sly smiles and cowed, embarrassed desperation.

Brownfield's father had no smiles about him at all. He merely froze; his movements when he had to move to place sacks on the truck were rigid as a machine's. At first Brownfield thought his father was turned to stone by the truck itself. The truck was big and noisy and coldly, militarily gray. Its big wheels flattened the cotton stalks and made deep ruts in the soft dirt of the field. But after watching the loading of the truck for several weeks he realized it was the man who drove the truck who caused his father to don a mask that was more impenetrable than his usual silence. Brownfield looked closely at the man and made a startling discovery; the man was a man, but entirely different from his own father. When he noticed this difference, one of odor and sound and movement and laughter, as well as of color, he wondered how he had not seen it before. But as a small child all men had seemed to merge into one. They were exactly alike, all of them having the same smell, the same feel of muscled hardness when they held him against their bodies, the same disregard for smallness. They took pride only in their own bigness, when they laughed and opened their cavernous mouths, or when they walked in their long fearsome strides or when they stooped from their great height and tossed him about in their arms. Brownfield's immediate horrified reaction to the man who froze his father was that the man had the smooth brownish hair of an animal. Thinking this discovery was the key to his father's icy withdrawal from the man, Brownfield acquired a cold nervousness around him of his own.

Once the man touched him on the hand with the handle of his cane, not hard, and said, with a smell of mint on his breath, "You're Grange Copeland's boy, ain't you?" And Brownfield had answered, "Uh huh," chewing on his lip and recoiling from the enormous pile of gray-black hair that lay matted on the man's upper chest and throat. While he stared at the hair one of the workers—not his father who was standing beside him as if he didn't know he was there—said to him softly, "Say 'Yessir' to Mr. Shipley," and Brownfield looked up before he said anything and scanned his father's face. The mask was as tight and still as if his father had coated himself with wax. And Brownfield smelled for the first time an odor of sweat, fear and something indefinite. Something smothered and tense (which was of his father and of the other workers and not of mint) that came from his father's body. His father said nothing. Brownfield, trembling, said "Yessir," filled with terror of this man who could, by his presence alone, turn his father into something that might as well have been a pebble or a post or a piece of dirt, except for the sharp bitter odor of something whose source was forcibly contained in flesh.

One day not long afterward Grange was drinking quietly at home, stretched out on the porch. Brownfield sat on the porch steps gazing at him, mesmerized by the movement of the bottle going up and down in his father's hand. Grange noticed him looking, and Brownfield was afraid to move away and afraid to stay. When he was drinking his father took every action as a personal affront. He looked at Brownfield and started to speak. His eyes had little yellow and red lines in them like the veins of a leaf. Brownfield leaned nearer. But all his father said was, "I ought to throw you down the goddam well."

Brownfield drew back in alarm, though there was no anger or determination in his father's voice; there was only a rough drunken wistfulness and a weary tremor of pity and regret.

Brownfield had told his cousins about the man, and it was then that they told him how his father was owned and of how their father escaped being owned by moving North. And now they had a nice new car every other year and beautiful plush furniture and their mother didn't pull nasty baits but worked instead for people who owned two houses and a long black car with a man in it dressed in green with gold braid. That man being their father, who had taken them one day for a ride in the car, so they knew what they were talking about. They had played with rich children, and, talking about them to Brownfield, who lived in a house that leaked, they sounded rich as well.

Angeline, his girl cousin, who eavesdropped as a matter of habit, told Brownfield impatiently that she and her brother Lincoln had heard their mother say that Brownfield's family would never amount to anything because they didn't have sense enough to leave Green County, Georgia. It was Angeline who told him that her mother said that Grange was no good; that he had tried to get his wife to "sell herself" to get them out of debt. Brownfield's mother and Angeline's were sisters.

"He even wanted her to sell herself to the man who drives the truck," Angeline lied.

"Or anybody else who'd buy her!" Lincoln said.

Lincoln began to dance around Brownfield. "You all are in debt twelve hundred dollars! And you'll never pay it!"

Angeline sniffed primly with her nose in the air. "My daddy says you'll never pay it 'cause you ain't got no money and your daddy drinks up everything he can get his hands on."

What did "sell" mean when it applied to his mama, Brownfield had wanted to know, but his cousins only giggled and nudged each other gravely but in apparent delight.

For Brownfield his cousins' information was peculiarly ominous. He tried to remember when his father's silence began, for surely there had been a time when his father cooed hopefully to him as he fondled him on his knee. Perhaps, he thought, his father's silence was part of the reason his mother was always submissive to him and why his father was jealous of her and angry if she spoke, just "how're you?" to other men. Maybe he had tried to sell her and she wouldn't be sold—which could be why they were still poor and in debt and would die that way. And maybe his father, who surely would feel bad about trying to sell his wife, became silent and jealous of her, not because of anything she had done, but because of what he had tried to do! Maybe his mother was as scared of Grange as he was, terrified by Grange's tense composure. Perhaps she was afraid he would sell her anyway, whether she wanted to be sold or not. That could be why she jumped to please him.

Brownfield got a headache trying to grasp the meaning of what his cousins told him. The need to comprehend his parents' actions seeped into him with his cousins' laughter. The blood rushed to his head and he was sick. He thought feverishly of how their weeks were spent. Of the heat, the cold, the work, the feeling of desperation behind all the sly small smiles. The feeling of hunger in winter, of bleak unsmiling faces, of eating bark when he was left alone before his mother returned home smelling of baits and manure. Of his mother's soft skin and clean milky breath; of his father's brooding, and of the feeling of an onrushing inevitable knowledge, like a summer storm that comes with high wind and flash flooding, that would smash the silence finally and flatten them all mercilessly to the ground. One day he would know everything and be equal to his cousins and to his father and perhaps even to God.

Their life followed a kind of cycle that depended almost totally on Grange's moods. On Monday, suffering from a hangover and the aftereffects of a violent quarrel with his wife the night before, Grange was morose, sullen, reserved, deeply in pain under the hot early morning sun. Margaret was tense and hard, exceedingly nervous. Brownfield moved about the house like a mouse. On Tuesday, Grange was merely quiet. His wife and son began to relax. On Wednesday, as the day stretched out and the cotton rows stretched out even longer, Grange muttered and sighed. He sat outside in the night air longer before going to bed; he would speak of moving away, of going North. He might even try to figure out how much he owed the man who owned the fields. The man who drove the truck and who owned the shack they occupied. But these activities depressed him, and he said things on Wednesday nights that made his wife cry. By Thursday, Grange's gloominess reached its peak and he grimaced respectfully, with veiled eyes, at the jokes told by the man who drove the truck. On Thursday nights he stalked the house from room to room and pulled himself up and swung from the rafters of the porch. Brownfield could hear his joints creaking against the sounds of the porch, for the whole porch shook when his father swung.

By Friday Grange was so stupefied with the work and the sun he wanted nothing but rest the next two days before it started all over again.

On Saturday afternoon Grange shaved, bathed, put on clean overalls and a shirt and took the wagon into town to buy groceries. While he was away his wife washed and straightened her hair. She dressed up and sat, all shining and pretty, in the open door, hoping anxiously for visitors who never came.

Brownfield too was washed and cleanly dressed. He played contentedly in the silent woods and in the clearing. Late Saturday night Grange would come home lurching drunk, threatening to kill his wife and Brownfield, stumbling and shooting off his shotgun. He threatened Margaret and she ran and hid in the woods with Brownfield huddled at her feet. Then Grange would roll out the door and into the yard, crying like a child in big wrenching sobs and rubbing his whole head in the dirt. He would lie there until Sunday morning, when the chickens pecked around him, and the dog sniffed at him and neither his wife nor Brownfield went near him. Brownfield played instead on the other side of the house. Steady on his feet but still ashen by noon, Grange would make his way across the pasture and through the woods, headlong, like a blind man, to the Baptist church, where his voice above all the others was raised in song and prayer. Margaret would be there too, Brownfield asleep on the bench beside her. Back home again after church Grange and Margaret would begin a supper quarrel which launched them into another week just about like the one before.

Brownfield turned from watching the road and looked with hateful scrutiny at the house they lived in. It was a cabin of two rooms with a brick chimney at one end. The roof was of rotting gray wood shingles; the sides of the house were gray vertical slabs; the whole aspect of the house was gray. It was lower in the middle than at its ends, and resembled a sway-backed animal turned out to pasture. A stone-based well sat functionally in the middle of the yard, its mossy wooden bucket dangling above it from some rusty chain and frazzled lengths of rope. Where water was dashed behind the well, wild morning-glories bloomed, their tendrils reaching as far as the woodpile, which was a litter of tree trunks, slivers of carcass bones deposited by the dog and discarded braces and bits that had pained the jaws and teeth of many a hard-driven mule.

From the corner of his eye Brownfield noticed that his father was also surveying the house. Grange stood with an arm across the small of his back, soldier fashion, and with the other hand made gestures toward this and that of the house, as if pointing out necessary repairs. There were very many. He was a tall, thin, brooding man, slightly stooped from plowing, with skin the deep glossy brown of pecans. He was thirty-five but seemed much older. His face and eyes had a dispassionate vacancy and sadness, as if a great fire had been extinguished within him and was just recently missed. He seemed devoid of any emotion, while Brownfield watched him, except that of bewilderment. A bewilderment so complete he did not really appear to know what he saw, although his hand continued to gesture, more or less aimlessly, and his lips moved, shaping unintelligible words. While his son watched, Grange lifted his shoulders and let them fall. Brownfield knew this movement well; it was the fatal shrug. It meant that his father saw nothing about the house that he could change and would therefore give up gesturing about it and he would never again think of repairing it.

When Brownfield's mother had wanted him to go to school Grange had assessed the possibility with the same inaudible gesticulation accorded the house. Knowing nothing of schools, but knowing he was broke, he had shrugged; the shrug being the end of that particular dream. It was the same when Margaret needed a dress and there was no way Grange could afford to buy it. He merely shrugged, never saying a word about it again. After each shrug he was more silent than before, as if each of these shrugs cut him off from one more topic of conversation.

Brownfield turned from looking at his father and the house to see his mother brush a hand across her eyes. He sat glumly, full of a newly discovered discontent. He was sad for her and felt bitterly small. How could he ever bear to lose her, to his father or to death or to age? How would he ever survive without her pliant strength and the floating fragrance of her body which was sweet and inviting and delicate, yet full of the concretely comforting odors of cooking and soap and milk.

"You could've gone," said Grange softly, to his wife.

"I don't know nothing about up Norse."

"You could learn."

"Naw, I don't believe I could." There was a sigh in her voice.

Brownfield came alive. So his cousins had been right; there had been talk about him and his mother going back with them to Philadelphia. Why hadn't they gone? He felt peeved and in the dark.

"I didn't know nobody *asked* us to go. *I* want to go up Norse." His cousins said only the greenest hicks from Georgia said "Norse" like that.

His mother smiled at him. "And wear your hair pressed down like a woman's? Get away from here, boy!"

Brownfield, an admirer of Uncle Silas, was not dissuaded. "I just wouldn't wear the headrag at night," he said.

"My poor sister Marilyn," his mother muttered sadly, "all bleached up like a streetwalker. The Lawd keep *me* from ever wanting to brush another woman's hair out of *my* face. To tell you the truth," she continued to Grange over Brownfield's head, "I don't even think it *was* real hair. I felt it when she took it off for me to try on. Just like the hair on the end of a cow's tail, and when you pulled a strand it stretched."

"I like it 'cause it swooshes," said Brownfield rhapsodically.

"That's 'cause you ain't got no sense," said Grange.

2

FIVE YEARS AFTER his cousins' visit, Brownfield stood on the same spot in the yard watching the approach of another vehicle. This time it was a big, gray high-bodied truck that he knew well. It rolled heavily over the road, blasting the misty quiet of the Sunday morning. The man driving the truck was not the one who usually drove it. As it came nearer Brownfield saw a brown arm dangling from the window. It was Johnny Johnson, a man who worked for Mr. Shipley. The truck stopped at the edge of the clearing and Brownfield's mother descended. She stood for a moment talking to the driver, then turned and came slowly and quietly toward the house. The truck made a noisy turnabout and disappeared back up the road. His mother took off her shoes and carried them in her hand. She walked gingerly and reluctantly over the dew. So intently was she peering at the ground she did not see Brownfield until she nearly bumped against him. He was taller than she, and bigger, and when she noticed him she jumped.

"'Morning," he said coolly.

His mother carried her shoes guiltily to her bosom, clutching them with both hands. Her beautiful rough hair was loose about her shoulders like a wayward thundercloud, with here and there a crinkly and shiny silver thread. Her dress was mussed, and the golden cross that usually nestled inside her dress lay jutting up atop her collar. Her eyes were haggard and blinked foggily at her son. She gave off a stale smoky odor. With nervous fingers she sought to thrust rumpled stockings farther inside her shoes.

"Oh," she said, looking toward the house, "I didn't see you standing there."

Brownfield stood aside, saying nothing.

"The baby all right?" she asked quickly, her knuckles sharp against her shoes.

"He all right," said Brownfield. He followed her into the house and watched as she stood over his little half-brother. The baby was sleeping peacefully, his tiny behind stuck up in the air. The baby was a product of his mother's new personality and went with her new painted good looks and new fragrance of beds, of store-bought perfume and of gin.

"Your daddy and me had another fight," she said, sinking down on the bed. "Oh, we had us a rip-rowing, knock-down, drag-out fight. With that fat yellow bitch of his calling the punches." She was very matter of fact. They had been fighting this way for years. Gone were the times she waited alone on Saturday afternoons for people who never came. Now when her husband left her at home and went into town she followed. At first she had determinedly walked the distance, or hitchhiked. Lately she had switched to riding, often in the big gray truck.

"I see he ain't back yet," she said.

Brownfield lounged in the doorway, hoping his job as babysitter was over.

"Said he wouldn't be back no more," his mother said, pulling her dress over her head and shaking it out. She chuckled spitefully. "How many times we done heard *that*. You'd think he'd be satisfied, me feeding him and her fucking him!"

Brownfield carefully closed his ears when his mother cursed. He knew his father was seeing another woman, and had been seeing one, or several, for a long time. It did not affect him the way it did his mother. He watched her roll down her slip and did not think to look away when it touched the floor. She turned to face him, eyes weary but defiant.

"What the hell you staring at?" she asked.

"Nothing," said Brownfield, and turned away.

His mother located the cross at the end of its chain around her neck and fingered it solemnly.

"I was just thinkin' about Uncle Silas and Aunt Marilyn," he said with his back to her.

"What you thinkin' about them for? I ain't heard from Marilyn since Silas was killed. Just think, tryin' to rob a liquor store in broad daylight! Marilyn always had a lot to say about her new icebox and clothes and her children's fancy learnin', but never did she breathe one word about Silas being on dope. All the time coming down here in they fancy cars and makin' out like *we* so out of fashion—I bet the Norse is just as much a mess as down here." She knelt by the side of the bed. "Give the baby a bottle of milk when he wakes up," she said from the floor. Within minutes after saying her prayers she was sound asleep.

Brownfield looked at the baby with disgust. Always it was his duty to look after the baby. It made him feel like a sissy. Fortunately the baby was sleeping deeply, for if he had awakened then Brownfield would have felt like giving him a pinch that would bring his mother flying from her bed, her curses and blows falling first on his, then on the baby's, head.

He was too big to play in the clearing, so instead he went to his box at the foot of his bed and brought out his new shoes, bought with money earned from spare-time work at the bait factory, and carried them outside. He sat on the porch steps polishing them with a piece of one of his father's old shirts.

As he stroked his shoes caressingly with the rag, Brownfield sank into a favorite daydream. He saw himself grownup, twenty-one or so, arriving home at sunset in the snow. In his daydream there was always snow. He had seen snow only once, when he was seven and there had been a small flurry at Christmas, and it had made a cold, sharp impression on him. In his daydream snow fell to the earth like chicken feathers dumped out of a tick, and gave the feeling of walking through a quiet wall of weightless and suspended raindrops, clear and cold on the eyelids and nose. In his daydream he pulled up to his house, a stately mansion with cherry-red brick chimneys and matching brick porch and steps, in a long chauffeur-driven car. The chauffeur glided out of the car first and opened the back door, where Brownfield sat puffing on a cigar. Then the chauffeur vanished around the back of the house, where his wife waited for him on the kitchen steps. She was the beloved and very respected cook and had been with the house and the chauffeur and Brownfield's family for many years. Brownfield's wife and children—two children, a girl and a boy—waited anxiously for him just inside the door in the foyer. They jumped all over him, showering him with kisses. While he told his wife of the big deals he'd pushed through that day she fixed him a mint julep. After a splendid dinner, presided over by the cook, dressed in black uniform and white starched cap, he and his wife, their arms around each other, tucked the children in bed and spent the rest of the evening discussing her day (which she had spent walking in her garden), and making love.

There was one thing that was odd about the daydream. The face of Brownfield's wife and that of the cook constantly interchanged. So that his wife was first black and glistening from cooking and then white and powdery to his touch; his dreaming self could not make up its mind. His children's faces were never in focus. He recognized them by their angelic presence alone, two bright spots of warmth; they hovered about calling him "Daddy" endearingly, while he stroked the empty air, assuming it to be their heads.

Brownfield had first had this daydream the week after his cousins told him about the North. Each year it had grown longer and more intensely real; at times it possessed him. While he dreamed of the life he would live as a man no other considerations entered his head. He dreamed alone and was quiet; which was why his mother thought baby-sitting an ideal occupation for him. But with the baby near, capable of shattering the quiet at any moment, Brownfield was cut off from deep involvement in the snow, in the cozy comfort of his luxuriously warm limousine, and in the faithful ministrations of his loving imaginary wife. He harbored a deep resentment against his mother for making it so hard for him to dream.

He finished his shoes. Piercing the silence now was the cry of his baby brother. Without hurrying, partially in his dream's afterglow, he stood, his hands holding the shoes carefully, palms up, so as not to smudge the shiny leather, and walked toward the box by his bed. It was a cardboard box and, like a small trunk, complete with cardboard shelves. He lifted the flap that was its top and placed his shoes with care a distance from his other possessions. There were a pair of new denim pants, a new green shirt with birds and Indians and deer on it, and a soft yellow neckerchief made of satin. He had bought the neckerchief from the rolling-store man. It cost a quarter and he was very proud of it.

The baby was still crying. Brownfield looked for a moment at his mother in the bed, who had pulled the quilt over her head. The wall around her bed was aflutter with funeral-home calendars, magazine pictures and bits of newsprint which she had cut out of the 1st Colored Baptist Christian Crusade. The baby looked hopefully toward the bed and then pathetically at Brownfield. With a harsh push of his fingers Brownfield thrust the bottle into the baby's mouth. The baby lay on its side, intently sucking, and looked at his big brother with swollen distrustful eyes. The baby was almost two years old but refused to learn to walk. Instead it allowed itself to be dragged about, propped up and ignored, until something caused it to scream. The baby's name was Star, but it was never called anything. It was treated indifferently most of the time and seemed resigned to not belonging. It had grayish eyes and reddish hair and was shadowed pale gold and chocolate like a little animal. From its odd coloration its father might have been every one of its mother's many lovers.

Margaret had not been impressed, ever, by her sister's Northern existence, or so she had repeatedly said to Brownfield. But she had grown restless about her own life, a life that was as predictably unexciting as last year's cotton field. Somewhere along the line she had changed. Slowly, imperceptibly. Until it was too late for Brownfield to recall exactly how she had been when he had loved her. It seemed to Brownfield that one day she was as he had always known her; kind, submissive, smelling faintly of milk; and the next day she was a wild woman looking for frivolous things, her heart's good times, in the transient embraces of strangers.

Brownfield blamed his father for his mother's change. For it was Grange she followed at first. It was Grange who led her to the rituals of song and dance and drink, which he had always rushed to at the end of the week, every Saturday night. It was Grange who had first turned to someone else. On some Saturday nights Grange and Margaret left home excitedly together, looking for Brownfield knew not what, except that it must be something strong and powerful and something they had thought lost. For they grew frenzied in pursuit of whatever it was. Often they came home together, still bright, flushed from fighting or from good times, but with the glow gradually dying out of their eyes as they faced the creaking floorboards of their unpainted house. Depression always gave way to fighting, as if fighting preserved some part of the feeling of being alive. It was confusing to realize but not hard to know that they loved each other. And even when Margaret found relief from her cares in the arms of her fellow bait-pullers and church members, or with the man who drove the truck and who turned her husband to stone, there was a deference in her eyes that spoke of her love for Grange. On weekdays when, sober and wifely, she struggled to make food out of plants that grew wild and game caught solely in traps, she was submissive still. It was on weekends only that she became a huntress of soft touches, gentle voices and sex without the arguments over the constant and compelling pressures of everyday life. She had sincerely regretted the baby. And now, humbly respecting her husband's feelings, she ignored it.

What Brownfield could not forgive was that in the drama of their lives his father and mother forgot they were not alone.

When Brownfield woke in the night his mother was gone. From his bed in the kitchen he could see his father sitting on the bed, cradling something in his arms. It was long and dark, like a steel rod, and glinted in the light from the kerosene lamp. Grange's face was impassive, its lines brooding. Placing the rifle on the bed he picked up his dusty black-green hat. He stood looking at the floor, his shoulders slumped, motionless. He looked very old. Ploddingly he moved about the room. He waited indecisively for his wife to return. He gazed at the baby asleep in its makeshift crib, a crate that had once been filled with oranges. He shrugged. Then he lifted his eyes toward where Brownfield's bed was, at one side of the kitchen, between the table and the stove. Slowly he walked into the kitchen, which was chilly and smelled of old biscuits, and which changed to a new rhythm of night with his entrance into it. The air was gently agitated by his movements. The sounds of the floor shifted with each step he took.

Brownfield pretended to be asleep, though his heart was pounding so loudly he was sure his father would hear it. He saw Grange bend over him to inspect his head and face. He saw him reach down to touch him. He saw his hand stop, just before it reached his cheek. Brownfield was crying silently and wanted his father to touch the tears. He moved toward his father's hand, as if moving unconsciously in his sleep. He saw his father's hand draw back, without touching him. He saw him turn sharply and leave the room. He heard him leave the house. And he knew, even before he realized his father would never be back, that he hated him for everything and always would. And he most hated him because even in private and in the dark and with Brownfield presumably asleep, Grange could not bear to touch his son with his hand.

"Well. He's gone," his mother said without anger at the end of the third week. But the following week she and her poisoned baby went out into the dark of the clearing and in the morning Brownfield found them there. She was curled up in a lonely sort of way, away from her child, as if she had spent the last moments on her knees.

3

"YOU CAN GET yourself a wife," said Shipley confidentially, "and settle down here in the same house. It might need a little fixing up, but I could lend you enough for that, and with a few licks here and there it ought to be good as new."

Shipley's hair was still like that of a sleek greasy animal, but now it was dingy white and thin. He looked at Brownfield from under brows that had faded from blond to yellowish-gray. His pale blue eyes struggled to convey kindness and largesse. Brownfield slid down from the truck knowing his face was the mask his father's had been. Because this frightened him and because he did not know why he should have inherited this fear, he studiedly brushed imaginary dust from the shoulders of a worn black suit Shipley had given him.

He had been shocked to see Shipley at the funeral, but soon guessed he had come hoping to catch Grange. Shipley did not take kindly to people running off owing him money, no matter that they had paid off whatever debts they might have owed many times over. Nobody had whispered a word against him while he stood looking down on the bloatedly sleeping mother and child. To most of the people at the funeral Shipley's presence was a status symbol and an insult, though they were not used to thinking in those terms and would not have expressed such a mixed feeling. Shipley squeezed out a tear for the benefit of the other mourners, and Brownfield had chuckled bitterly to himself. The tear wasn't necessary: pity was scarce at his mother's funeral; most of the people there thought she had got what she deserved. Shipley's crocodile tear was the only one shed.

Brownfield himself had sat, limp and clammy, wishing he were a million miles away. His mother as she was in the last years got none of his love, none of his sympathy and hardly any of his thoughts. The idea that he might continue to live in her house aroused nothing but revulsion. He knew too that the minute he accepted money from Shipley he was done for. If he borrowed from Shipley, Shipley would make sure he never finished paying it back.

"Don't know but what we might can build you a new house," said Shipley, thinking that with Brownfield's muscles he could do a grown man's work. Shipley believed with a mixture of awe and contempt that blacks developed earlier than whites, especially in the biceps. He thought too that as long as he had Brownfield there was a chance of getting Grange. Believing that Brownfield was choked up from grief and from his generous offer Shipley continued speaking to him on an encouraging plane.

"After all, if you marry one of these little fillies on my place she's going to want to smell some new wood. Why, I can't stop by a house on the place without the womenfolks waylayin' me; talking about me fixing up the house they already got or wanting me to build 'em a new one."

He fished about for sympathy, while Brownfield stood looking at the ground.

"But the main thing is"—Shipley smiled kindly—"we want you to stay here with us. And we don't hold it against you what your daddy done. We'll just wipe that off the books." He continued to smile but eyed Brownfield shrewdly from under his brows. "Of course, I believe you said you didn't know which way he was headed?"

"No, sir," said Brownfield, from a great hollow distance.

"Well," said Shipley sadly, as if a great wrong were being done him but one which he would not allow to dissuade him from future acts of kindness, "you think about all we discussed. And take the day off and get yourself straightened out. I tell you this much, I think we going to work out fine; and I know my boys will be glad to have somebody they already know to work with them when they take over Shipley's Farm and Bait." He leaned out of the truck, the hand dangling from the end of his coat sleeve like a papery autumn leaf. "You and me will start out fresh," he said, "and remember, the North ain't all people say it is. Just remember that."

When Brownfield looked up, Shipley and his truck were gone. He was left in the familiar clearing. Scornfully, shaking the ice from his gut, he spat on Shipley's ground. His mind raced headlong into the realm of his dream. The fear of Shipley that had tied his tongue disappeared as the urge to sample his new freedom grew. He would be his own boss. From the forlorn and empty house he took only his box. As he left the clearing a thousand birds began wildly singing good luck.

Part II

Part II

4

HE WALKED IN the direction the sun was going. He walked all day without stopping, except to throw a rock into a stream and to watch squirrels play across the tops of trees, twisting and flying among the branches as if they had wings. Under his feet the earth, being moist with spring, became sunken; he stopped to watch as the print of his foot sprang back to smoothness on the moss along the streams. Rivers and creeks crisscrossed his route, and everything he saw in the woods delighted him. When it became dark he made himself a bed in a shed in a big field, a shed used for storing cotton to keep it dry after picking. The shed was empty now, but he found a few discarded croker sacks outside. On these he lay down and went to sleep.

After walking a few miles next morning he was very hungry. He walked past farmhouses that were big and painted white, with shrubs and flowering trees around them. When he saw a baked gray two-room shack he quickened his pace and walked for its flat dry yard.

There was a woman standing in the back yard over a rusty black pot. Her fire was kept going with rubber tires and refuse. The air around her was smelly and smoky. She was stirring her boiling clothes with a long lye-eaten stick. She took the stick out of the water and shook it as Brownfield came up to her. She looked about quickly to locate three small children, who were playing with car tires all over the yard, and didn't say a word or even seem to notice him until he spoke.

"'Morning," he said.

"All right . . . how're you?" she answered in a low, singsong voice.

"Nice bright morning, ain't it?"

"Shore is," she said and stopped.

"My name Brownfield—Brownfield Copeland—and what might yourn be?"

"My name Mizes Mamie Lou Banks glad to know you." She stuck out a bleached and puckered white palm and they shook hands.

"I wonder if a starving man might ax a lady for a little somethin' to eat?" said Brownfield, looking sideways at her as if she were not the lady he meant.

"Why," she said, putting down the stick, placing it across the pot, "you is just a boy, ain't you?"

"Yessem, I reckon," he said, unconsciously hanging his head.

"You runnin' from any white peoples? If you is," she continued, not looking at him but down at her pot, "you best to go on in the house where can't none of them see you if they's a mind to pass. They's some grits on the stove 'n some eggs if you knows how to cook. I got my washin' to do, 'n if you *is* runnin' from the white folks I ain't seen nothing but potash 'n lye this morning, 'n that's the truth." She smiled very slightly, at least her mouth quivered about the corners. There was a chunky bulge in her bottom lip.

"Thank you kindly, ma'am, I ain't runnin' but I shore is hongry. Fact of the matter is, I'm kinda lookin' for my daddy."

"Was the white folks after him too?" she asked. "Or did he just run off?"

"It was both."

"Well, I can't picture nobody runnin' *back* this way."

Brownfield nodded and walked to the door she shook her fingers at and went in. While he was cooking the eggs she came through the house to get more dirty clothes. He thought she must be a washerwoman, she was washing so many clothes.

"Hep yourself now," she said. There was something stern in her kindness. He thought that if she had ever been good-looking it must have been when she was no more than eleven or twelve.

"Oh, I got plenty."

"I tell you, a growin' boy can eat it up like a brand-new stove."

"You got children bigger'n them outdoors?"

"Oh, five more, but they all be gone up Norse." She said it proudly, as if she were saying she sent them off to Harvard. "They says they couldn't just hang round here and hang round here." She paused a minute, going to the china closet for butter and putting it down next to his plate. "Don't know if I blames them neither." She was a very thin woman with knobby cheekbones and dark circles under her eyes. She had no more figure than a stick, and wore a man's pair of overalls and a tight checkered headrag. "For all I know somebody just might be feeding my old hongry younguns up there in

Chicago. I swear, they could eat up yere 'bout a whole hog at one dinner." She sighed and walked outside with the clothes.

Brownfield thought perhaps he would go to Chicago, or maybe even New York City. Maybe he would just keep walking and walking and then hop a freight and wake up in the morning in a place where people were nice and had manners. He wouldn't even care if they didn't have manners, if they didn't try to lure him into debt and then cause him to turn into stone whenever they came around. He stopped chewing a moment to think about what his mother had said about up Norse; and he remembered that his cousins said that up Norse was cold and people never spoke to one another on the street or anything. His father had once said that being up Norse ruined Uncle Silas and Aunt Marilyn, being so cold and unfeeling and full of concrete, but even while Grange said this his eyes had shown a fascination with the idea of going there himself.

"Say, you know. I done heard some things about up Norse," Brownfield said, after he had eaten and come outdoors again. "They say it ain't as good as folks make it out to be."

"Maybe not, maybe 'tis," she said, stirring her pot, spitting snuff juice into the fire. "I wouldn't be saying I knows. But I declare it so out of fashion round here you'd think most any other place would be better."

"Yessem," he said, thinking what was so confounded bad about people not speaking to you if there was no Shipley around to see that you never made any money of your own. "Yessem." He looked about the bleak yard and at the house that seemed about to cave in. "You just might have somethin' there."

She continued to stir the pot, stoke up the fire and bustle about the yard.

"They daddy work round here?" he asked, pointing to the three small children, who were busy rolling car tires.

"Well, I tell you," she said, standing up from putting more rubber around the pot and resting her back by swaying it, "one of they daddies is dead from being in the war, although he only got as far as Fort Bennet. The other one of they daddies is now married to the woman what lives in the next house down the road. If you stands up on your tippy toes you can jest about see her roof, sort of green colored. I thought she was helpin' me get another husband and all the time she was lookin' out for herself. But I am still her friend. The other one of they daddies was my last husband, by common law, but he dead too now, shot by the old man he was working for for taking the chitlins out of a hog they kill." She looked at the children and frowned. "But they is so much alike, just to look at; they git along right well together."

"Reckon they going to grow up and go on up Norse too?" he asked, looking at the children. They had bad colds and snot ran down their lips like glue.

"I don't know," she said, stirring her pot. "The Lawd knows I loves them, but when they does grow up I hope they has sense enough to git away from round here."

"Well, I thank you kindly for that good breakfast."

"Aw, don't mention it. 'N if you gets hongry runnin' back the other way drop in again." She gave him a grave, boastful, wry and conspiratorial smile. "I also hope you finds your daddy."

"Bye, you all," he said, waving to the children, who stopped playing to stare at him.

"Bye-bye! Bye-bye!" they piped like birds, running after him to the edge of the highway, and yelling "Bye-bye!" long after he had turned the curve and was out of sight. He heard their mother call "Y'all *come* back here before you hit by a car!" and the voices stopped abruptly; then the only sound was his footsteps against the grainy damp shoulder of the road.

5

AFTER WEEKS OF indecisive wandering, of worrying that Shipley might be following him, of breakfasting with dozens of secluded families in hollows and clearings deep in trees, Brownfield abandoned all hope, for the present, of reaching Chicago or New York. He had spent several days looking for a slow freight to hop but had not even found railroad tracks. He had no idea which direction he should follow to go North; unlike thousands of his ancestors he had never heard of the North Star. Often at night he gazed at the sky, searching for an omen. To gaze hopefully at the sky was in his blood, but nothing came of it.

On the last morning of wandering he breakfasted with a family of women, whose various husbands and boy friends were off hunting. With their own men away the women lavished attention on Brownfield. They drew water for his bath, pressed his new shirt and yellow satin tie, and gave him a shoe box for his things, which they said would be easier to carry than the trunklike box he had. Brownfield watched as the youngest girls tore the old box to bits. Then he felt truly that it was time to quit, that he had come far enough, and that where he was by nightfall he would stay. At least for a while. As he told the women shyly, he "needed a little chance to catch his breath."

Resplendent in his new Indian-bird-and-animal-decorated shirt, daring in the yellow satin necktie, awkward in stiffly starched denims and highly lustered shoes, Brownfield set out in the new direction the women showed him. He mumbled, almost inaudibly, that he was "kinda" looking for his daddy. That made parting gayer somehow, his walking away less bleak. He liked the women, all temporarily menless, without cares; he liked commanding their uninhibited attention.

When he described Grange to them they looked at one another and smiled and smiled; but they would not say if they had seen him. They only insisted that Brownfield take a certain road, and no other, which ran a certain way, and which would bring him by dusk to a certain peaceful town.

6

He reached the town when the sun was setting. There were two streets, lightly graveled, which formed the upper corner of a square. To Brownfield's right, within the square, off the main street, rose the solid brick dimensions of the county courthouse. Directly ahead of him, in a circle of grass in the middle of the street, stood a stone soldier, his bayoncted rifle lifted, his intrepid but motionless foot raised to advance northward. On both sides of the street there were stores. Brownfield met buggies and two cars and a few storekeepers on foot. Raucous boys from the blacksmith's shop rushed past in leather aprons; one of them looked with fleeting envy at Brownfield's tie. Except for this glance Brownfield entered the town unnoticed.

He had never seen more than thirty people at once before, unless they were working in a cotton field, and he was amazed at the diversity of clothing people wore. There were storekeepers in black suits, their helpers in threadbare blue. He saw a few white women leaning on the arms of their husbands, fussy-looking in frills and wide hats. He saw black women trudging home from the day's nannying, their uniforms remarkably starched and ironed, their aprons still on. He saw a mixed group of black people walking determinedly, eyes down, heads down, for the very end of the second street. On a hunch, Brownfield followed them.

Soon losing sight of this group, Brownfield turned left off the street in the direction of some shacks. In a few minutes he stood in front of the local Negro bar and grill. It was a small wooden structure with a bare, hard, cleanly swept yard. Its sides were covered with tin and wooden posters, some of them advertising Brown Mule tobacco, Red Cherry snuff and laxatives; the rest advertising Cajun whiskey, Old Joe and Grape Beer.

He could tell what each thing was because he was thoroughly familiar, as was every black person in the county, with all of these products. No father came to town on Saturday evening without bringing home at least one. If tobacco, on him; if whiskey, mostly inside him.

The juke joint, when he imagined how it must jump with light and life at night, fascinated Brownfield, and he thought he would try to get a job there. He had no money, and knew he would need some if he decided later to push on to Chicago.

His mother and father had come to such places, perhaps this same one, and when they had fought and argued in public it was usually among the kind of people who would frequent such a place. But this thought only heightened Brownfield's interest in the night spot, which, in the dull gray dusk, held all the latent tension of an important club. Sighing and feeling young and incapable, he squared his shoulders and walked in.

There were twelve small tables with black-flowered oilcloth covers on them arranged neatly around a potbellied stove, in which a fire was burning low. The smell of chitlins, pig's feet and collard greens was strong and thick coming from somewhere in back behind the counter. There was a box in the corner for keeping beer cold, and kerosene lamps around the walls. A gramophone, like those he had seen in catalogues, was pushed against one side of the counter, its big horn turned outward like a gourd that had been cut off at one end. A murky silence with a near-undercurrent of voices that went with the cooking food, enveloped him; he was over-whelmed already by the gracious aspects of town living that he saw.

A heavy cantaloupe-colored woman with freckled cheeks and gray-green eyes looked him up and down and said, "You kinda *young*, aincha, cutie?" She eyed him in a way that made his palms sweat, and he was sure she had no intention of hir-ing him.

"But I can do your cleaning, and help move things around. I'm strong," Brownfield said, rubbing his hands on his pants. "I can do your chopping."

At that the woman looked interested and smiled a sly little smile.

"Does good choppin', does you?" she asked.

"Yessem."

"No need to yessem me," she said lazily. "The name is Josie. *Fat* Josie." She looked at Brownfield as if she expected him to have heard the name before. During the pause a thin, very black young woman slid by.

"This here's my daughter, Lorene." Josie reached out abruptly, arrested the woman, and pulled her unwilling and muscled arm close beside her, holding it in a pinch. The woman, darting her eyes at Brownfield, snatched her arm from her mother's grip, then looked from one to the other of

them with baleful scorn. She was cursed with the beginnings
of a thick mustache and beard. Her hard, malevolent eyes
were a yellowish flash in her dark hairy face. She was sinewy
as a man. Only her odor and breasts were female. She reeked
of a fishy, oniony smell.

"Yep," said Josie, chuckling at the look on Brownfield's
face and watching her daughter slouch off, "that's the pride of
her mama's heart."

Lorene turned and hissed something vile, her tongue
showing through her lips like a snake's. With one hand she
yanked at her waistband. Brownfield looked down with as-
tonishment as her slip disappeared under her short tight skirt.
Her legs were even more hairy than her face.

When he looked at Josie she was running her tongue over
her teeth, her eyes small brassy points between the fat.

"You sort of gets a thrill from the thought of plowin'
through all that hair, don't you?" she asked, shamelessly grinning while Brownfield stammered.

Confounded by her, Brownfield pushed his shoe box farther under his arm and turned away.

"*Wait* a minute," the woman wheezed. "What's your
name?"

"Brownfield."

"Brown*field*?" the woman cackled. "Shit. Brownfield
what?"

"Copeland," said Brownfield weakly.

Josie was fingering his tie. She was so close he could feel
her breath. Suddenly she drew back.

"Where you *from*?" she asked suspiciously.

"Green County," said Brownfield. "What county's this?"

"Baker." She took the shoe box from him and pushed him
to a table in the back.

"Now," she said, "tell me just how you happened to turn up *here*."

"What's the matter with here?" he asked.

"I don't know. Maybe that's what you come to tell me," she said.

By nine o'clock that night he was installed washing dishes and chopping wood, scarcely believing his luck, and listening to the thoroughly arousing music that came from the magic gramophone. Josie had clucked sympathetically as he told of his unfortunate life with Margaret and Grange. She was deeply interested in what he had to say about Grange and when Brownfield spoke of him Josie fidgeted with her hands and nibbled her lips. After his story she fixed him a supper and pulled him along behind her upstairs to her room. There she fitted him with an apron, standing behind him and reaching around and under his shoulders to get at the halter.

"How come you so curious about the Copelands?" Brownfield had asked.

"Oh," Josie had said, "it just seem like to me I had done heard that name before." Then—looking down the front of his trousers—"But on a heap *bigger* man."

And he said "Ma'am?" In his excitement over having the job, he did not think that his father might indeed have passed exactly this way; through the town, through the tavern, and even through Josie. And then she had laid her arm on his, her skin like dry cracked honey, and said in a sporty way, "Never you mind, Sugar, I'm just talkin' *to* myself."

In the weeks to follow he found her a devouring cat, voracious and sly, wanting to eat him up, swallow him down alive. Thoughts of his father ceased to come to him as he was led into her incredible softness; thoughts of moving northward melted from him in the snug forgetfulness of her experienced warmth. What she had said about the much bigger man with the same name didn't begin to haunt him until it was too late. His contented existence could not have anticipated a day when he would see Grange once more, not in New York or Chicago, but in the very room in which the majority of his nights were to be spent. Grange, not bewildered or rich in the North but crazy and well-to-do in the South, in Baker, in Josie's room, in Josie's arms, disgusted with everything, caring for nothing, but for some reason wanting to take the great lusty insatiable cat up to the altar.

7

JOSIE HAD VIOLENT DREAMS. Once she had gone to Sister Madelaine for help. Sister Madelaine said her dreams had to be told, and Josie could never do that.

"They just embarrasses me so bad, Sister," she said. "When I prays in church the other womens laugh at me. They don't know how I've suffered; if they did they wouldn't laugh at me."

"That's your feelings about it anyhow. But listen, they say you should lay your burdens at the feet of the Lord. They say He'll listen." Sister Madelaine stifled a yawn. "But you have to tell *Him* the truth; that's the only catch there. Else, even *He* can't help you."

"I have laid them everywhere, believe me that is the truth. Starting years ago I went to everybody that would listen. Including Him. But the more I lays them down the heavier they gets. All around me is a great big hush, like before a storm, and when I dream it is just to let witches ride me."

Sister Madelaine raised an eyebrow. "My colleged son will tell you there is no such thing as witches riding people. From

Morehouse he learns it is indigestion. Something you ate, the way you are laying in the bed. The circulation of your blood stops and you can't move. While you lay there sweating and not able to move you have nightmares, and when you wake up you think a witch has been riding you. According to my son you wouldn't need a fortuneteller, you'd need a dose of salts."

"*He rides me,*" Josie cried, pleading for belief. "I seen him do it."

"Who?"

"Now," said Josie, "I can't tell you that."

"Well," said Sister Madelaine, handing Josie a cup of tea, "you wouldn't go to a doctor with a pain in the behind without telling him a mule kicked you, would you? I am a fortuneteller, but I ain't God. I got limits. Also a boy in college."

Josie took a sip of tea and handed over some bills.

Sister Madelaine paced, her Indian-chief profile to Josie.

"That theory about witch-riding belongs wholly to my educated child. I don't argue with him to keep peace in the family. But I ask you, what kind of business could I have built up if I *didn't* believe in witches? I know they are real because I have had to shed a few of my own. My son has learned they are *not* real in college, where everybody believes in a man called Freud who uses old couches. Well, *I* don't believe in couches! But what do youngsters know about anything?"

She stopped pacing and looked down at Josie. There was never pity in Sister Madelaine's eyes, just a steady, beady waiting. This unnerved Josie, who thought of the fortuneteller as of another species than herself. She could not bear to look Sister Madelaine straight in the eye.

"Everyone who is straddled by a witch knows the identity of the witch," Sister Madelaine said with her back to Josie. "If you can call his name," she said, as Josie was leaving, "you will be cured."

After Josie was gone, Sister Madelaine scribbled a short note to her son, put it in an envelope, together with the money Josie had paid her, and then sat back reflectively in her chair, savoring the last drops of her tea.

8

JOSIE HAD NOT been able to say his name. She even told herself she did not remember him. She did not know why he came to her while she slept, drenching her in perspiration, racing her heart with fear, holding her immobile with his weight, like judgment, across her chest. For her father had been a heavy man, and it was her father who rode Josie, stifled through the night.

Her father. How did she remember him? A question asked slowly, always in bewilderment, to dull the unforgotten impression of one cruel night over thirty years ago. Her last night in her father's house as a young girl. The night that was to have changed her life of sin back to its original country righteousness.

She had thought her father agreed to let her back into his house. He had not refused her gifts to his other children or to himself or to Josie's mother. And Josie had worked hard to buy them. She had thought, *at last* I will go home to stay, to be again a child, be again sixteen, and near his heart and hand.

It happened on her father's birthday. Josie came walking

down the road, dusty-shoed, into the hard swept yard. Her father was on the porch, a shabby dais of power, not knowing about the party she planned for him. She carried small bundles, but had hidden away larger ones the night before. His deep solemn eyes followed her up the steps and into the house. He did not speak. But his eyes seemed to glow with promise and there was a bemused smile on his lips. She thought she was about to be forgiven.

"Do you think he'll let me come back?" she asked her mother, who, like her daughter, was big with child. The money Josie put into the party for her father would be the last she would earn before she delivered. Her mother's answer was a prayer in silence, a frightened and hopeful *cautious* nod of the head. Her mother was a meek woman, and though she rarely agreed with Josie's father she never argued with him.

Josie had come early to prepare the food, mix the drinks— corn liquor, sugared water, crushed mint leaves —and to greet her father's guests. They knew her shame but would come, fearing her father in his stiff sobriety and decency, but depending on his abundant Christianity, the same that he preached to them, to help him forgive. Not only Josie, but them.

For themselves, those who had fucked his daughter, they had paid when possible and felt only a very limited twinge of conscience when they knew she used that money to try to buy back her father's love. And he took the new pipe, the slippers, the big brass watch, and they watched him wear them, and listened to his thoughts on crops and the weather, and saw the amused yet baffled horror in his eyes.

At the party they sat in a semicircle around him and watched him ignore her.

"You want some of this, Pa?" "You want some of that?"

And the big questioning eyes over the big thrusting stomach that none of them owned. Josie took more of the liquor for herself and moved out from them on its floating haze, and when she fell clumsily on her back within the curve of the all-male semicircle (the wives of the men had, of course, not come) it was then and only then that her father rose from his chair, from the garish cushion of war, with birds and cannon and horses and red roses, that she had bought him with the money, that he rose and, standing over her, forbade anyone to pick her up.

Her mother stood outside the ringed pack of men, how many of them knowledgeable of her daughter's swollen body she did not know, crying. The tears and the moans of the continually repentant were hers, as if she had caused the first love-making between her daughter and her daughter's teen-age beau, and the scarcely disguised rape of her child that followed from everyone else. Such were her cries that the men, as if caught standing naked, were embarrassed and they stooped, still in the ring of the pack, to lift up the frightened girl, whose whiskied mind had cleared and who now lay like an exhausted, overturned pregnant turtle underneath her father's foot. He pressed his foot into her shoulder and dared them to touch her. It seemed to them that Josie's stomach moved and they were afraid of their guilt suddenly falling on the floor before them wailing out their names. But it was only that she was heaving and vomiting and choking on her own puke.

"Please, sir," someone said from the intimate circle, "let her *up*. She in a *bad* way."

They saw that Josie had seemed to faint, her dark dress pulled up above her knees. Knees turned out. Arms outstretched. She was like a spider, deformed and grotesque beneath the panicked stares of the gathered men. Stares that were only collectively horrified and singly aroused. They had seen her so stretched out before.

"Let 'er be," growled her father. "I hear she can do *tricks* on her back like that."

Such was the benediction of Josie's father, the witch who rode her breathless in her middle age. Lorene had almost been born beneath his foot. As it was she was born into a world peopled by her grandfather's male friends, all of whom frequented the little shack on Poontang Street where "fat Josie" (she grew large after the baby) did her job with a gusto that denied shame, and demanded her money with an authority that squelched all pity. And from these old men, her father's friends, Josie obtained the wherewithal to dress herself well, and to eat well, and to own the Dew Drop Inn. When they became too old to "cut the mustard" any more, she treated them with jolly cruelty and a sadistic kind of concern. She often did a strip tease in the center of their eagerly constructed semicircle, bumping and grinding, moaning to herself, charging them the last pennies of their meager old-age savings to watch her, but daring them to touch.

9

A WET GURGLE came from Josie's throat. An alien force seemed to be pressing her into the mattress. She drew her breath shudderingly, her body rigid. She was building up pressure for a scream. Brownfield poked her dutifully and after a minute she opened her eyes. She lay breathing heavily, trembling.

"You all right?" he asked. "You want some water or something?"

"God help," said Josie.

"What *is* this dream you keep having?" asked Brownfield. "You gets just as stiff and hard as a dead person. Except you sweat. You kind of vibrates too, like there's a motor on right there where people say the heart is."

For a year Brownfield had been asking about the dream. Josie never talked. They lay in bed between crisp white sheets. On Josie's side the crispness had become moist and limp with sweat. Brownfield lit the lamp and placed it on the table near her head. He stood, naked and concerned, gazing down on her face. Josie's face was heavy and doughy, lumpy and creased from sleep, wet from her dream. She had the stolid, anonymous face of a cook in a big house, the face of a tired waitress. The face of a woman too fat, too greedy, too *unrelentless* to be loved. She could grin with her face or laugh out of it or leer through it, but she had forgotten the simple subtle mechanics of the smile. Her eyes never lost their bold rapacious look, even when she woke from sleep terrified, as she was now.

Josie, Brownfield was sure, had never been young, had never smelled of milk or of flowers, but only of a sweet decay that one might root out only if one took the trouble to expose inch after inch of her to the bright consuming fire of blind adoration and love. Then she might be made clean. But Brownfield did not love Josie. He did not really wonder, therefore, that she told him almost nothing about herself, although she constantly pumped him for details of his own life. To shock him once she had told him a strange tale about how his father had stopped at the Dew Drop Inn on his way North, and stayed with her, and loved her. Brownfield had laughed.

"If he love you so much why ain't he here with you right now?"

Josie had retreated in tears, and the next day pretended she'd made her story up.

"Thank *God* I ain't poor," Josie murmured from the bed. "And thank the good Lord I takes care of myself without the help of strangers, *which,* in a matter of plain speaking, ain't got a pot to piss in nor a window to throw it out of." She took the liberty occasionally of reminding Brownfield of his penury. Now she took his pillow from his side of the bed and cradled it in her arms like a lover.

"Listen," she said, "my side of the bed's wet."

Brownfield stumbled next door without a word, into Lorene's room and, not caring to sleep on the floor, he climbed unhesitatingly into Lorene's bed.

10

THE FIRST TIME Brownfield saw Mem, Josie's "adopted" daughter, he had been balling Josie and Lorene for over two years. Mem had been away at school in Atlanta, an errant father paying her bills. She was Josie's sister's child. Her mother was dead.

"She died and left me the *sweetest* li'l burden," Josie occasionally allowed as how to impressionable friends.

"That girl have to buy *books* that cost as much as a many of us pays for dresses!" Josie would smile proudly and with malicious aforethought at some of her less well-off acquaintances. For her "business" in the lounge paid off, and she didn't mind letting people think she was putting Mem through high school.

Mem's father, Brownfield learned, was a big Northern preacher with a large legitimate family. He had met Josie's sister one summer when he came South to preach revival services in Josie's father's church. They had fallen in love and Mem was conceived. The preacher went back North to his family and Mem's mother was put out of her father's house.

Josie took her in until Mem was born, and shortly afterward she died.

"Of course, my sister sort of snatch that preacher from me on the rebound, you understand." Josie smiled coyly, insistently, at Brownfield. "But it were really *me* he actually love."

According to Josie, the only reason Lorene didn't go to school ("of course, I were anxious and well off enough to send her") was because she was too stubborn to go. However, by the time she was fifteen Lorene was the mother of two baby boys. Living in the lounge with her mother's boy friends always after her, she was tripped up from the start by the men underfoot, and was the fastest thing going, next to her mother, in town. It had not taken Brownfield long to see that Lorene had her kind of crush on him (anything her mother tried appealed to her), and that Josie more than liked him. At seventeen he was well set up between the two of them and the lounge was as much his as theirs. Or so they were quick to assure him.

He got along well with them both and turned his back when they fought over him. Lorene, a smoke-cured slattern who doused herself with cheap perfume and wore her hair a bright new penny red, was as flattering a lay as her mother. For although she looked more like somebody's brother than anybody's girl, she had a reputation for toughness that earned her an abundance of respect from youngsters who hoped to grow up to be like her. She was noted for her expert use of the razor, and it was said that she had once cut up a customer's wife and then run the customer out of the room while his wife almost bled to death. Brownfield enjoyed her also for her language, as when she said of the customer and his bleeding wife, "I was just tryin' to *catch* that nigger and tell him to get that bleeding brood sow off my floor. I ain't gonna kill *my* ass mopping up after these nasty folks." Brownfield was happy until he got his first look at Mem.

Mem was cherry brown, not yellow like Josie or dark and hairy like Lorene. She was plump and quiet, with demure slant eyes. When she came home from school she was barely noticed. She stayed upstairs when the lounge was rocking, and when she did come down she kept right on out of the house and out walking, just walking, in the woods. Brownfield tried to talk to her but she answered him shyly, her eyes on the ground, without interest, it seemed to him, and went her way, with him more and more turning to look after her. He had never known anybody to go walking, "just walking," in the woods, unless they expected to walk up on a good stick.

"Who the hell she think she *is*?" he asked Josie, frowning at what he couldn't understand. "I can't stand for women to go away for two weeks and come back talking proper!"

Part of what he meant was "walking proper," for Mem certainly had a proper walk. For a while her walk alone mystified him, intrigued him, and in every way set his inquisitive itch on edge. He was not averse to making his person available to all members of the family.

"Aw, quit your going on and get on in this bed," Josie purred, looking more like a fat caterpillar every day. "Ain't no need for you looking at *that* one, she ain't got no real itch in her pussy. She can't do for you what I can do."

Brownfield responded to her soft, sinful old hands by taking her to bed.

"When's you and me going to get married, lover?" Josie asked, while Brownfield realized that Mem's bed was just on the other side of the wall, about a foot from her benevolent "mother's."

In moments of spitefulness, Lorene tried to tell Brownfield that what Josie had said about Grange and her was true. It didn't make any sense to Brownfield that his father and Josie might have been lovers. Besides, what did he care if he now plowed a furrow his father had laid? Josie's old field had never lain fallow. And after Mem came, what Lorene or Josie told him about anything didn't matter. He was interested only in Mem. How to penetrate her quiet strangeness occupied his whole mind.

11

WHAT HE FELT always when he thought of Mem was guilt. Shame that he was no better than he was. Grime. Dirt. He thought of her as of another mother, the kind his own had not been. Someone to be loved and spoken to softly, someone never to frighten with his rough, coarse ways. But he could never successfully communicate his feelings to her; he did not know the words she knew, and even if he could learn them he had no faith that they would fit the emotions he had. She could read magazines and books, and he could only look at the pictures in them and hazard a guess at what the print meant. Often, when they were thrown together in the house and she walked outside on the porch to keep from being inside alone with him, he followed and tried to talk to her. She would smile and speak a few words, never harsh, about his carryings on with Josie and Lorene. He expressed an interest in wanting to read and write, and she offered to teach him. He caught on quickly to small things, and they spent many afternoons, before the Dew Drop Inn opened, on the steps outside with her old school books. When she began teaching grade school in the fall she took him along with her class. Or tried.

"In the first place," she would begin, in an intense prim way Lorene and Josie scoffed at, "if you have two or three words to say and don't know which word means two or more, it is better to just not use 's' on the end of any of the words. This is so because the verb takes on the same number as the subject. You understand? Well, all I'm saying is 'I *have* some cake,' *sounds* better than 'I *haves* some cake.' Or, 'We have a friendship,' is better than 'We *haves* a friendship.' Now is that clear?" And she would look at him, properly doubtful, wrinkling her brow. And he would nod, yes, and say over and over happily in his mind, We haves a friendship! *We*, Mem and me, haves us a friendship! and he would smile so that she would stop her frowning and smile too.

She was a good teacher. He had never had one. He learned to write his own name, to recite the ABC's, and to write his name and her name linked together, all in a flourish, without lifting his hand from the paper. When she began to teach at school he sometimes sat on the porch by the open door and listened to her clear voice directing the small children, and he concentrated on what she said, as much for the subject matter (which taught him how to spell chicken, goat, cow, hog) as for the pleasure of hearing her speak. She did not sound at all like Josie and Lorene, who talked like toothless old women from plain indifference. Mem put some attention to what she was saying in it, and some warmth from her own self, and so much concern for the person she was speaking to that it made Brownfield want to cry.

In his own mind he considered himself perfect for Mem, if only because he loved her. But much of the town saw things differently, including Josie and Lorene, who were so jealous of their Cinderella that Brownfield became afraid for her (although he was hardly royalty, unless they considered him Prince Stud). Besides, Mem had never told him she cared for him.

But what really began to bother Brownfield was that since he became the man of the establishment, he had not felt it necessary to draw a salary. He was constantly dependent on Josie or Lorene for money, which they gave him readily enough, but with the understanding that he must work for his living and in exactly the ways they specified. And so he stood it around the house as long as he could, screwing Josie and Lorene like the animal he felt himself to be, especially when he stood next day in the same room with Mem, whose heart, pained, was becoming readable in her eyes. There was no longer any joy in his conquest of the two women, for he had long since realized that *he* wasn't using them, *they* were using him. He was a pawn in a game that Josie and Lorene enjoyed. Sometimes he felt he was the link they used to prove themselves mother and daughter. Otherwise they might have been strangers. They existed for the simple pleasure of flirting with each other's men, and then of fighting it out in the street in front of the lounge, where every man in the district soon learned that if you wanted a piece of pussy you had only to make up to one of them to have the other one fall in your lap.

For a while it was grand being prize pawn; for both women, fast breaking from the strain of liquor, whoredom, moneymaking and battle, thought they truly loved him—but as a clean young animal they had not finished soiling. Their lives infinitely lacked freshness. They were as stale as the two-dollar rooms upstairs. Innocence continued to exist in him for them, since they were not able to see anything wrong in what they did with him. He enjoyed it and after all he was nobody's husband.

And if guilt feeling did exist, as perhaps it did on Sunday mornings in the Baptist church, when they outdressed all the women in town and outshouted half of them, it was a minimal and momentary uneasiness, fanned into a pleasurable passion of repentance by inflamed readings from the Scripture. They shouted out their sins in paroxysms of enjoyable grief. The righteous cleanliness of their souls hardly outlasted the service.

12

MATTERS CAME TO a head for Brownfield when he saw Mem walking for the first time with a man, a teacher like herself. Suddenly he felt he might be passing up a great chance. He felt injured by her choice. Had Mem bypassed him because he was not a well-taught man? His pride was hurt. Gloomily he thought of his poverty and his dependence on Josie and Lorene. All he owned were the clothes on his back and they were none too new.

One night he spied on Mem and her upright, clean-living beau and knew he must have her for his wife. And coming in that night, with him standing in the unlit doorway gazing out at them, Mem brushed past him with tears in her eyes. That was the first time he knew she loved him, and that she was forcing him out of her life by womanly design, and that if he didn't do something soon she would be lost to him. He caught her in his arms as she was going up the stairs and vowed in words and kisses never to let her go.

The next day he went out into the country, to a plantation not far from where he was born, to a man he had heard was fair. They talked of farming on shares for two years, or until Brownfield could make enough money to take his bride northward.

The next week Mem and Brownfield left Josie and Lorene still fighting each other over him, each claiming the other had pushed Mem on to "ketch" him. Brownfield borrowed a wagon from the man he was now working for, and Mem sat beside him on the splintery wooden seat.

"We ain't always going to be stuck down here, honey. Don't you worry," he promised her while she sat quietly, holding her veil in her warm brown hands, and looking and smiling at him with gay believing eyes, full of love.

13

THREE YEARS LATER when he was working the same farm and in debt up to his hatbrim and Mem was big with their second child, he could still look back on their wedding day as the pinnacle of his achievement in extricating himself from evil and the devil and aligning himself with love. Even the shadow of eternal bondage, which plagued him constantly those first years, could not destroy his faith in a choice well made. For Mem was the kind of woman who sang while she cooked breakfast in the morning and sang when getting ready for bed at night. And sang when she nursed her babies, and sang to him when he crawled in weariness and dejection into the warm life-giving circle of her breast. He did not care what anybody thought about it, but she was so good to him, so much what he needed, that her body became his shrine and he kissed it endlessly, shamelessly, lovingly, and celebrated its magic with flowers and dancing; and, as the babies, knowing their places beside her as well as life, sucked and nursed at her bosom, so did he, and grew big and grew firm with love, and grew strong.

They were passionate and careless, he and Mem, making love in the woods after the first leaves fell, making love high in the corncrib to the clucking of hens and the blasting of cocks, making love and babies urgently and with purest fire at the shady ends of cotton rows, when she brought him water to the field and stood watching with that look in her eyes while he drank and leaned an itching palm against the sweaty handle of his plow. As the water, cooling, life-giving, ran down his chin and neck, so did her love run down, bathing him in cool fire and oblivion, bathing him in forgetfulness, as another link in the chain that held him to the land and to a responsibility for her and her children, was forged.

Part III

Part III

14

IT WAS A YEAR when endless sunup to sundown work on fifty rich bottom acres of cotton land and a good crop brought them two diseased shoats for winter meat, some dried potatoes and apples from the boss's cellar, and some cast-off clothes for his children from his boss's family. It was the summer that he watched, that he had to teach, his frail five-year-old daughter the tricky, dangerous and disgusting business of handmopping the cotton bushes with arsenic to keep off boll weevils. His heart had actually started to hurt him, like an ache in the bones, when he watched her swinging the mop, stumbling over the clumps of hard clay, the hot tin bucket full of arsenic making a bloodied scrape against her small short leg. She stumbled and almost fell with her bucket, so much too large for her, and each time he saw it his stomach flinched. She was drenched with sweat, her tattered dress wringing wet with perspiration and arsenic; her large eyes reddened by the poison. She breathed with difficulty through the deadly smell. At the end of the day she trembled and vomited and looked beaten down like a tiny, asthmatic old lady; but she did not complain to her father, as afraid of him as she was of the white boss who occasionally deigned to drive by with friends to watch the lone little pickaninny, so tired she barely saw them, poisoning his cotton.

That pickaninny was Brownfield's oldest child, Daphne, and that year of awakening roused him not from sleep but from hope that someday she would be a fine lady and carry parasols and wear light silks. That was the year he first saw how his own life was becoming a repetition of his father's. He could not save his children from slavery; they did not even belong to him.

His indebtedness depressed him. Year after year the amount he owed continued to climb. He thought of suicide and never forgot it, even in Mem's arms. He prayed for help, for a caring President, for a listening Jesus. He prayed for a decent job in Mem's arms. But like all prayers sent up from there, it turned into another mouth to feed, another body to enslave to pay his debts. He felt himself destined to become no more than overseer, on the white man's plantation, of his own children.

That was the year he accused Mem of being unfaithful to him, of being used by white men, his oppressors; a charge she tearfully and truthfully denied. And when he took her in his drunkenness and in the midst of his own foul accusations she wilted and accepted him in total passivity and blankness, like a church. She was too pure to know how sanctified was his soul by her silence. He determined at such times to treat her like a nigger and a whore, which he knew she was not, and if she made no complaint, to find her guilty. Soft words could not turn away his wrath, they could only condone it.

He was expected to raise himself up on air, which was all that was left over after his work for others. Others who were always within their rights to pay him practically nothing for his labor. He was never able to do more than exist on air; he was never able to build on it, and was never to have any land of his own; and was never able to set his woman up in style, which more than anything else he wanted to do. It was as if the white men said his woman needed no style, deserved no style, and therefore would get no style, and that they would always reserve the right to work the life out of him and to fuck her.

His crushed pride, his battered ego, made him drag Mem away from schoolteaching. Her knowledge reflected badly on a husband who could scarcely read and write. It was his great ignorance that sent her into white homes as a domestic, his need to bring her down to his level! It was his rage at himself, and his life and his world that made him beat her for an imaginary attraction she aroused in other men, crackers, although she was no party to any of it. His rage and his anger and his frustration ruled. His rage could and did blame everything, *everything* on her. And she accepted all his burdens along with her own and dealt with them from her own greater heart and greater knowledge. He did not begrudge her the greater heart, but he could not forgive her the greater knowledge. It put her closer, in power, to *them*, than he could ever be.

His dreams to go North, to see the world, to give Mem even the smallest things she wanted from life died early. And in his depression he saw in his submissive, accepting wife a snare and a pitfall. He returned to Josie for comfort after his "mistake" and for money to pay his rent, leaving Mem to carry on the struggle for domestic survival any way she chose and was able to manage. He moved them about from shack to shack, wherever he could get work. When cotton declined in Georgia and dairying rose, he tried dairying. They lived somehow.

Over the years they reached, what they would have called when they were married, an impossible, and *unbelievable* decline. Brownfield beat his once lovely wife now, regularly, because it made him feel, briefly, good. Every Saturday night he beat her, trying to pin the blame for his failure on her by imprinting it on her face; and she, inevitably, repaid him by becoming a haggard automatous witch, beside whom even Josie looked well-preserved.

The tender woman he married he set out to destroy. And before he destroyed her he was determined to change her. And change her he did. He was her Pygmalion in reverse. The first thing he started on was her speech. They had begun their marriage with her correcting him, but after a very short while this began to wear on him. He could not stand to be belittled at home after coming from a job that required him to respond to all orders from a stooped position. When she kindly replaced an "is" for an "are" he threw her correction in her face.

"Why don't you talk like the *rest* of us poor niggers?" he said to her. "Why do *you* always have to be so damn proper? Whether I says 'is' or 'ain't' ain't no damn humping off *your* butt."

In company he embarrassed her. When she opened her mouth to speak he turned with a bow to their friends, who thankfully spoke a language a man could understand, and said, "Hark, mah *lady* speaks, lets us dumb niggers listen!" Mem would turn ashen with shame, and tried to keep her mouth closed thereafter. But silence was not what Brownfield was after, either. He wanted her to talk, but to talk like what she was, a hopeless nigger woman who got her ass beat every Saturday night. He wanted her to sound like a woman who deserved him.

He could not stand having his men friends imply she was too good for him.

"Man, how did you git hold of that *school*teacher?" they asked him enviously, looking at his bleached and starched clothing and admiring the great quantities of liquor he could drink.

"Give this old blacksnake to her," he said, rubbing himself indecently, exposing his secret life to the streets, "and then I beats her ass. Only way to treat a *nigger* woman!"

For a woman like Mem, who had so barely escaped the "culture of poverty," a slip back into that culture was the easiest thing in the world. First to please her husband, and then because she honestly could not recall her nouns and verbs, her plurals and singulars, Mem began speaking once more in her old dialect. The starch of her speech simply went out of her and what came out of her mouth sagged, just as what had come out of her ancestors sagged. Except that where their speech had been beautiful because it was all they knew and a part of them without thinking about it, hers came out flat and ugly, like a tongue broken and trying to mend itself from desperation.

"Where all them books and things from the schoolhouse?" Brownfield asked one day when he wanted to see if she'd learned her place.

"I done burned 'em up," she said, without turning from a large rat hole she was fixing in the bedroom floor.

For a moment he felt a pang of something bitter, as if he had tasted the bottom of something black and vile, but to cover this feeling he chuckled.

"I were just lookin' for something to start up a fire with."

"Take these here magazines," she said tonelessly, pulling

some battered *True Confessions* from under her dress. She thought he had seen the bulge of them under her arm, but he hadn't. He reached out a hand for them and with a sigh she relinquished all that she had been to all she would become now.

Everything about her he changed, not to suit him, for she had suited him when they were married. He changed her to something he did not want, could not want, and that made it easier for him to treat her in the way he felt she deserved. He had never had sympathy for ugly women. A fellow with an ugly wife can ignore her, he reasoned. It helped when he had to beat her too.

There was a time when she saved every cent she was allowed to keep from her wages as a domestic because she wanted, someday, to buy a house. That was her big dream. When she was teaching school they both had saved pennies to buy the house, but when he was angry and drunk he stole the money and bought a pig from some friends of his who promised him the pig was a registered boar and would be his start in making money as a pig breeder. Mem cried when he came home broke, with the pig. Then the pig died. The second time she saved money to buy the house he used it for the down payment on a little red car. She was furious, but more than furious, unable to comprehend that all her moves upward and toward something of their own would be checked by him. In the end, as with the pig, his luck was bad and the finance company took the car.

The children—there were two living, three had died—did not get anything for Christmas that year. On Christmas Eve they sat around and watched him until he ran out of the house to see if Josie would give him money for a drink. When he got home he woke the children and cried over them, but when he saw they were afraid of him he blamed Mem. When she tried to defend herself by telling him the children were just frightened of him because he was drunk he beat her senseless. That was the first time he knocked out a tooth. He knocked out one and loosened one or two more.

She wanted to leave him, but there was no place to go. She had no one but Josie and Josie despised her. She wrote to her father, whom she had never seen, and he never bothered to answer the letter. From a plump woman she became skinny. To Brownfield she didn't look like a woman at all. Even her wonderful breasts dried up and shrank; her hair fell out and the only good thing he could say for her was that she kept herself clean. He berated her for her cleanliness, but, because it was a small thing, and because at times she did seem to have so little, he did not hit her for it.

"I ain't hurting you none," she said, pleading with something in him he kept almost suppressed, and he let the matter drop.

"Just remember you ain't white," he said, even while hating with all his heart the women he wanted and did not want his wife to imitate. He liked to sling the perfection of white women at her because color was something she could not change and as his own colored skin annoyed him he meant for hers to humble her.

He did not make her ashamed of being black though, no matter what he said. She had a simple view of that part of life. Color was something the ground did to flowers, and that was an end to it.

Being forced to move from one sharecropper's cabin to another was something she hated. She hated the arrogance of the white men who put them out, for one reason or another, without warning or explanation. She hated leaving a home she'd already made and fixed up with her own hands. She hated leaving her flowers, which she always planted whenever she got her hands on flower seeds. Each time she stepped into a new place, with its new, and usually bigger rat holes, she wept. Each time she had to clean cow manure out of a room to make it habitable for her children, she looked as if she had been dealt a death blow. Each time she was forced to live in a house that was enclosed in a pasture with cows and animals eager to eat her flowers before they were planted, she became like a woman walking through a dream, but a woman who had forgotten what it is to wake up. She slogged along, ploddingly, like a cow herself, for the sake of the children. Her mildness became stupor; then her stupor became horror, desolation and, at last, hatred.

Strangely, Brownfield could bear her hatred less than her desolation. In fact, he rather enjoyed her desolation because in it she had no hopes. She was weak, totally without view, without a sky. He was annoyed when she despised him because out of her hatred she fought back, with words, never with blows, and always for the children. But coming from her, even words disrupted the harmony of despair in which they lived.

For Brownfield, moving about at the whim of a white boss was just another example of the fact that his life, as it was destined, had "gone haywire," and he could do nothing about it. He jumped when the crackers said jump, and left his welfare up to them. He no longer had, as his father had maintained, even the desire to run away from them. He had no faith that any other place would be better. He fitted himself to the slot in which he found himself; for fun he poured oil into streams to kill the fish and tickled his vanity by drowning cats.

15

EACH SATURDAY EVENING Brownfield was at the Dew Drop Inn lounge. Josie welcomed him; it was like home. Having been lovers they were now much more. They were comrades. They shared confidences. Lorene had migrated North, and Josie ran the lounge alone, except for two very young and talented girls who had Lorene's old room.

Brownfield and Josie spent a great deal of time talking. About Mem and her self-righteousness, about Brownfield's error in marrying her, and about Josie and her fears and dreams and the cruel tricks fate had played on her. They talked of Josie's driving will to survive and to overcome. Her need to avenge herself on those who wronged her. They talked about Brownfield, about how numb he felt when he allowed himself a fleeting remembrance of his mother. They talked about Margaret and her bastard baby, Star. They talked for hours and hours about Grange.

"Your mammy was a *fool*, boy. Thinkin' she could keep Grange by making him jealous of other mens," Josie's chin shook the slightest bit.

"You tried the same thing," said Brownfield, "in his *absence*. Or do you plan to tell me I got the job here just 'cause you liked my face?"

"Oh, but I weren't *tryin'* to make Grange *jealous*," said Josie.

"No?"

"No." Josie's chin fairly quivered. "I were tryin' to *kill* the son of a bitch!"

For some reason Brownfield laughed. "It wouldn't have killed him, seeing you with me. He never cared no more for me than a stranger."

"You don't understand yet how the thing go, do you?"

"I know enough."

"Ain't you the lucky one, then," said Josie. "Now set down and listen."

Brownfield sat down in a familiar blue chair, facing Josie, who was propped up in bed.

"It was some weeks before *you* come," said Josie, "that me and Grange made all our plans to leave Georgia. We was goin' up to New York. To Harlem, the black folks' city, where we owns *every*thing! Ain't that something? We was goin' to go away and never come back. You may wonder what I was planning to do with Lorene," she said, looking at Brownfield. "Well, just between you and me, I was goin' to *dump* Lorene. She been a chain round my neck long enough. If it hadn't been for her me and your daddy would have *been* together in the first place. Grange and me started goin' to church them weeks he was here. And I want you to know he *promised* me he was goin' to take me with him; and then he sneaked off and I ain't seen him from that day to this one!"

Josie leaned her head back against the pillows, her eyes on

the ceiling. In a minute, in a lower, more careless voice, she continued.

"Oh, Grange and me goes back a long ways. Since *way* before you was born. Way before he even met your mama."

Brownfield was not surprised. He had waited to know this part of his father's life.

"Where you keep yourself all that time?" he asked. "I never heard nobody at home talk about no Josie."

"You remember tellin' me 'bout that fat yellow *bitch* your mammy use to mention?"

"You don't *mean* . . ." said Brownfield, still not very surprised.

"Nobody else but." Josie wore a red silk kimono with blue and purple dragons on the sleeves. She ran a pudgy hand down into the cleavage of her dress.

"Lemme tell you," she said, "Grange never would have married Margaret if he hadn't been pushed into it by his damn 'respectable' family. His African Methodist Episcopal brothers and they mealy-bosomed wives couldn't stand the thoughts of having me in the family; I weren't *good* enough for him. Never mind I built up a establishment with my own hands and figured out how to git rich with my own brain. I still wasn't good enough. Nothing would do the family but that your daddy marry Margaret. The only thing she had that I didn't have was a unused pussy. But it didn't stop me and Grange from being together. He didn't have the heart to leave your mammy outright. But every Saturday evening, by the *clock,* you could find Grange Copeland right where you is now."

"So he come here, and you took . . . *care* of him?" The chair he was sitting in felt uncomfortable. Brownfield got up and paced.

"Yes," said Josie, proudly. "I took care of him, 'cause he was *mine*. I didn't pity your mammy *one* bit."

"Mama was okay," said Brownfield. "At least she put herself out of the way. I wondered why she done it like that. Looked like to me at the time she knowed something I didn't."

"She knowed plenty," Josie sneered. "Knowed she wouldn't do for your daddy what Fat Josie would do. You think she could come up with any idees of how to git Grange out of debt? And with half the men in the county after her tail? The *thought* never crossed her mind! Then, when it *did* strike her, *she forgot to charge!* Shit."

"Well," said Brownfield, embarrassed, "it been ten years almost since he left here. Long enough for me to done run up *on* you, run away *from* you, and run back *to* you." He turned to face her, seeing the new gray hair she had not had time to blacken, seeing the deepened wrinkles everywhere.

"You might as well stop sleepin' with me," he said softly, feeling so grown up and knowledgeable he could hardly bear it. "Grange ain't coming back. If you still want to give him a little shock you got to go all the way up Norse to do it. I ain't no good to you."

Josie read the sickness in his eyes.

"But, *lover*"—she smiled maternally, loosening her robe and coming to hold him—"ain't you found out *yet* that I also likes you for your*self*?"

16

As THE YEARS PASSED, Brownfield got in the habit of thinking of Grange as someone he had never closely known. He didn't refer to him as Father, but as Grange. This made Josie seem not such a burden and lessened the feeling Brownfield often had that Josie had made a fool of him, pretending she cared for him, a boy whose manhood meant only one thing and went easily to his head, when all the time she was eating her heart out for Grange.

He would never forget Josie's face the night Grange returned to Baker County. How fear, self-condemnation, guilt and *joy* flushed through her as she hastily pushed Brownfield away; pushed him away as if he were as odious as a toad, as inconsequential as some kind of harmless lizard. For all her boasting that she wanted to "kill" Grange, she would have spared him that moment if it cost her her life. Brownfield wanted one day to see her damned for that stricken and guilty look on her face.

They had been lolling on the bed, rubbing and feeling each other, Josie in her slip. They were speaking of their insatiable passion for each other, a subject they brought up whenever he became impotent with her. He was often unable, after Mem, to make love to Josie; the thought of Mem and her perpetual tired grayness shriveled him up. He and Josie talked about their passion, about the old days, and Josie made up lies to tell him about Mem. And sometimes, by pretending to believe something nasty about his wife, something lowdown enough to go home and beat her about, he could succeed in making love to Josie. Josie didn't care how she got his passion up, she just wanted it up. With him covering her she released her mind from its memories of betrayals; she forgot the terrors of her recurring dream, and she entered a world of gentleness and contentment. Her face became that of a pure and guileless fat girl; she was innocent, uncomplaining, real.

Even so, Brownfield never really shared sex with Josie, not in the complete, sustaining way he had with Mem. Josie took and he took. She was either stirred to a single-minded vileness, when she swore at him and used foul descriptive words, or she passed into a safe solitude. A solitude to which Brownfield was genuinely happy to send her, for then he thought of his screwing as an act of kindness, and he wanted to be kind. Josie's nightmares, witnessed over the years, had moved him. The least he could do, he thought, was help her sleep.

But that night he had had no chance to help her sleep. Grange, graying, bushy-haired, and lean as a wolf, came through the bedroom door. Curses erupted from Brownfield. His first impulse was to knock his father down. But he realized immediately, and it made him sob, that he was still afraid of him. He might still have been a child from the fear he felt. So instead of fighting his father, Brownfield cursed him and cried and left one of his socks near Josie's bed. Grange stood against the wall near the door gazing from Brownfield to Josie and finally resting his eyes on Josie.

Brownfield put his arms around Josie's neck. His tears dripped onto her bosom. But Josie looked beyond him, over his shoulder; for the final time she pushed him away.

Forgetting about Brownfield, Grange and Josie shut him out. Josie wriggled into a somber wrapper, dabbed at her neck and throat with moist hands, and looked at Grange with eyes that said she'd die on the spot if he wanted her to. As Brownfield staggered away, angry and shaken, heading for a drunk, they hardly moved, frozen by some strange commitment to each other that Brownfield had not even been aware of. They did not fear him, for all his threats. Nor did he seem to matter to them in any way at all. In two weeks Grange and Josie were married.

Part IV

Part IV

17

VERY EARLY on the morning of Ruth's arrival into the world, at about five o'clock in the morning on a gray drizzly Thursday in November, Mem awakened Brownfield and asked him to get the midwife, who lived some eight miles away. Brownfield was sleeping off a drunk and could not rouse himself, although he tried, before seven o'clock, and by then Ruth had popped out by herself. Brownfield woke finally, groggy, with a sense of something new having been added, to find his wife surrounding a small bundle, shivering on the bed. His own cot, nearer to the fire than Mem's bed, blocked the little heat that came from a smoldering hickory log in the fireplace. He was apologetic and sorry for his neglect and tried to make up for it with various cooing pleasantries directed at his small daughter, but Mem was in no mood to have Ruth subjected so soon to the foul after-aromas of puke-smelling brew.

"Git out of my sight," she whispered, turning from him to warm the baby with what heat she could call her own.

It was toward this charged atmosphere that Grange walked, laden with meat, collards, candy and oranges. Brownfield, embarrassed, uneasy and fuzzy, got up and walked out to meet him. Grange was stepping briskly down the road freshly and neatly dressed, bashfully smiling.

"Aw, *Grange*," Brownfield stammered in greeting, as his father came up to the edge of the yard.

Brownfield was angered to see the packages in his father's arms. This intrusion of goods—Grange never set foot in his son's house without a load of eatables and wearables—made Brownfield wish more than ever to see him someday on the rack.

"*You* shouldn't have did that, Grange," he said sheepishly, smiling but gritting his teeth; hating himself for wanting to see what was inside the bundles Grange thrust into his hands. He realized self-pityingly that he was ravenous and hadn't eaten a meal in two days.

"That's all right," Grange mumbled, patiently waiting for his son to lead him into the house. Brownfield sniffed at one of the bags in his hands. It contained fruit, a treat the children would love, another reason for adoring their grandfather. It was only at Christmas that Brownfield's children got apples and oranges and grapes. As a child Brownfield had never seen a grape. He clutched the bags in a confusion of feeling. He was hungry, he was suffering from a malaise of the spirit, he was jealous of his children's good fortune. He wished he did not have children down whose gullets the good fruit would go; he wished he were a child himself.

Brownfield was not as tall as Grange, who had to bend his head to his chest to enter the room where Mem and Brownfield slept. In winter, usually, they all slept in the same room. Brownfield, Mem, Daphne and Ornette; because it was impossible to heat two rooms in such a hole-filled house. It was impossible, really, to heat one room; but when four people slept together in one small room and kept a fire going they could manage not to freeze to death before summer.

To see his wife and children through his father's eyes— knowing of the farm and the snug house Grange and Josie owned—made Brownfield eager for his family to appear warm and happy and well-cared for. One look at the walls of the room they were in made it clear no one could ever be warm in it. The walls had been covered, probably neatly at one time, with paper bags. Bags cut open along one side and flattened out, sides overlapping. But the bags hung down now, here and there, in rustling flaps; the wind had pushed them loose. Where the flaps hung down from the ceiling one could look directly up into the loft and in several places straight through the loft into the sky. In the window frames without panes someone had tried to put in neat square pieces of cardboard, but the rain, coming down against these squares at a slant, made the bottom half of them wet and the same wind that pushed the flaps aside to reveal the holes in the roof forced aside these pieces of cardboard, and puddles of icy water were collected on the bare gray floor.

Grange, as he entered, took in the sorry condition of the room in a glance and could not withhold a sigh. A sigh Brownfield heard and understood immediately as condemnation. Brownfield thought of the money his father had brought back from the North—enough to buy a farm, enough to marry Josie, enough to lend Brownfield some on the condition that he stop drinking!—and thought maybe now was his chance to get more of what his father seemed so willing to give his family. Money. Accordingly, Brownfield whined, "Just poor folks, that's us." He wiped the hardened matter from the corners of his eyes and bade his father sit down on the little cot which was his bed, now that Mem used all of the double one.

Grange looked about him silently. The fire sputtered and went out. Brownfield made no move to relight it. Grange took off his coat and started to work over the fire. He was outraged to find there was no more wood.

"*How* can you not have *wood* and your *wife* 'bout to pop?" he asked.

Brownfield looked over his shoulder at his wife's folded pallet. Not wanting the children to see the blood she had folded it as neatly as a newspaper and had tied it with string. There was a sheet hanging before Mem's bed. It formed a curtain which would have protected her children from the sight of childbirth. Brownfield thought what a blessing it must have been to Mem that the baby was born at night while Daphne and Ornette slept and wind and rain muffled her sounds of struggle.

Brownfield could not, dared not, tell his father that Mem had already had the baby, and without help from him or from anybody. He only hoped his father would soon leave and not try once more to "explain," as he so often tried to do, his reasons for deserting his own family. Grange felt guilty about his son's condition and assuaged his guilt by giving food and money to Brownfield's family. He never gave money directly to Brownfield, who had drunk up the first sum Grange had given him. After that there was no second chance. Grange had no faith in him, Brownfield correctly assumed. But, having laid aside his bundles, Grange was in no mood to leave. He wanted to talk to Mem, see if she needed anything for the baby, whose birth, Grange thought, was so near.

"Why, she *sleep*ing," Brownfield said, hoping his father

would hurry out. But Grange, looking into the fireplace, rubbing his hands, spoke of unimportant things like the weather and then of what was pressing on his heart.

"Like I been trying to tell you, ever since I come back, there's a lot I *done* I didn't *agree* with. It was the times, I reckon. You could work so *hard*, for nothing. And as tight as times was they started tightenin' up some more. I was worked so hard, I tell you the truth, my days had done all run together. There wa'n't no beginning nor no end."

Brownfield stared bitterly at the floor.

"Margaret's days all run together *too*, after *you* left." He said his mother's name thickly, with abundant emotion, though he disliked the memory of her last days as much as ever. Brownfield felt he had been abandoned by Grange's desertion to whatever wolves would take him; not at the time of his leaving, nor while Brownfield was living at the Dew Drop Inn, but in married retrospect, seen through Brownfield's own miserableness in the life he convinced himself he was courageous enough to *accept*. He did not really care what his mother had felt at all.

Grange looked at Brownfield, Brownfield looked at him. Josie's shadow came between them. She kept them from becoming what they had never really been anyhow, father and son. That was her revenge.

"That'll have to be a strong chile to be born in here. And it'll have to be kin to the Eskimos or it'll freeze to death. Well," Grange said, rising finally, "when Mem wake up tell her I'll send Josie over to help out, or maybe I might just come back myself." Grange stood, looking toward the bed. "Lawd knows the *whole* business is somethin' of a miraculous event. Out of all kinds of shit comes something clean, soft and sweet smellin'."

"If you think it so *sweet smellin'*, you *take* it," said Brown-field, seeing his baby with entirely different, unenchanted and closely economic eyes.

Behind the muslin sheet Mem lay, huddled against her baby. The baby, unwashed, was moist and sticky against the soft cloth that was wrapped around her. Mem had been dry-ing the film of wetness from her when Grange came in. Fear-ing the sharpness of the cold she stopped, and now, instead, rubbed the baby softly up and down its hardly moving body. The window near her bed let in sporadic bursts of damp air. In the middle of the night she had asked Brownfield to cover it with a quilt, but the only quilt he could use, he said, was the one on his bed, or the one on hers.

The wind came through the window, moving the newspa-pers under the bed. Weakly Mem called out to her husband.

"What you say you want, honey?" he asked, coming to peer at her from around the curtain. Grange also came. Mem heard the intake of Grange's breath as he stood beside Brown-field, looking down on her, seeing the bundle, rooted in disbelief.

"You no-good, *sorry,* good-for-nothing *tramp,*" he said, pushing Brownfield aside and impatiently bending to move Mem's bed closer to the fire.

"It won't move," said Mem, glancing fearfully at her hus-band. "It just set up on some blocks."

Her eyes were sunken and hazy from her long night. Meekly her eyes pleaded with Grange to go away, to leave them alone. She watched him anxiously as he moved about the room, burning the pallet, which, made of newspapers and old clean rags, burned well, despite its spots of slimed wet, and then taking out the slop jar that was so filled with the proof of how her night was spent.

Grange took down the makeshift curtain, ordered Brownfield to make up his bed and go out for wood, and prepared the baby for the eyes of her two sisters.

"I'm all right, I'm just fine," Mem said, when Grange reached for the thin quilted covers of her bed.

With a great show of control, Grange took the wood Brownfield brought in and put it on the fire. Thankfully he watched it begin to burn.

"At least you got sense enough to know wet wood won't burn," he said. Brownfield stood at his elbow with an amused and belligerent smirk.

"Got it off the barn," he said.

"Brownfield, git me a little warm water to drink or maybe a little coffee," said Mem. Grange had raised her head and placed his own coat across her shoulders.

Grange had always liked Mem. He had known her when she was a child, playing behind the lounge. Lorene was always making her cry and run and hide in the woods. Grange had been glad when Josie told him that Brownfield had married her. He thought a good wife would mellow Brownfield, even if she was kin to Josie. Though Mem had none of Josie's hardness.

On the night he had returned to the Dew Drop Inn and found Josie with Brownfield he discovered the bitterness his son felt toward him, the resentment, the hate; but he had hoped Brownfield's own experience as a family man and sharecropper would change that. But now, looking at Mem after eight years with Brownfield was like seeing some old mangy aunt of the girl Brownfield had married. Mem's hair, which had been so thick and black, now pressed against her pillow gray as charcoal. Much of it had fallen out. Grange felt, among all the other reasons for her being laid so low, his own guilt. That was why he spent so much time with her and his grandchildren, and brought them meat and vegetables, and gave them money on the sly, and reaped in full the anger of his wife and the unflagging bitterness of his son.

Brownfield was handing Mem a cup of barely warm coffee.

"I know that's what she asked for," said Grange, "but surely there's somethin' to *eat* in this house. I mean like some *soup* or something."

Brownfield walked calmly to the door, his face set, and tossed the coffee out into the yard.

"I give her what she ask for, what more you want?" He sat down solidly in front of the fire, not willing now to give her anything. His face was as sulky as a child's.

From the provisions he'd brought Grange made a stew. When Daphne and Ornette crawled out of their damp covers in the next room it was to the hot spicy smell of the stew and to the warming leaps of a good fire. At first Brownfield would not touch the stew. He grudgingly watched his children fall all over their grandfather. Soon, though, he began to eat, his hunger caring nothing for his pride.

"My trouble is," he told his father, "I always *could* do *without* childrens." He watched Daphne and Ornette take turns examining the baby's tiny fists. "I didn't like having to baby-sit that brat *you all* dumped on me." Brownfield looked his father in the eye.

"I never liked my brother—you know that—'cause *you* didn't like him neither. I seen you pinch him when you thought nobody was looking. Looks like back then the whole *business* just about made you puke—takin' care of Margaret's bastard, and *me* too."

Grange hung his head and endured in silence.

18

To his three daughters Brownfield gave the dregs of his attention only when he was half drunk. To him they were not really human children, although his heart at times broke for them. He could not see them as innocent or even as children. He scolded Ornette, who had come a year after Daphne, with the language he would use on a whore. And the baby, Ruth, he never touched.

As they grew older, Daphne, the only one who could remember the scanty "good old days" before Brownfield began to despise them, took the baby and Ornette out under the trees and told them of how good a daddy Brownfield had once been. Brownfield overheard her whispering her stories into the baby's ear, as if she wanted her little sister to grow up believing that the few greedily cherished good times with Brownfield had also been her own.

Part V

Part V

19

BROWNFIELD DID NOT believe Mem would be able to find a house. He had not found a decent house the first and only time he had looked for one. What was more, he did not believe she had been looking for one.

"You get through telling all them old dried-up friends of yours that I just got kicked out on my ass and you already out looking for a *mansion* to live in—for a change?"

He reached out an arm and grabbed her quickly around one wrist.

"Ow, Brownfield," she said, dropping her shoes.

"I ought to make you call me Mister," he said, slowly twisting the wrist he held and bringing her to her knees beside his feet. "A woman as black and ugly as you ought to call a man Mister."

"I didn't find no house today," she whimpered dryly, because she was so tired and her feet hurt. "And I didn't see *no-body* but people that was renting."

He shoved her and she knocked over her flower boxes, spilling flowers and dirt. She scrambled shakily to her knees, then to her blistered and callused feet, sniffling and putting a wrinkled hard hand to her head. Her daughters stood at the battered screen watching, their baby sister in their arms.

We ought to jump on him and kill him dead, Mem thought, as she avoided her children's eyes, took the baby, Ruth, into her arms, and went into the house.

"Goddam rib-ridden *plow*horse," Brownfield muttered spitefully, propping his legs against the rotten railing of his sagging front porch.

20

AT THE END of the second feeding, when he was putting the scoops back into the feed bags, Captain Davis came in and stood in the doorway chewing and spitting, acting half-interested in what Brownfield was doing and half-interested in emphasizing that he owned the cows and the barn and everything else in sight. He just stood there, with his shirt sleeves pinned up and his bald head mottled, being boss man.

"I told Mr. J. L. you was going to be looking for a place right soon," he said. He turned his head down at a slant and watched Brownfield tie up the feed bags. His lips pursed tightly when a few grains of feed spilled on the concrete.

"I told him he could probably do worse than you if he's in the market for a field and dairyman."

Brownfield's hands stopped momentarily tying the bags. "Yassur?"

He made as if to straighten all the way up but managed to stand stooped a little so that he felt small and black and bug-like, and Captain Davis, with his sparse white hair, seemed a white giant that could step on him.

"Yassur?" he said again, while Captain Davis's eyes swept the ceiling and roamed over the rumps of his cows. Slowly.

Damned one-arm son of a bitch, Brownfield thought, as he stooped motionless, looking up at the tall white man and waiting to shift his eyes the moment the captain turned his face to him.

Why don't he say what he going to say, 'stead of acting like I got all goddam *day* to hear 'bout his slave-driving son. Let him get his own motherfucking help 'stead of trading *me* off! As the captain turned, Brownfield averted his eyes. A vacant obliging smile wavered on his face.

"'Course you won't be living as easy as you do here," Captain Davis said as his eyes came down to the level of Brownfield's and Brownfield dropped his own, being careful to maintain a smile that was both alert and respectful.

"You interested in this, Brown?" the old man asked, clearing his throat and spitting between them, not bothering to turn his head. "I already told Mr. J. L. you was."

"Yassur!" Brownfield said, taking out a large print handkerchief and wiping his hands. Paying special attention to between the fingers. He thought about what Mr. J. L. was like; stingy and mean, not to be trusted around black womenfolk, and shuddered. He did not want to work for him. He remembered how he and Mem had come to work for Captain Davis. Captain Davis's brother had sent them after he had finished with Brownfield and his wife had died and there was no further need for Mem. In return Captain Davis had let his tractor go for a season. The swap had been made exactly as if he and his family were a string of workhorses.

"I be much obliged to you for putting in a word for me." Brownfield nodded up and down still smiling but with his eyes carefully averted. He thought about turning down the offer but when the words of refusal came to his lips he found they would not come out. He cleared his throat and prodded the ground in front of him with his foot as if he would speak, but no words came out, only a hesitant grunt that sounded like further strangled acceptance.

"What you say, Brown?" Captain Davis asked in impatiently severe tones. He turned his tall frame in the doorway so that the sun made a halo of his thin ring of white hair. Looking for a brief second into his light blue eyes Brownfield stood speechless.

"Yassur," he said finally, hypnotized by the old man standing in the sun.

Captain Davis shrugged his gaunt white shoulders and walked away toward his white house with the bright red chimneys.

Pity how you got to look after 'em, he thought, as he wrapped his good hand round his stub.

21

HE WAS LATE and had not told her he would be; still they had not dared to begin supper without him. Daphne was looking at a page full of bathroom fixtures, staring nearly cross-eyed in the light of the kerosene lamp that hung from a cord over the table.

"Is this the kinder toilet we going to have, Ma?" Ornette asked, looking dazzled over Daphne's sharp elbow at all the sparkling fixtures.

"Look at them shiny *toilets*!" she whispered urgently, her spread fingers touching four commodes, excitement making her voice rough and burpy. Daphne nudged her playfully with the elbow she kept between the Sears, Roebuck catalogue and her sister.

"Why don't you get on out the way, girl!" she said, and tried to hog the book, but Ornette clamped a grubby fist on a corner of the book, covering, except for a bright corner, a deep white bathtub filled with greenish blue water like that in the white swimming pool in town.

Mem, her knees spread under the table and her battered

hungry face cracking every once in a while in a grin, supervised the turning of the pages.

"Wait a minute, Daphne, I ain't through looking at these sinks and dishracks!" she said sharply, when Daphne wanted to race on ahead to the warming glowing pictures of multicolored light bulbs and fancy lamps.

"Is us going to have 'lectric lights in our new house?" Ornette asked breathlessly, caressing the slick pages of the catalogue. The yellow glow of the lamp encircled Mem and her homely children in soft kindly light, making them look good to one another. The baby, Ruth, too small to be interested in home furnishings, gurgled and cooed in her box by the stove. In vain did she compete for her mother's attention.

"I ain't promising nothing," Mem said, laughing at Ornette's big serious eyes and running one rough hand over her head. "I ain't saying what's going to be," she continued, "but the Lord *wills* we going to have 'em!" She said the last flatly, almost to herself, hearing the back door open and shut and feeling the draft caused by Brownfield's entry and seeing the lamp flicker and almost go out.

"Why ain't supper on the table?" Brownfield demanded as soon as he walked in.

"We didn't know *when* you was coming, Brownfield," Mem said softly, pulling herself out of her chair so fast she scraped her bony knees. Meekly she hovered over the stove stirring and taking up peas and ham hocks. She placed a heaping plate in front of Brownfield and backed into the stove, getting food for herself and the children. Brownfield saw she had burned herself turning around clumsily, and he smiled as he plowed into his peas, sending them scattering across the table, down his shirt front, and down his throat.

Ornette sat dazed, watching her father pick up his meat

with his hands and tear at it, sending the juice flying over the tablecloth Mem was proud to make white. When her father was eating Ornette could not think of him as anything but a hog. She blinked her eyes as he said to her over a mouthful of peas and bread, "What you looking at me for?"

Her eyes quickly riveted to her own plate and she began slowly to eat, trying very hard not to hear the whistling noise her father made as he sucked at the meat and gobbled the peas.

Mem ate with her head down, passing the food up to her husband the moment she thought he might like some more. Daphne sat completely squelched, nervously chewing and beading her dress under the table, as close to her mother's side as possible. She hallucinated vividly that Brownfield ate so many peas he swoll up and burst. She saw herself helping gleefully to bury him and then watched in horror as the huge twisting and congested pea vines began to come up. Aloud, she began a strange blank-eyed whimper.

"What's the matter with *you, stupid*?" Her father's eyes were on her, intense and hard, like the eyes of a big rat.

I wish he'd get swoll up and die! she thought behind her alerted but sad and empty face. I wish he'd just *do* that for us so we could *bury* him!

"What's this I hear about some *new* house?" Brownfield asked, finally, chewing noisily and sweating from eating so vigorously. He grunted slyly as if choking back a laugh. "We going to move over on Mr. J. L.'s place."

He was pleased to feel the weight of their tense and silent response.

"I ain't," Mem said. "I ain't, and these children ain't." She stiffened her thin tough neck for his blow. But he only laughed and kept eating, stabbing at stray peas with round wads of cornbread.

"Get me some water," he grunted to Ornette, who pretended she was fetching slop for a hog.

"Yassur," she mumbled with her head down, going to the icebox.

"You should have got some ice from the iceman yesterday," Mem said, smelling the reek from the box.

"You ought to have stayed at home yesterday instead of traipsing off all over creation looking for a mansion to live in. If you acted like a woman with some sense we'd a had ice." He rolled his eyes to indicate her foolishness and coughed in her face without turning his head.

A shiver of revulsion ran through his wife. "He's just like a old dog," she thought, guiltily urging her nervous children to eat their fill.

He had once been a handsome man, slender and tall with narrow, beautiful hands. From trying to see in kerosene lamplight his once clear eyes were now red-veined and yellowed, with a permanent squint. From running after white folks' cows, he never tended much to his own, when he had any, and he'd developed severe athlete's foot that caused him to limp when the weather was hot or wet. From working in fields and with cows in all kinds of weather he developed a serious bronchitis aggravated by rashes and allergies.

He was not a healthy man. When he first started working with cows his hands broke out and the skin itched so that he almost scratched it off. It was only after years of working every day milking cows that the itch gave up, and by then his hands were like gray leather on the outside, the inside scaly and softly cracked, too deformed for any work except that done to and for animals. The harder and more unfeeling the elephant-hide skin on his hands became the more often he planted his fists against his wife's head.

I ain't never going to marry nobody like him, Daphne swore to herself, watching the big ugly hands that smelled always of cows and sour milk.

"It's all settled," said Brownfield, belching loudly and digging under the table between his legs. "We going to move over to Mr. J. L.'s come next Monday and," he spoke menacingly to Mem, "I don't want any lip from you!"

"I already told you," she said, "you ain't dragging me and these children through no more pigpens. We have put up with mud long enough. I want Daphne to be a young lady where there is other decent folks around, not out here in the sticks on some white man's property like in slavery times. I want Ornette to have a chance at a decent school. And little baby Ruth," she said wistfully, "I don't even want her to *know* there's such a thing as outdoor toilets."

"You better git all that foolishness out your head before I knock it out!"

"I ain't scared of you," his wife lied.

"When the time comes, you'll see what you do, Miss Ugly," he said, and pinched her tense worn cheek. Even as he did it he knew dull impossible visions of a time when that cheek was warm and smoothly rounded, highlighted and sleek. It was rare now when it curved itself in a smile.

"Me and these children got a *right* to live in a house where it don't rain and there's no holes in the floor," she said, snatching her cheek away. From long wrestles in the night he knew she despised his hands. He held one gigantic hand in front of her eyes so she could see it and smell it, then rammed it clawingly down her dress front.

If I was a man, she thought, frowning later, scrubbing the dishes, if I was a man I'd give every man in sight and that I ever met up with a beating, maybe even chop up a few with my knife, they so pig-headed and mean.

22

"'EVENING, BROWN," she said solemnly the following after-noon, Wednesday.

"'Evening, Ugly," Brownfield said, crossing the porch and eying her with suspicion. He detected a sad meager smile be-ginning to work itself across her broad lips. The sun across her hair made him notice how nearly gray it was. She was hanging there in the doorway, her ugly face straining between deep solemnity and sudden merriment. It had been years since he'd seen her look anything near this excited.

"What you turning that idiot look on me for?" he asked, facing her, his hand on the screen door. He had never despised her as much. Was she looking like she was going to be this ugly when I married her? he asked himself, as the face in front of him spread itself out in a funny-shaped pie and Mem laughed soft and deep, as she used to laugh when they were first married and not one day passed without some word of deepest love.

"We got us a new house," she said, as if she were drop-ping something precious that would send up delightful bright

explosions. "We got us a new house in *town*!" she whispered
joyously.

He looked around to see the children also with wide
spreading mouths, looking just like their mother.

"I know we got a new house," he said patiently, "but it's
going to be over on Mr. J. L.'s place, and nowhere else!"

"Oh, nooo," she said gaily, still laughing in her rough,
unused-to-laughing way. "This house has got sinks and a toilet inside the house and it's got 'lectric lights and even garden
space for flowers and greens. You told me yourself," she said,
laughing harder than ever, "that old man J. L.'s place done fell
down on one side and is anyhow all full of hay." Talking
about the house seemed to make her dizzy. She fell into a
chair, placing her hands to her eyes as if to clear her head.
"Besides," she said, suddenly sobered, "it don't cost but
twenty dollars a month to rent and you can make enough at
a factory in town to pay that much: factory work'll keep you
out of the *rain*. A school is close by for the children and the
neighbors look like nice people. And on top of that . . ." She
started to list assets of the house again. Her eyes lit up, then
went dull and tired. She had spent all day looking for the
house. "Besides all them things," she said tonelessly, and resigned as she stood up, "I told the man we'd be there to start
living in that house Monday morning. I signed the lease."

"You *signed* the lease?" He was furious. He could not,
even after she'd tried to teach him, read or write. It had gone
in with the courting and out with the marriage. "I ought to
chop your goddam fingers off!"

"I'm real sorry about it, Brownfield," said Mem, whose
decision to let him be man of the house for nine years had cost
her and him nine years of unrelenting misery. He had never
admitted to her that he couldn't read well enough to sign a

lease and she had been content to let him keep that small grain of pride. But now he was old and sick beyond his years and she had grown old and evil, wishing every day he'd just fall down and die. Her generosity had shackled them both.

"*Some*body had to sign the lease, Brownfield," she said gently, looking up into his angry eyes. "I just done got sick and tired of being dragged around from dump to dump, traded off by white folks like I'm a piece of machinery." She straightened her shoulders and drew her children to her side, the baby, Ruth, in her arms. "You just tell that old white bastard—Stop up Your Ears, Children!—that we can make our own arrangements. We might be poor and black, but we ain't dumb." There was a pause. "At least *I* ain't," she said cruelly, burying her face in her baby's hair.

"I guess you know that up there in town you wouldn't be able to just go out in the field when you're hungry and full up a sack with stuff to eat. I hope you know what you doing too, going out there pulling up all the greens and things just when we leaving the place."

"They sell food in the grocery stores there in town," said Mem, not slackening her work. "And I planted these greens myself and worked them myself, and I be damn if I'm going to let some sad-headed old cracker that don't care if I starve scare me out of taking them!"

"If you had any sense you'd know it don't look right," said Brownfield, raising himself up on an elbow. "Here we is moving off to Mr. J. L.'s place next Monday and you goes out and strips the fields on Thursday." He turned his gaze on her callused feet. "My ma always told me not to git myself mixed up with no ugly colored woman that ain't got no sense of pro*pridy*."

"I reckon if your ma was black, Brownfield," Mem said, putting a hand on her hip, "she found out a long *time* ago that you can't *eat* none of that."

"You don't surely think that I intends to move to town," Brownfield said slowly, turning his back as if he were about to fall off to sleep. He smiled at the wall. "I'm a *man,* and I don't intend working in *no*body's damn factory."

Daphne and Ornette looked at their parents through a sudden darkening blur. They came and stood in the kitchen door behind their mother, silently watching.

"You hear that, Woman!" Brownfield swung up and placed his feet with a stamp on the floor. "We moving exactly when and where I say we moving. Long as I'm supporting this fucking family we go where I says go." He bullied his thin wife murderously with his muddy eyes. "I may not be able to read and write but I'm still the man that wears the pants in this outfit!" He towered over her in a rage, his spittle spraying her forehead.

I don't have to stand here and let this nigger spit in my face, she thought more or less calmly, and for the first time very seriously. Who the hell he think he is, the President or somethin'.

"You do what you want to, Brownfield," she said, swiftly stepping out of range of his fist. "You do exactly what you want and go precisely where you please. But me and these children going to live in that house I leased. We ain't living in no more dog patches; we going to have toilets and baths and 'lectric lights like other people!"

"I reckon you think you ain't going to need somebody to *pay* for all them toilets and baths and 'lectric lights, you chewed-up-looking bitch!" Brownfield broke past his defensive children and grabbed Mem by the shoulder, spinning her round.

"Let me tell you something, man," Mem said evenly, though breathing hard, "I have worked hard all my life, first trying to be something and then just trying to be. It's over for me now, but if you think I won't work harder than ever before to support these children you ain't only mean and evil and lazy as the devil, but you're a fool!"

"Who the hell you think'd hire a snaggle-toothed old *plow mule* like you?" He was sweating and felt his hands beginning to itch. "You ought to look in the glass sometime," he said, clenching his fists. "You ain't just ugly and beat-up looking, you's old!"

I ain't thirty, she wanted to say, but instead she said, "I know what I look like and I know how old I am." It seemed impossible that she could face him and not weep. "And neither one of them knowledges is going to keep me from getting me a job so we can move on in that house Monday morning."

"I'd like to see you *try*, Bitch," he cried on his way out, shoving her and pushing against his daughters. Ruth woke from her nap with a yowl from the noise. Mem dried her and lifted her high along her shoulder.

"And this one is going to grow *up* in 'lectricity and gas heat!" she said tremblingly, giving her baby small tearful kisses all around her fuzzy head.

23

"HOW'S MEM?" Captain Davis asked pleasantly Friday noon when Brownfield was on his way home for lunch. "How she feel about moving over to Mr. J. L.'s? I told J. L.'s wife about her shortbread. Ummm Um," he said magnanimously, "she sure can cook!"

"Oh, she fine!" Brownfield said with enthusiasm. "She fine, and she all ready for the big move over to Mr. J. L.'s." He could not breathe normally and felt black and greasy under the man's cool gaze.

Ought to pick up a rock and beat it into his old bald head that hell naw me and Mem don't want to go work for his crazy motherfucking son! What the hell he think, we both of us crazy or somethin'! He smiled broadly at Captain Davis and clasped his hands together behind his back. His knees under his overalls leaned shakily against each other.

"We both right sure it going to work out fine," he said hopelessly, making his face as pleasant as possible and bland, "just fine."

"See you do your work good," the old man said sharply, clearing his throat and turning in the direction of his house. "You and Mem ain't bad hands," he said almost as an after-thought. "Glad to be keeping you in the family!"

But this is 1944! Brownfield wanted to scream; instead he said "Yassur," and waited until Captain Davis was three yards away before he moved. "I ought to stick my feed knife up in him to the gizzard!" he whispered, nervous sweat running down his sides. He walked home slowly, kicking rocks and bushes.

24

"BROWNFIELD, I GOT me a job in town," Mem said, sitting herself down on the porch railing and dangling her hard skinny legs. Brownfield sat in silence; behind his head he could feel the two children standing there hiding big grins behind their eager apish faces.

"I got me a job in town that pays twelve dollars a week!" Mem spoke softly but with excitement in her voice. She said it like a bird might talk about first flying.

He continued to say nothing, but his hands gripped the bottom of his chair so hard his fingers ached.

"Twelve dollars a week is more than *you* makes, ain't it, Brownfield?" asked Mem, who had never been told her husband's wages. Her ugly mouth crinkled happily at the corners. Slowly she let the crinkling go and watched him silently for a while. Her children came to stand beside her, all of them looking at Brownfield.

"You coming with us or no?" she asked, without much caring in her voice. "If you is," she went on, "you got to get a job and pull your weight. If you ain't, we going on ahead anyhow."

They left him sitting there with his feet up on the railing, looking every one of his relatively few sick old years, with another dozen added on.

25

SATURDAY NIGHT FOUND Brownfield, as usual, liberally prepared for his weekly fight with Mem. He stumbled home full
of whiskey, cursing at the top of his voice. Mem lay with her
face to the wall pretending to be asleep.

"You think you better than me," he cried. "Don't you?
DON'T YOU! You ugly pig!" He reached beneath the bedclothes
to grab her stiffly resistant shoulder.

"You wake up and *look* at me when I talk to you!" he said,
slurring the words, bending close enough to kiss her with his
foul whiskey-soaked mouth.

"You and them goddam sad-looking high and mighty
brats of yours, that you done turned against me!" He said the
last with an angry sob in his throat. As if he cared. Mem said
nothing, lay so silent it was as if she were not breathing
or thinking or even being, but her tired eyes rested directly
on him with the tense heated waiting that many years of
Saturday-night beatings had brought.

"I'm sick and tired of this mess," she said, rising abruptly,
waiting for the first blow to head or side or breasts. "Shit!" she

said, flinging the covers back, looking frail as a wire in her shabby nightgown. "I'm sick of *you!*"

No sooner had the words fallen out in a little explosive heap than Brownfield's big elephant-hide fist hit her square in the mouth.

"Don't you interrupt me when I'm doing the talking, Bitch!" he said, shaking her until blood dribbled from her stinging lips. The one blow had reduced her to nothing; she just hung there from his hands until he finished giving her half-a-dozen slaps, then she just fell down limp like she always did.

"You going to move where I says move, you *hear* me?" Brownfield yelled at her, giving her a kick in the side with his foot. "We going to move to Mr. J. L.'s place or we ain't going nowhere at all!" He was hysterical. Mem lay with her eyes closed.

"You listening to me, Bitch!" Mem opened her eyes like someone opening up the lid of a coffin. "I ain't *going* to Mr. J. L.'s place," she said quietly. "I done told you that, Brownfield." Hesitantly she moved her hand up to wipe blood from her chin. "I have just about let you play man long enough to find out you ain't one," she said slowly and more quietly still. "You can beat me to death and I still ain't going to say I'm going with you!"

"You goddam wrankly faced black nigger slut!" Brownfield said, beside himself. "You say one more word, just one more little goddam *peep* and I'll cut your goddam throat!" He fumbled in his pocket for his knife and reached down and grabbed Mem in a loose drunken hug. Mem closed her eyes as he dropped her abruptly against the bedpost and gave her a resounding kick in the side of the head. She saw a number of blurred pale stars, then nothing else.

In the next room, with tears trickling so slowly they made them want to sneeze, Daphne and Ornette held their trembling skinny arms around each other and licked their warm red tongues over each other's salty homely eyes and wished nothing so hard as that their father would trip over his own stumbling feet, fall on his open knife and manage somehow to jab his heart out.

There was a restless whimper from Ruth. "You reckon he going to come in here?" Ornette asked her sister, thinking of ways to run and also of ways to be a man and protect her.

"He come in here," Daphne whispered with a grown-up coldness in her voice, "he come in here, you let him grab you for a minute while I run in the kitchen and get the butcher knife." She ran her tongue carefully down her sister's cheeks tracing her tears. "If by time I get back he done hit you just one time—I'm going to cut his stanking *guts* out!"

Huddled there under the bed they heard the birds begin chirping at dawn. They fell asleep dreaming in chilly exactness of killing that would set them free.

Brownfield did not dream. He just dropped out of his mind, and the late Sunday morning sun stabbed at his eyelids as if it were a gangman's pickax. Stretching his body, he felt he had been undressed. He spread his body leisurely over the bed and reached out a hand to grab his woman for the morning.

"*Open your eyes!*" Mem's voice was as even as a dammed-up river. Slowly he stopped turning and opened his eyes, squinting them stickily to keep out the light. Mem was propped up against the wall on her side of the bed, holding a shotgun. At first he saw only the handle, smooth and black and big, close to his head like that. One of Mem's long wrinkled fingers pressed against the trigger. He made a jump, half toward her, half away from her. He felt a sharp jab on his body down below the covers, the shooting pain caused him to wince and thrash on the bed.

"Don't you move a inch," Mem said lazily, controlling the cool hard gun barrel down between his thighs. He broke out in a quick cold sweat, and his eyes rambled frantically and dizzyingly over the room.

"*What's the matter with you, Mem?*" he asked hoarsely, his mouth tasting like somebody'd died up in it. Weeks ago. "What in the Lawd's name is troubling you this Sunday morning?" He looked around the room. "Where is the children, Woman?" he asked, expecting to see them. "Ain't you got no sense of what's decent?" Mem began to chuckle low in her throat. Oh, my Lawd, Brownfield thought, and began to tremble underneath the sheet, that kick in the head I give her last night done run her crazy! Mem gave a light jab at him with the gun, her whole hand wrapped around the stock. Brownfield cried out in pain and moved his big thick hands slowly downward.

"You move one more one hundred per cent of a half of a *half* inch," Mem said, putting her other hand lower down on the gun, "you move just a teeny weeny little bit more *Mr.* Brownfield, and you ain't going to have nary a ball left to play catch with."

"Aw, Mem." He began to whine. "Honey, you ain't got no cause . . ."

"Shet up," Mem said, staring at him with purple-circled eyes. "The children is out to church for the day. They grandpa came by and I even let him take the baby. Ain't nobody here but us chickens. Ain't nobody round to know or care whether one of us gits fried."

"Oh, Lawd," Brownfield began to moan in prayer.

"Call on the one you serves, boy!" Mem said, chuckling dryly at his terror. "Call on the one you serves."

Brownfield thought irresistibly of Captain Davis; the tall old cracker just popped into his mind like he was God or somebody.

"Captain Davis won't let you git away with nothing." He began to babble and to throw up.

"Don't you let none of that mess drop on this bed!" Mem said when she saw his hand going to his mouth. He leaned his head over the side of the bed and let it all out on the floor. He was a long time vomiting the dead-smelling stuff and fell back worn out and weak. He almost forgot Mem and the gun, his head was spinning so.

"Now you can just git on down there with it," Mem said, wrinkling her nose from the smell. "I don't want you laying up here with me! Go on, git down there!" she said, jabbing him again with the gun. Brownfield slid down onto the floor, slipping on the rotten vomit and falling wetly on his naked behind on the outskirts of the stagnant yellow pool. He'd never felt this sick in his life. Mem watched him from the bed with a cold and level eye. She uncovered the full length of the big gun and pointed it where she had before. Brownfield lay back for a moment, then quickly crouched over his groin, shielding himself from her. She was grinning mirthlessly. Like a skinny balding gorilla, he thought.

"To think I put myself to the trouble of wanting to git married to you," she said. "And to think that I put myself to the trouble of having all these babies for you and you didn't even go out but once to git the midwife, *you was too drunk* or the weather was too *cold!*" Her left hand stroked the long barrel of the gun.

"You reckon Captain Davis really would give a good

goddam if I shot you, Brownfield?" she asked. "What you reckon he'd *say*? Now Mem, I bet he would say, whoever heard of anybody going around shooting somebody else's *balls* off? Why, you *colored* people—you never heard tell of any *white* people going around shooting each other's balls off. Shame! Shame! He'd be thinking, *I always said niggers is crazy*! And this here Mem Copeland proves me right, going around shooting her husband's balls off, for Lawd's sake. 'Course, he'd go on, spitting on the ground like he created the dirt himself, far as I'm concerned with that Brownfield Copeland, I never knowed he *had* any!" Mem carried on her talk with her eyes opening and almost shutting like she'd seen Captain Davis do when he didn't want to look at her or Brownfield. Which was every time he had to talk to them.

"Nobody ever give a shit about you but me, you mean old fool! Don't you know that yet!"

"You ugly black hound!" Brownfield whispered weakly, trying to pull himself back in control. Mem swung the stock of the gun with both hands and laid a gash an inch wide right across his forehead. Dark red blood began dripping down over Brownfield's naked stomach, trickling down on the floor, making the weathered floorboards deep red and yellow. He began to cry.

"Long as you live—and that won't be long the rate you going—don't never call me 'out my name!" Mem sat calmly, watching the blood drip. "To think I let you drag me round from one corncrib to another just cause I didn't want to hurt your feelings," she said softly, almost in amazement. "And just think of how many times I done got my head beat by you just so you could feel a little bit like a man, Brownfield Copeland." She squinted her eyes almost shut staring at him.

"And just think how much like an old no-count *dog* you done treated me for nine years." She tightened her grip on the gun. Brownfield's body began to tremble in deep convulsive shudders. "Woman ugly as you ought to call a man Mister, you been telling me since you *beat* the ugly into me!" his wife said, and moaned.

"Mem," he whined, assuming weakness from her altered face, "you know how hard it is to be a black man down here." Tears and blood and vomit ran together down his shaking legs. "You knows I never wanted to be nothing but a man! Mem, baby, the white folks just don't let nobody *feel* like doing right."

"You can't stand up to them is what you mean, ain't it?" asked Mem, regaining her composure and propping up her chin with her right palm, holding the gun in her left hand. "Look at you now, crying like a little baby that's going to be whipped for peeing in his pants."

"Lawd, Mem, you knows how hard I try to do the right thing. I don't make much money, you knows that. And the white folks don't give us no decent houses to live in, you knows that. What can a man *do*?" he asked, holding his head up like a whipped hound. "What can a man do!"—planning to reach up and snatch the gun. Mem put both hands back on the gunstock and crossed her bony knees.

"He can quit wailing like a old seedy jackass!" she said, hitting him over the head with the gun. Brownfield skidded in the mess on the floor and lay too weak to move.

"The thing I done noticed about you a long time ago is that you acts like you is right where you belongs. *All* the time!" She climbed from the bed and stood on the floor at his feet.

"Now I'm going to say this here just one more time; I realize at last that you is just a weezy little bit hard at understanding anything. But you best to git this straight. Me and
my children is moving to town to the house I signed that lease
on. We is moving in with you or without you." She kicked a
clean spot on his limp left leg. "You hear me, boy?" Brownfield groaned and nodded his head.

Serves me right for gitting mixed up with a crazy woman!
he thought weakly, feeling pain shoot through the calf of his
leg.

"If you intend to come along I done made out me some
rules for you, for make no mistake it's going to be my house
and in my house what the white man expects us to act like
ain't going to git no consideration! Now, first off you going to
call me Mem, Mrs. Copeland, or *Mrs. Mem R. Copeland*. Take
your pick. And second, you is going to call our children
Daphne, Ornette and baby Ruth. Although you can call any
one of them 'honey' if you got a mind to. Third, if you ever
lays a hand on me again I'm going to blow your goddam
brains out—after I shoots off your balls, which is all the
manhood you act like you *sure* you got. Fourth, you tetch a
hair on one of my children's heads and I'm going to crucify
you—stick a blade in you, just like they did the Lawd; if it
was good enough for him it's good enough for you. Fifth, you
going to learn to eat your meals like a gentleman, you ain't
going to eat like no pig at my table. You going to use spoons
and knifes and forks like everybody else that got some sense.
Sixth, I don't care about your whoring round town, but don't
you never wake me up on Sunday morning grabbing on me
when you been out all Saturday night swinging your dick.
Seventh, if you ever use a cuss word in my new house I'm
going to cut out your goddam tongue. Eighth, you going to

take the blame for every wrong thing you do and stop blaming it on me and Captain Davis and Daphne and Ornette and Ruth and everybody else for fifty miles around. Ninth, you going to respect my house by never coming in it drunk. And tenth, you ain't never going to call me ugly or black or nigger or bitch again, 'cause you done seen just what this black ugly nigger bitch can do when she gits mad!" Mem backed off a step. "Now git your ass up," she growled, "and wash yourself off!"

Brownfield started slowly to his feet, head hanging, body slick with sweat and blood and vomit, eyes bleary with fear. He was still crying forcefully, his nose dripping all over him. "And when you've cleaned yourself off you come back here and git up this mess. When my children come back from church with their granddaddy they going to find a model daddy, and if they don't you and me is going to know the reason why! You hear me, Brownfield?" Mem said, keeping the gun leveled at him. Brownfield's throat was too choked to speak. He stumbled toward the kitchen.

"You hear me, I say, Boy!?" Mem ran up behind him catching him across the back of the head with the gun barrel. His knees buckled, but he caught hold of the door casing. He could not raise his bloodied eyes to her steely yellow ones.

"Yes, ma'am," he mumbled, cowering against the door, not looking up. "Yes, ma'am," he said again, sobbing, as Mem set the gun down in a corner with a weary hand.

Part VI

26

BROWNFIELD LAY IN WAIT for the return of Mem's weakness. The cycles of her months and years brought it. The first early morning heavings were a good sign. Her body would do to her what he could not, without the support of his former bravado. The swelling of the womb, again and again pushing the backbone inward, the belly outward. He surveyed with sly interest the bleaching out of every crease on her wrinkled stomach. Waiting. She could not hold out against him with nausea, aching feet and teeth, swollen legs, bursting veins and head; or the grim and dizzying reality of her trapped self and her children's despair. He could bring her back to lowness she had not even guessed at before.

27

IN THE CITY HOUSE, a "mansion" of four sheetrocked rooms, no holes, a grassy yard and a mailbox on the porch, he lay low in his role. He played his conversion by terror long after the terror was gone and was replaced by a great design to express his rage, his humiliation, his deep hatred.

During the day at his job in a frozen pie factory, he was in a rage against his own contentment. It did not seem fair to him that the new work should actually be easier than dairying or raising cotton or corn. True, there was the boring placing of trays of peach pies on the assembly line, but after tramping for years after white folks' cows, the monotony soothed him. The even coolness of the building almost made him forget the stifling heat of the fields. His hands were drier now, for he could and did wear rubber gloves whenever there was wet work to do. He enjoyed pouring the mixture for the pies into the big vats, and liked regulating the hoses for water into the pressure cookers, and looked forward every day to washing up the big shiny, always new, utensils.

At the new house too there was a feeling of progress. An indoor toilet with a white tub, a face bowl, mirror and white commode. Now he could shit, and rising, look at himself, at the way his eyes had cleared themselves of the hateful veins and yellow tigerish lines, without much odor or rain, and much like a gentleman; or, as he invariably thought of it, like a white man.

He was cowed into wielding a paintbrush against dingy walls, planting bushes, attempting to fix the faulty wiring. For there were electric lights, and he was sometimes moved to read (look through the pictures of) the catalogues his wife got in the mail. The pictures of the new clothes and the guns and the boats and everything looked extra good in the clear light. He woke in the mornings now to the warmth of an almost noiseless gas heater; and the refrigerator, another example of Mem's earning power, although not new by some years, had nothing to do with melted ice or spoiled food.

If he had done any of it himself, if he had insisted on the move, he might not have resisted the comfort, the feeling of doing better-ness with all his heart. As it was, he could not seem to give up his bitterness against his wife, who had proved herself smarter, more resourceful than he, and he complained about everything often and loudly, secretly savoring thoughts of how his wife would "come down" when he placed her once more in a shack.

And when they became reconciled again in a happiness similar to but not very near in depth to what they had known as newlyweds, it was only Mem who looked forward to a less destructive and less inhuman future. He could not see beyond his emotion. He held himself back and, even when desperately—for there was a passion in them that often served as affection—still making babies, he planned ahead. Planting a seed to grow that would bring her down in weakness and dependence and to her ultimate destruction. Like the nonfighter she essentially was, Mem thought her battle soon over. She was not evil and he would profit from it.

What replaced the desire to heal old wounds was the desire to wipe them out as if they had never been.

When he considered his wife's poor health, which he did in some tight lonely hours, her boniness, her rotted teeth (and those knocked out by him and the two coated in gold by a dentist who assumed she wanted glittering gold), he could not face what he could remember of how she had been. Round and plump, a mouth of pure white when open—he and they had robbed her of her smile. Now, when she guffawed hoarsely at some tiny joke, corralling the slight intensity of the funny to her innermost heart, he could see himself reflected in the twin mirrors of her eyeteeth; and he wanted one dark gigantic stroke, from himself and not the sky, to blot her out.

28

WHAT A SLY and triumphant *joy* he felt when she could no longer keep her job. She was ill; the two pregnancies he forced on her in the new house, although they did not bear live fruit, almost completely destroyed what was left of her health. Yet, how sad he was somewhere inside that he should still be strong and free to rove about while she spent so much time nursing her feet, attending her children's colds, trying to reassure them they would not have to move back to the country because she could still find work in town. But it was hopeless, her dream for herself and for them was slipping away. She had tried so hard, and even her husband, she thought, had started to respect her again. She didn't ask herself if she loved him. They were at a kind of peace; in the house in town he no longer struck her. The children went to school with happy faces. The baby was trained on an indoor commode.

All of her confidence wore away with her health as Brownfield watched, gloating and waiting. She could not believe he had planned it. She thought he had behaved well, considering everything, which was what he wanted her to

138 · Alice Walker

think, until he was ready to reveal the plot to her. And then there came the day when she could not even get out of bed to look for work.

It had been raining for several days. Mem had tried every day to find something, anything, in factory, shop or kitchen. But perhaps the employers thought she looked too thin, probably tuberculous, and would not hire her. Each day she had come home beat.

The children took their cue from her silence, and they, sooner than she, knew the danger of their father's rising to rule them again now that their mother was sick. And sure enough, on this day, while Mem coughed and shivered, the blow fell.

"Why ain't the heat on?" she wheezed, when Brownfield came home from work.

"'Cause ain't nobody paid the bill."

"Well, why ain't *you* paid it?"

"'Cause it's your house, you pay the damn bills."

Mem groaned and turned her face to the wall. Ruth walked over to her and tried to play patti-cake with her face, but her mother pushed her away. She had turned the color of ashes, as if she'd seen a ghost.

"But you got a duty too," she told her husband. "You can't just let these children freeze to death."

"The rent ain't paid either." He began taking all his clothes from the chifforobe behind his wife's bed.

"How long?" All of their eyes were upon him, frightened, frozen as if he held the lungs that controlled their breathing.

"Since you bought all that medicine and spent all that money that you ought not have on you and the kids. I reckon that been two months ago." And then he pulled his trump. From his pocket he drew an eviction notice, flung it on the bed. "You read so damn good maybe you can tell me what all this here's about."

His wife picked up the eviction notice and read it through, trembling. Horrified, pale, weak, she looked at her husband packing his clothes.

"What you doing?"

"Gitting ready to move out."

"But—*move!*" She looked around at their smart little house and the things she was buying on time. She looked at the clean blue walls, the polished wood floor, the window sills full of evergreens.

"But where can we move? We ain't made no plans. Why didn't you pay the rent? You make enough money." Then, "We was *sick,* we all had flu; that's how come I spent all the money last month." She was becoming hysterical; the girls sat along the side of the bed, in a cloud of her VapoRub, but she was not mindful of them. "Where in the *world* do you expect us to move now?" she asked again, weakly, pathetically, trying to show strength she no longer had.

"Why," he said, and sniggered in spite of himself, "can't you make one of your eddicated guesses? *We* going to move over on *Mr. J. L.'s place!*"

It was like an overwhelmingly bad dream, and Mem fainted and was loaded half conscious into the cab of the truck that came to move them. She had no chance to pack, to cover her things from the weather, to say good-bye to her house. She was too weak to argue when the friends he got to help him move broke her treasured dishes, tore her curtains, dragged the girls' dresses through the mud.

They arrived at the house he had reserved for her "come down" in the middle of the night, and even his skin prickled at the sight of it. Mr. J. L. had promised that someone would clean it out, but it was still half full of wet hay. There were no panes in the windows, only wooden shutters. Rain poured into all three of the small rooms, and there was no real floor, only tin, like old roofing, spread out to keep the bottom of the hay bales from getting soggy.

"Git out, git out, this is your new home!" Brownfield shouted. They acted afraid to touch the ground. The house was not far from the highway, but there was a darkness about it, a crippled abandoned look.

"No—I can't." Mem drew back from his hands but fainted again. When she awoke she found herself stretched out between her girls on the hay, with all her newly acquired furniture stacked haphazardly around her. Brownfield had gone back to town with his friends and the girls said they had had to struggle hard to make the friends give them all the furniture. Brownfield had been intent on giving it away, they said.

29

"I DONE WAITED a long time for you to come down, Missy," he said when he came home, reeking of alcohol for the first time in almost three years. "This is what I can afford and this is what you going to have to make do with. See how you like *me* holding the upper hand!" He was enjoying himself in a sort of lunatic way.

"You was going to have your house, straight and narrow and painted and scrubbed, like white folks. You was going to do this, you was going to do that. Shit," he said, "you thought I fucked you 'cause I wanted it? Josie better than you ever been. Your trouble is you just never learned how not to git pregnant. How long did you think you could keep going with your belly full of childrens?" He stood glowering down at her. There was no electricity in the house, but it was nearly morning and they could see enough of each other to know that Brownfield's mask was decidedly off.

"Miss high-'n-mighty, you come down off your high horse now," he could not help giggling, she was so incapable of doing anything.

"You come down off your high horse now," he said again, laughing out loud, thinking how she looked like she was going to die.

"Brownfield, I'm sick," said Mem, "but I ain't going to ask you for mercy and I ain't going to die and leave my children. Even in this weather you brought me out in I ain't going to catch pneumonia. I'm going to git well again, and git work again, and when I do I'm going to leave you."

"Ain't no stopping you, is it? You a real red-hot ball of fire, ain't you!" He continued to laugh. "You *skeleton," he* said, stopping in the middle of a laugh and gazing at her from under his hat, "you can't do nothing but lay up there and *moan.* And if you could get your ugly ass up I wouldn't let you go nowhere, make a fool out of me, have people laughing at me!"

"You really think you can stop me?" she asked, knowing her children trembled at her saying anything that might provoke him.

"I'll stop you," he said, looking over at something that was covered in plastic.

"You can't stop much with a gun."

"I can stop *every*thing for you, Bitch. I can stop *you!*"

Daphne whimpered, Ornette cried, Ruth alone merely looked on with all the bewilderment and disgust of a small child. The three girls did not know their father. They too thought him capable of change. They thought he had changed. They thought it had been a matter of less work, fewer worries, gas heat and electric lighting. They had misjudged him because they were so young and because they knew nothing of most of his persistent memories. They saw now only that they had made a mistake; and knew their father was not so much changed as changeable. He could put on a front to fool the trusting.

"You know what," piped Ruth seriously from behind her blanket-covered bale of hay. Her father turned away from them; Daphne tried to shush her. "Hey, I say do you know what," she said again loudly, in her best fearless voice, though the pit of her stomach quivered. Her father turned toward her. She was his youngest, barely four. "You nothing but a sonnabit," she said, and quickly covered herself with her blanket so she wouldn't feel the first really hard blows Brownfield ever gave her.

30

AT THIS HOUSE, the only one of her father's choices she would ever recall with any degree of clarity, Ruth saw the comings and goings of her fourth and fifth and sixth birthdays. When she was five she began school, tagging along each morning with Daphne and Ornette. J. L.'s house—her mother always said to friends who had never visited them at their new location, "We haves that old house of Mr. J. L.'s"—was a place of icy kitchen water buckets in winter, and in summer flashing rainstorms uncovered sharp bits of colored glass in the back yard along with pieces of rusty tin and fragments of scarred linoleum. In the summer the house gave off a quiet hot musty smell and *hum*, like droning flies, and the air around it was full of motes thrown up from the trampled dust of dung and rotting hay.

There was a spring down the hill behind the house where they got their water; a little beyond it was a pigpen. The wild grass grew high beside the woodpile, near which leaned an ancient corncrib gray with weather and full of old plowshares and funnels and dried horse liniment in motley green bottles with tattered rag stoppers. Dozens of sharecropping families had lived in the house and had left their various odors of sweat, hogslop and discomfort deep in its rotting wood.

Daphne and Ornette found J. L.'s house unbearable and complained all the time with their eyes. It was a great fall for them, after the house in town, to have to tote water up to the house from the spring and suffer through muddy trips to the odorous outhouse when it rained. They had thought such days gone forever. Being little more than a baby, Ruth was less stricken by the move, although she knew it made her mother unhappy and therefore hated it. But there was much in the straw field behind the house to occupy her. And she enjoyed the cool greenness of the ferns and water lilies that grew beside the crayfish-inhabited spring.

Daphne was nine when they moved into J. L.'s house and Ornette was eight. The big gap between Ornette's age and Ruth's was because of the babies that had died. When Ruth was four Mem became pregnant again, and for a brief time afterward there was a baby in the house. Daphne and Ornette liked to hold him in their arms for Ruth to see. Daphne, always the inventive one, made up stories about the baby's future. He would be a doctor, she said, and run a big hospital in town, and marry one, maybe two (if the first one didn't work out) of his nurses. He was small and still and gray. Ruth thought he looked more like a possum than a child. He curled himself in sleep and, with his grayish red-rimmed eyes and the yellowish fuzz of his hair, which was more white than yellowish, he seemed a phantom baby, not the real thing. Ruth could never imagine him becoming anything. She could not even imagine that he would eventually grow on the food he was fed, much as she herself had grown. His cry was a thin pitiful thing. Nevertheless, in moments of small loneliness, when Daphne and Ornette claimed she was too much a baby to play with them, Ruth contemplated having a tough bouncy little brother to play with and perhaps to boss around. In the main, though, it was hard to tell he was in the house he was so quiet. He slept a great deal. They did not miss him very much when he died. Daphne and Ornette cried and whispered between themselves that somehow the baby had frozen to death because when they saw him lying dead he was all blue. But with school and play and the routine of living in J. L.'s house, the pale little brother was rapidly forgotten.

After his death Mem took a job that kept her away from home all day. She became a maid in a house in town. Ruth could not really understand why her mother left her again. When they had lived in town she had had her fill of being left with strange women, big snuff users with dusty bosoms and thin nervous girls with no prospects who were short with her. Daphne told her that Mem worked so that one day they would be able to leave the county, leave Georgia and leave Brownfield. Ruth did not know about the first two, but the idea of leaving her father pleased her.

Daphne knew more than Ornette. She called herself the Copeland Family Secret Keeper. What this meant was that at every opportunity she talked about how Brownfield had played with her when she was little. How he had bought her candy. How he had swung her up in his arms. How he had sung and danced for her. Ornette and Ruth were jealous of her memories and appropriated them for themselves. Daphne's memories of Brownfield as doting father became theirs, although the Brownfield they pretended to remember had no relation (except for Daphne) to the one they knew. To "remember" Daddy when he was good became their favorite game. When Brownfield overheard Ornette babbling to Ruth about some extraordinary kindness he had done her ("he bought me a dress" or "he fixed my dolly") he did not think anything of it except that Ornette was going to turn out to be an incorrigible liar. They knew he did not understand their game and that made it all the more fun; their "good" daddy would have understood, they said, which proved Brownfield was nothing compared with him.

Daphne was more forgiving than Ornette. Her temper became murderous only when Brownfield abused Mem. When Brownfield beat Daphne she tried to endure it by keeping her mind a perfect though burning blank. She tried so hard to retain some love for him, perhaps because of her memories of an earlier time, that she became very nervous. She jumped at the slightest noise or movement. Because she was so jumpy Brownfield teased her and called her names. He told her she was stupid and crazy. He swore at her, called her Daffy instead of Daphne, and pinched her sides until they bruised. Through it all she bravely stood, seeking to hide her trembling as best she could. She despised the house because it was impossible to clean and because she, more than Ruth or Ornette, had some idea of the struggle Brownfield had forced upon Mem. She hated it because it was cold in winter and she could never get warm; she must tremble summer and winter. Somehow she kept her feeling for her father separate from her hatred of the house. How she did it Ruth and Ornette never knew. They saw Brownfield less charitably than Daphne because they saw him only as a human devil and felt wherever he placed them would naturally be hell. They were as afraid of him as Daphne was, but in a more distant, impersonal way. He was like bad weather, a toothache, daily bad news.

Ornette was jolly most of the time. A loud, boisterous girl, sassy and full of darting rebellion. She was fat and glossy. Her skin had a luscious orange smoothness and felt like a waxed fruit. Of the three children Brownfield appeared to like her least. He thought she would grow up to be a plump, easy-going tramp and was telling her so constantly by the time she was eight. Ornette learned to toss her head at him. When she was seven she refused to go to church or to say her bedtime prayers. She had a flexible sexual vocabulary at eight and a decided interest in pussies and bowwows at nine. Her opinion of the house was that it was a barn and that only the stupidest cows lived in worse. She could not be depended upon to sweep the floor or even to pull the proper kind of straw with which to make a broom. She liked to sit in the middle of the straw field and sing rhythm-and-blues tunes she'd heard on the radio. Mem, pulling straw and binding it into brooms as she moved across the field, would listen to Ornette's songs almost dreamily. She did not scold her. Ornette was bold with her mother, thought her a hag and of little account. She thought Mem had married beneath her and should have married instead a teacher or a mason or anybody with land of his own and a fine house. She did not respect Mem. Occasionally she stole pennies from Mem's purse.

Mem's grief over losing the "decent house" was not a sign around her neck. She recovered from the illness that had caused her to lose it and with grim determination attended to roof leaks and rat holes in this house. She fixed sagging shutters and cleared away the rubbish that choked the weeds in the front yard. She did not do as much work on this house as she had on the ones before it. She tried to see that it was fairly clean, or as clean as she and Daphne could make it, that it did not leak overmuch, that the rats did not stay in control of it, as they had when she and her family moved in, and dispiritedly she threw a few flower seeds in the moist rich soil around the woodpile. Never again did she intend to plant flowers in boxes or beds.

Part VII

Part VII

31

WHEN RUTH STRUGGLED sleepily to open her eyes the morning of her first day at Grange's house, the big grandfather clock on the mantel made a last clinking echo across the chilly bed and sitting room. She sniffed, for her nose felt stuffy, and snuggled into the long warm back in front of her, but that back slid gradually away from her and stood stretching by the side of the bed. She heard footsteps shuffling up to the front of the room. She sighed, blinked her eyes, and turned over. The person on the other side of her was lying snoring with her face turned toward her and her breath was onions and dandelion weeds. Ruth turned over and lay drowsily in the warmth vacated by the person who had got up. She was aware of a feeling of oddness and insecurity, as if she had been on a long journey during the night; the morning air smelled different to her somehow, and when she opened her eyes to peer over the covers she could not recall having fallen asleep in this room. She looked around. There was a chifforobe in the corner, brown wood around yellow-glazed drawers, with cut-glass handles, a stuffed sofa the color of fuchsia geraniums under the window opposite the bed; and on the wall there were several old-fashioned pictures of people in top hats with waxed mustaches and kinky though slickly pomaded hair worn with a part in the middle. One of the pictures was of an ashen, sickly looking woman who might already have been dead when her picture was made. This was a tinted drawing of Ruth's grandmother, Grange's first wife, Margaret.

Ruth's mind, reluctantly becoming alert, was unwilling to set her straight about where she was, but it finally came to her in a prickly little rush that she was at her grandfather's house and that it was his wife, Josie, who slept beside her. She tried to remember having gone to bed here the night before but could not.

From the front of the room she heard the swift flare of flame as her grandfather put kerosene on the fire, and the sound of her stepgrandmother's snores was an abandoned droning in her ears. Without rustling the covers or making any sounds of being awake, she began to remember.

The night before had been Christmas Eve. Ruth had been going to get a tricycle for Christmas, or she had thought she was. But her mother had kept saying that this whole year had been a very hard one for Mr. Santa Claus, mainly because Mrs. Santa Claus had died (or run away) and Mr. Santa Claus didn't feel much like making anything, especially not toys; for it would hurt him to see everybody else making merry while he sat in a corner at the North Pole just crying his eyes out. The most it was best to look for, she had said to Ruth and Ornette and Daphne, was oranges and maybe some peppermint sticks.

Brownfield had come in from town that night very drunk. He was raving so badly that Daphne had taken Ruth and Ornette and they had hidden in the chicken house. Ruth remembered how all the chickens began to squawk and how they all smelled so fresh, not good-fresh, but fresh in the way raw meat smells. They had got dodo all over their hands and faces crawling around in the chicken house, but Daphne made them sit down in a rotten-smelling corner while she peeked out at the house through a crack. Once they had begun to giggle loudly because Ornette, who was in the fifth grade, said that a boy at school was always trying to pull her bloomers down during recess. But Daphne slapped them both hard across the face. She was trembling violently. She never cut up like they did because she had some kind of fits once in a while and was always serious. Until she slapped them they had thought the whole thing something of a joke. A rough one, but with some fun in it. It seemed to them that Brownfield was nearly always mean and unruly and drunk.

Usually, though, he didn't come home but would spend the night fighting in the juke joints in town. Most of the time he would get beaten up by whomever he picked a fight with and then they would take pity on him and force him to let them drive him home, with him shouting, slurring, "I got my goddam *pride, I* is!" then falling asleep on the way. They would dump him lifeless and foul-smelling or sometimes singing onto the porch. Thump! He would land on the porch, and if it woke them up Ruth and Ornette would laugh at him under the covers.

Daphne felt strongly tensions in the house to which Ruth and Ornette were oblivious. She was always having to look out for them, because Brownfield, even when sober, would beat and kick them. They hated him while he was doing it, but not between times, and spent whole days playing contentedly under the trees behind the house where not even the vaguest consideration of him followed.

Mem tried hard to control him when he beat them. She always said, "Brownfield, you ought not to carry on this a-way. You *know* you won't be able to look yourself in the face when you gets old and the children done gone." To which he would answer with a lick against her head or a kick against her legs.

Only Mem was working. He had been fired from his job with J. L. They rented the house. The rent money came from Mem's salary. She made seventeen dollars a week, which seemed like a fortune to them, in its lump sum. What she made from six days of work was far more than Brownfield had made as J. L.'s dairyman and cotton farmer. Brownfield hinted to his drinking buddies that he made Mem go out and work for him, but she never left the house in the morning without him trying to pull her back. Sometimes he would be lying in bed watching her get ready for work, and just as it was time for her to step out of the house he would reach out and grab her arm and try to get her to lie down with him.

"Aw, come on, honey," he would say, "how about laying down here with your pore ol' man?" His mattering yellowed eyes would be still and deadly.

And Mem would say, furrowing her brow and looking around at the children, who immediately stopped whatever they were doing whenever he put his hands on her ("Why he want her to git in the bed," they'd ask themselves suspiciously, "can't he tell it *day*time?"), "You ought to turn loose my arm, Brownfield, you know I got to get to work." She would be looking down at her shoes, which were white, like nurses' shoes. Then she would pull herself loose and disappear almost running down the road.

And Brownfield would say, "Shit. All these fucking womens can think about is they goddam *jobs*. One of these days

I'm going on over to Jay-*pan*, where the womens know what they *real* job is!' And he would spit at the cold fireplace or throw a shoe at one of them, usually knocking over a jar of leaves or a picture from a magazine which Mem had put up against the bare cracked walls.

The three of them would dress hurriedly, grab the pieces of bread that were in the warmer on the stove, biscuits from last night's supper, and run out the door to the school.

"You ain't going to learn nothing *use*ful," he would say, lounging on the bed with his hands behind his head, "not unless they teaching *plow*ing!" His words had hurt Ruth at first, unbearably hurt her. But one day she surprised him trying to mouth some of the simpler words in her speller. When Brownfield saw her looking at him he threw the book at her. She dodged it and, though feeling somehow sad, she ran laughing out the door. In the first grade she knew envy when she saw it.

The dustiness of the hen house made them sneeze, and their father staggered onto the porch and looked out at the bushes around the house. He cursed, holding his shotgun in the air, and hobbled back into the house.

It became apparent to Ruth and Ornette, finally, that they were not engaged in a game. Fear at last hit them and, seeing the gun in his hand and knowing without being told that he was waiting for their mother, they began to cry.

Daphne, always brooding and nervous so that if you walked into a room behind her and said "Hey!" she was likely to go into convulsions, was holding her stomach. She did this whenever she was upset or confused. She had bad sickness once a month and would cry and cry, and one time, when she was holding her stomach and crying, with sweat popping out like grease bubbles on her face, Brownfield had kicked her right where her hands were. He was trying to sleep, and couldn't because of the noise, he said.

Mem had taken Daphne to the clinic, but the nurse said she didn't see anything wrong with her, except that she was nervous. Mem had said that she knew the child was nervous and wanted the nurse to tell her what to do about it, but the nurse was busy talking to another nurse about changing her hair color, and both nurses ignored Mem, who was standing there exasperated, holding a quivering Daphne by the hand. Daphne was particularly frightened of white people; she did not fear them because she found them to be particularly cruel, she had very limited dealings with them; she was afraid, childishly enough, of their ghostliness, the shadowless lightness of their faces, the twinkling vacuity of their marble eyes. She could believe they were pure, free of passion, odor or blood, and that they belonged, as she did not, to a horrible God. Her fear encompassed the world and included darkness, buildings, ancient trees and flowers with animal names. She was afraid of the world; but it was she who protected her sisters; she who stood trembling and barely able to stand underneath her father's fist, while Ornette and Ruth ran yelling and crying from Brownfield, out through the back yard and into the woods.

Now she told them, with her voice shaking, that she was going to walk to town to try to head Mem off. She said maybe she could keep her from coming home while Brownfield was drunk. They wanted to go with her but she said she could go faster if they stayed behind. They watched her sneak out, ashy and dark, without a sweater. It was hailing lightly. She skittered out and down the highway like a lean brown rabbit. The black night, grayed down with white hailstones, soaked her in against the wet highway.

Left in the hen house Ornette cried silently and Ruth sat shivering with cold, looking out through a crack at the yard. The hen house was to the front of the front yard, a leaning musty building made of slabs and pieced out with scraps of rusty tin. In summer sparse patches of green grass grew in front of the door, but now in winter the whole area was slushy and wet and slippery with ice. The house sat back from the highway about thirty yards; a narrow road filled with sharp gravel turned off the highway, ran risingly up, and stopped abruptly in front of the door. The outside of the house had changed little since they moved in. There was an old weather-beaten bush with purple flowers in summer and nothing but thorns in winter that stood misshapen by the wind on the far side of the yard. The porch sank heavily at one end and rose off its foundation on the other. Around the porch on the end next to the hen house there were bits of old rusty screen with great jagged holes punched in. The steps were two logs that Mem had cut from a stout tree, then halved and pushed into the dirt. The house was made of thin gray boards with no re-inforcement on the inside. Mem had lined the inside with cardboard boxes, and when the wind rose and came through the cracks outside it caused the cardboard to strain and throb as if it were alive.

Ruth could see a light on in the room where her parents slept, the room that was also the living room. The house had three rooms altogether, one of these a kitchen. They were bet-ter off than some people, for they did not have to share a bed-room with their parents, and though their room was small it was private. That is, you could hear through the walls, but at least you couldn't see through them. Sometimes the shadow of her father loomed against the window as he looked out into the night. Ruth shrank down in the dust. She and Ornette were not completely knowledgeable about why they were sitting there nearly frozen in the hen house, but they knew they were afraid and too afraid to trust being anywhere else.

Occasionally Mem walked or hitchhiked to and from town, but sometimes the husband of the woman she worked for would drive her in his long blue Chrysler. He was a strange sort of man, according to Mem, for he insisted on paying her seventeen dollars a week, which was five dollars more than the usual rate of pay for domestics. He was from the North and was dying, it was said, from cancer of the mouth. Some said he was a Jew, but they did not know quite what it was that made him different—his eyes didn't make you look at your feet like the eyes of other men—and they did not very much care. Mem was fond of him because he let her take home magazines and sent books to Daphne and Ornette. She did not like his wife, however, who was a Southern belle and whose father owned a big plantation outside of town. She was all the time mentioning how "cute" colored children were and giving them pennies, Ruth hated her because she called Mem, "Mem, my colored girl."

Ruth was startled to hear the sound of a car stopping down by the highway. She heard the low murmuring of her mother's voice—she would be thanking him for the ride— and then she heard her heavy footsteps trudging up the drive. She looked out the crack to see if Daphne was with her but did not hear her mother talking to anyone as she came up, and she thought that in the car her mother and the white man had not seen her on the road. Soon Ruth was able to see the outline of Mem's figure.

Mem did not quit work until six o'clock and then it was dark. She was carrying several packages, which she held in the crook of both arms, looking down at the ground to secure her footing. Ruth wanted to dash out of the chicken house to her, but she and Ornette sat frozen in their seats. They stared at her as she passed, hardly breathing as the light on the porch clicked on and the long shadow of Brownfield lurched out onto the porch waving his shotgun. Mem looked up at the porch and called a greeting. It was a cheerful greeting, although she sounded very tired, tired and out of breath. Brownfield began to curse and came and stood on the steps until Mem got within the circle of the light. Then he aimed the gun with drunken accuracy right into her face and fired.

What Ruth remembered now with nausea and a feeling of cold dying, was Mem lying faceless among a scattering of gravel in a pool of blood, in which were scattered around her head like a halo, a dozen bright yellow oranges that glistened on one side from the light. She and Ornette were there beside her in an instant, not minding their father, who had already turned away, still cursing, into the house. They were there looking at the oranges and at the peppermint sticks and at everything. It occurred to Ruth sadly that there really was no Santa Claus. She was Santa Claus. Mem. And she noticed for the first time, that even though it was the middle of winter, there were large frayed holes in the bottom of her mother's shoes. On Mem's right foot the shoe lay almost off and a flat packet of newspaper stuck halfway out. Daphne ran up screaming and threw herself across her mother's legs. She began to rub Mem's feet to make them warm.

What happened after that Ruth did not know, and now she did not want to know. She buried her face in the pillow and began to whimper. Why had her mother walked on after she saw the gun? That's what she couldn't understand. Could she have run away or not? But Mem had not even slowed her steps as she approached her husband. After her first cheerful, tired greeting she had not even said a word, and her bloody repose had struck them instantly as a grotesque attitude of profound, inevitable rest.

"She sleeping, Ruth, ain't she?" Ornette had asked, trying to see closed eyes where there were none at all.

"Hyar, hyar," her grandfather said, coming to her and sitting beside her on the bed, "we don't want to wake up the old lady, now does us?" She shook her head, sobbing softly with her arms around his neck. He had been drinking already and smelled of corn liquor, but his strong tobacco-and-corn-smell was soothing, and he patted her thoughtfully on the back.

"I might could tell you a right interestin' story 'bout old Br'er Fox. But you wouldn't listen. . . ." He looked sadly down at her. "Naw, I knows you wouldn't listen, and ain't no need of me saying nothing *no*how. I don't know what I'm talking about. Shit, baby gal, we just got troubles on top of troubles, and there ain't no trouble like losing your ma." He shook his head. "Lawd, and that's the truth, and"—looking at his wife—"say, I shore do wish my wife would shet her goddam mouth, her snores about to drive me crazy."

Ruth looked at him carefully and long. His eyes were moist and his cheeks quivered.

"Don't look at *me*," he said sourly. "I don't know no more about *any* of it"—throwing his arm up indicating everything in the world—"then you!" And she was never to hear him seriously claim, even in a boast, that he did.

32

GRANGE WAS A tall, gaunt man with a thick forest of iron-gray hair that whitened shade by shade over the next few years until it was completely white, completely pure, like snow. His mouth was unusually clean-looking, although he chewed tobacco, smoked, used snuff, drank anything strong, and rarely brushed his teeth. Sometimes he would go after them with the end of his nightshirt, but Ruth could never see how that could keep them so sound and white. For the longest time after she saw them grinning at her from a jar on the back porch, bubbling, she thought he just took them all out once in a while for a boiling. She knew her own cavity-weakened baby teeth only came out one at a time.

He was immensely sick at times. There were days of depression when he spoke of doing away with himself. There were times when she could tell he needed her to tell him to pull himself together. He would lie immobile on the floor, dead, and she would be drawn to him to try the magic of her hugs and kisses. She soon learned to overlook the differences between them. They got along well for grandfather and child and trivial complications in their relationship did not develop. Grange never spanked her and would probably have beaten up anyone who tried to do so. Even Josie was not allowed to touch her. Poor Josie, she was never even allowed to scold.

"You don't know nothing about raising no child," Grange said when Josie tried to make her do anything. "Look what a mess you did on your own young 'un!" Josie would sulk, but Grange's was the final word.

At the beginning Ruth was jealous of Josie, for she thought maybe Grange found her pretty. But Grange also thought his wife was not very nice, and he said so, often and loudly. He said she lived like a cat, stayed away from home too much. Josie was one of those fat yellow women with freckles and light-colored eyes, and most people would have said she was good-looking, *handsome*, without even looking closely. But Ruth looked closely indeed, and what she saw was a fat yellow woman with sour breath, too much purple lipstick, and a voice that was wheedling and complaining; the voice of a spoiled little fat girl who always wanted to pee after the car got moving.

Ruth sensed that Josie was none too happy to have her with them. "What do I know about plaiting hair on a eight-year-old kid?" Josie had asked Grange one day when Grange wanted her to wash and braid Ruth's hair. "I notice you cut Lorene's hair rather than take up time over it," Grange had replied, "but this my *grand* girl, you do hers up or I pulls yours off." Ruth had snickered that day while Josie, fuming, braided her hair. She and Josie were not to be friends, it seemed.

Before she moved in with them, Grange had spent his days fishing, sunning, whittling. After she came he began to grow cotton. Ruth could play in the fields beside him all day during the summer, though she was not allowed to pick the cotton. She wanted to, because it was so soft and light and looked so pretty early in the morning with the dew glistening on it. Why Grange forbade her she could not understand. Josie, who was asked to pick, said she would not if Ruth did not. "You may have talked me into helping you buy this damn *farm*," Josie sneered, "but if I ever picks another boll of cotton I hope somebody rush up and have me committed." With one long sack and his own two hands Grange was left to manage his cotton. Ruth was allowed to ride on the back of the truck when the cotton was taken to the gin. That is, she was allowed to ride on the back of the truck while they were on the dirt road which led to the highway. Each time, as they approached the highway, Grange stopped the truck and either sent her back home or put her inside on the seat next to him.

"You not some kind of field hand!" he muttered sharply when she said she'd love to ride on top of the cotton all the way to town.

"But Grange, my goodness, can't I ride as far as the *bridge*?" she asked the first time. He seemed too annoyed at the thought to answer her. She began to get the feeling she was very special. At school she avoided the children whose parents let them ride on the back of trucks—"Grinning niggers for the white folks to laugh at!" she scoffed. And the children in turn quickly learned what hurt her most. They called her "Miss Stuck-up" and when that produced no effect, "*Mrs*. Grange."

The time she did manage to spend atop the truck was supremely happy. From that high perch she could see, it seemed to her, miles and miles across fields and forests and on into the sky. A sky which was benign and cloudless in those days. More often than not she and Grange left Josie at home. Ruth rarely thought about Brownfield; when she did, Grange was quick to assure her that Georgia jails were among the best.

Grange also raised vegetables in his garden in front of the house. You could sit on the front porch and watch the tomatoes grow. He would cut big coarse cabbages at the stem with a flat dull knife and balance one like a crown on her head. He raised carrots and tomatoes and peas, and in fall, after the peas had dried in the sun, they sat up late at night gossiping and shelling them. Josie, who hated all kinds of work, farm or otherwise, would get up reluctantly from telling long tales about the "olden days" or her younger days and wash fruit jars so that in the morning Grange could help her can, "put up" the peas.

It was at times of such domesticity that Ruth felt keenly Josie's objection to her and mourned the loss of her mother. Memories that might have been tossed aside by a child more innocently brought into a new home with new sources of play, came rushing back at odd moments of wakefulness, more usually in dreams. The long fall days, languid and slow and heavy, of gathering in, and then of putting up, brought to mind the good memories she had of her mother, when they had seemed to prosper in the hot summers, canning and making potato hills, and winter held no fear for them.

Other grownups she saw never mentioned her parents. They acted as if they did not, or had not, existed. Josie was a clam when she was asked a simple question about them, or asked simply to remember. But Grange was drawn to discuss them. He said they should not be forgotten, especially Mem, who was a saint. He liked to use some reference to Mem's thriftiness or her hard-working goodness as a beginning to a list of comparisons he made between her and Josie. He would

be carried away by his vivid recollections of Mem and re-
proach his wife viciously because she was not the kind of
woman his son's wife had been. Josie would begin to cry, or
pretend to suffer.

"You lazy yaller heifer!" he would start out, "and don't
you come saying nothing defending to me. You no-good slan-
derous trollop, you near-white strumpet out of tallment, you
motherless child, you pig, you bloated and painted cow! Look
to your flopping udders hanging out in mass offense! You
lustful she-goat! Close up your spreaded knees before this innocent child and my gray head!" But he became unsure of
himself when she began to cry. "Shit," he would mutter, finally. "What you standing over there with your damn mouth
hanging open for *any*way. Come here and set on my goddam
knee when I'm talking to you!" At first such scenes of forgiveness were frequent and at times they were very happy. Josie
would come placidly over to him, chewing her gum, wetting
her purple lipstick with her sly little tongue, her tears vanished. And Grange would mumble from deep in her dress
front, "Ah, me oh my, here I is. *Lost* again."

Ruth did not always sleep with them. Grange was gentle
but firm.

"It ain't healthy for a heap of peoples to sleep in the same
bed, don't you know. Anyways, it all right for just two. If they
be grown."

Shut away from them, turning restlessly on her bed, Ruth
tried to fathom the mystery of her grandfather's contempt for
and inevitable capitulation to Josie. When she could not fall
asleep Mem came back to confront her; Mem, whose hands
were callused and warm, whose lips were chapped and soft,
and whose eyes were restored to their look of tough, gentle
sadness and pain.

33

GRADUALLY, SULKILY, Josie faded into the background, and Ruth and her grandfather became inseparable. They did not plan it this way; but always they were together; where Grange went, Ruth went, what he did, Ruth did. Josie, having sold her lounge to help Grange pay for the farm, had no place to go and none of her old friends came to see her. Ruth and Grange halfheartedly tried to interest her in their pursuits, but the farm held no attractions for Josie; she thought of herself as a city woman. She brushed them off, and they were happy to be brushed off. They left her muttering and pacing the floor, filing her purple nails.

In the wintertime, a few days before each Christmas Eve, Grange began his preparations for making ambrosia. He was an uneducated man, but he still remembered that somebody, some old white lady's daughter no doubt, had once told him that ambrosia was what all the gods used to eat before there just came to be one God, which they had now, that never did eat anything. "That's 'cause He done got stocked up while He was creating Hisself," was Grange's short explanation.

To make ambrosia you needed fresh, hand-shredded coconut and pineapples and oranges. Probably something else
went in, a shot of whiskey or wine, but Ruth remembered
mostly the oranges and coconuts. Grange's sister, who lived in
Florida, would send these in one large and one small crate,
along with so many grapefruits the whole house looked like a
fruit stand. Grange liked to put out every piece of fruit on a
"high place," like the mantel or the tops of dressers and chif-
forobes, and when children came to visit—and they were allowed to come only at Christmas—he had a generous way of
reaching behind him or over his head and producing a bright
orange or grapefruit. Then he would grin at the small bewildered visitor and say, as if he had forgotten the words at the
beginning, "Hocus-pocus on *you,* boy!"

The next thing you needed to make ambrosia was a big
churn. Grange had two, one milk-white with a lovely faded
drawing of a blue bull near the top, and a brown earthen one.
They had belonged to Josie's mother, and Grange said that she
had liked to use the white one during the week and the brown
one on Sunday. In remembrance of her—her wide-eyed picture was among those in the front room—they used the
brown churn for the Christmas ambrosia.

Grange and Ruth and Josie would sit around peeling oranges and shredding coconut until two o'clock in the morning. Of course, the whole business could have been finished in
an hour, but Grange would stop ten or fifteen times during
the process to tell a story, or the truth about something or
somebody. He knew all the Uncle Remus stories by heart, although he could make up better ones about a smart plantation man named John. John became Ruth's hero because he
could talk himself out of any situation and reminded her of
Grange.

Grange thought that Uncle Remus was a fool, because if he was so smart that he could make animals smart too, then why the hell, asked Grange, didn't he dump the little white boy (or tie him up and hold him for ransom) and go to Congress and see what he could do about smartening up the country, which, in Grange's view, was passing dumb. "Instead of making the white folks let go of the stuff that's rightfully ours, he setting around on his big flat black ass explaining to some stupid white feller how too much butter in the diet make you run off at the be-hind! We needs us a goddam statesman and all he can do is act like some old shag-assed *min*strel!"

He would reminisce about his boyhood, which was filled with all sorts of encounters with dead folks and spirits and occasionally the Holy Ghost, which he said was the same thing as a sort of chill, and which, if you didn't watch out, could turn into the soul's pneumonia.

He told stories about two-heads and conjurers; strange men and women more sensitive than the average spook. He said they could give you something to wear under your hat that'd make your wife come back (if she ran away), or make her run away if you were sick of her. He told about how one old juju man who, people claimed, could turn into a bat, had actually cured him of a bad case of piles by giving him a little bag of powder to dust down in the stool. "What's piles?" Ruth asked. "A serious grown-up disease," he answered.

He said there was a two-headed lady in town named Sister Madelaine. She had changed herself from a white colored woman to a gypsy fortuneteller. "Why she do that?" asked Ruth. "'Cause she didn't want to be nodody's cook," said Grange. She was a powerful woman, according to Grange, but not as good as the two-heads he had known when he was a boy. Two-heading was dying out, he lamented. "Folks what can look at things in more than one way is done got rare."

Ruth's favorite story was about how he came to join the church.

It happened one spring when he was seven or eight years old. And it was during a revival. He had already begun getting into fights with the white children who lived down the road, usually "beating the stuffing out of them" to let him tell it. His mother, a pious and diligent house servant for most of her life, never seriously attempted to make him stop fighting (she would say gently that she didn't want to break his spirit), but instead urged him more and more toward the "bosom" of the church. Grange could never say bosom without looking down the front of Josie's dress. Anyway, he had resisted with everything in him, for he hated revivals, hated church, and most of all hated preachers. His mother, gently persuasive and getting nowhere with him, was trying to convince him to join the church one night when her brother, Grange's Uncle Buster, came to visit. He was built like a keg around the chest, and mean. Grange didn't like him because he had seen him knock his wife, Grange's aunt, through a plate-glass window. Hearing his sister's mild, obviously ineffectual pleadings, the uncle grabbed Grange roughly by the shoulder and gave him a long lecture on receiving the Holy Ghost, and about how good it was to be saved and how if he would just open up his heart the "pue" light would just come aflying and aflooding in. In short, he said that if Grange didn't get religion that same night he would get a horsewhipping when he got home.

Grange punctuated his tales with mirthful explosive laughs, which startled them, though they were expected. He was very good at these stories and liked to watch their eyes fasten on him, lit to glowing points of light from the crackling fire, which from time to time he spat into with unusual delicacy and accuracy. Ruth even liked the spitting, the pursing of the slick, finely molded dark brown lips against, for a minute, the clean white of his teeth, then the stinging buzz of the irons in the fire as they were hit, the momentary halting of the fire, the sound of steam rising quickly, and the sputtering consummation of the spit by the flames, for which they all waited, staring into the fire without letting out their breaths.

Grange had been placed harshly, or as he put it, "sheved down," on the mourner's bench. All around him the revival spirit was evident. In the first place, around the "brothers"—every one of them saved—there hung the heady aroma of spirits; mostly corn liquor or home-made wine. At the beginning of the service all these brothers were sitting as stiff as ramrods, and that evening all of them, in order to keep from falling off their benches, fastened their eyes on Grange, who was sitting dejectedly on the hard wooden bench. His Uncle Buster was one of them, and Grange fancied he could smell his breath of peach-peel brandy clear across the church.

The sisters were all got up in their best. "They wore these long-tailed dresses then," said Grange. "In them days you could break your *neck* trying to see a little leg." They wore lots of red and yellow and green, and their hair was straightened to a "fare-thee-well." Grange grinned. "If a lizard had fell on one of them heads he was bound to slip off and break a claw!" Before the preacher started to preach they sat around gossiping like so many peacocks. "Lawd, how *you*, Sister So-an'–so! Chile, you shore does look good enough to eat!" Or, "You hush your mouth, girl, you ain't got no 'leven chilren. You looks jest like a sprang chicken!" They'd be spitting out of windows and into the stove, each one trying to show some ankle under her dress tail. But as soon as the preacher got up in the pulpit they started right in with "O Sinner!" which they did mournful things to, all the while looking at Grange and looking sad.

At the end of the sermon the preacher started calling for converts. ("Calling for what, convicts?" quizzed Ruth. "Same thing," Grange said, without stopping his story.) Two or three formerly unsaved and happy teenagers filed up front with their heads bowed. They'd probably stole something the night before, Grange said. The church began to rock with song, the sisters were shouting and the preacher stood in the pulpit dripping with sweat. Every once in a while he swiped at the top of his bald head with his handkerchief. The same handkerchief, Grange had noticed, that he was spitting into all during the service. He could feel his mother looking piteously at him, for he knew she wanted him safely enchurched more than she wanted anything in the world. He wanted to get the Holy Ghost too, for he was deathly afraid of the whipping Uncle Buster had promised him.

Looking at his mother, he thought about his uncle, and looked over in the amen corner for him. He was still there, but while the church throbbed with life and the spirit of the Lord had everybody else almost climbing the walls, Uncle Buster was fast asleep. Well! There he snored, with a long sliver of saliva collecting on his vest pocket. Grange looked, enthralled; for intently digging around in the trash that had collected around Uncle Buster's mouth was a huge fat housefly. The kerosene lights made the fly's wings shine like amber gems. His busy activity around Uncle Buster's mouth was like that of a housewife sweeping out a corner, or of a greedy little boy eating stolen pie. It was then that Grange made his bargain with the God of the AME church.

Watching Uncle Buster's wide-open mouth, around which the big fly played, he said to himself that if the fly got inside

Uncle Buster's mouth, *and if Uncle Buster swallowed it,* he would jump right up, claim he had found the Holy Ghost and join the church. He had decided the Holy Ghost was never coming on its own. As soon as he had done this, said Grange, the fly very cautiously sneaked into Uncle Buster's mouth, and Uncle Buster, waking to find everybody in the church gazing in his direction, or so it must have seemed to him, snapped together his ponderous whiskered jaws, and in a pious self-righteous gulp, downed the fly! He immediately began to heave and turn a sickly color; and when Grange, at that moment, rose and started up to shake the preacher's hand, Uncle Buster passed him with one hand clapped most firmly over his mouth. Grange said his mother had cried and shouted and was in general happy from then on.

And that was how come, Grange said, he was a member of the church but did not believe in God. For how could any God with self-respect, he wanted to know, bargain with a boy of seven or eight, who proposed such a nasty deal and meal.

During the latter part of the story Ruth bounced in her chair with laughter. And when she and Grange sat in church together they quite often giggled like silly girls over their own conventional absurdities, one of which was going to church. To preachers and church-going dandies alike, they were the dreaded incarnation of blasphemy. But it was funny, what they witnessed every Sunday—the placid, Christ-deferential self-righteousness of men who tortured their children and on Saturday nights beat their wives.

34

JOSIE SAW THEM dancing together once, in the small log cabin Grange had built Ruth as a playhouse. It was on Ruth's tenth birthday and she was dressed from head to toe in brand-new clothes. Josie was furious. Grange had not bought clothes for her since they'd been married. And he had never, after Ruth came to stay with them, taken the trouble to dance with her.

"It ain't decent!" she cried, while Grange and Ruth danced breathlessly all around her. "And with your heart already full of holes!" They continued to dance, the music coming bluesy and hoarse from Grange's straining throat. When he sang he seemed to be in pain. But Ruth knew nothing of the physical condition of his heart. She knew she was in it, and that seemed enough.

"What's she talking about your heart?" she asked. But Grange was caught up in his lament. Ruth thought her grandfather a very sexy sort of old guy. He was tall and lean and had a jutting hip. When he danced you couldn't tell if his day had been bad or good. He closed his eyes and grunted music. His songs were always his own; she never heard them sung over the radio. His songs moved her; watching him dance made her feel kin to something very old. Grange danced like he walked, with a sort of spring in his knees. When he was drinking his dance paced a thin line between hilarity and vulgarity. He had a good time. His heart, to Ruth, was not an organ in his body, it was the tremor in his voice when he sang.

They danced best when they danced alone. And dancing taught Ruth she had a body. And she could see that her grandfather had one too and she could respect what he was able to do with it. Grange taught her untaught history through his dance; she glimpsed a homeland she had never known and felt the pattering of the drums. Dancing was a warm electricity that stretched, connecting them with other dancers moving across the seas. Through her grandfather's old and beautifully supple limbs she learned how marvelous was the grace with which she moved.

Josie began to leave them every Sunday. She went into town to visit the jail where Brownfield was kept. Grange did nothing to detain her, or if he did Ruth knew nothing of it. Ruth, however, was startled by this turn in events. She could not imagine anyone being fearless enough to see her father. Josie had brought them word that Brownfield had changed since he was in prison, and that they would hardly believe it was him when they saw him. Ruth had assumed she would never see him again; she had even hoped he would be done away with. Josie made her afraid that her father would be out of prison very soon. However, as week followed week and Josie's visits became less extraordinary to her, Ruth began to relax and to enjoy her grandfather, who, now that Josie spent her time cooking chickens and baking pies for Brownfield, was all her own.

"Do you ever think how selfish and spoiled you is?" Josie asked her one day, her face oddly contorted.

"I don't know what you mean," said Ruth. Grange had promised to take her to the picture show, and she was in a hurry to get dressed. She honestly did not realize that she never thought of Josie as her grandmother, and never, never thought of her as Grange's wife.

"You didn't want to go to the show with me and Grange?" asked Ruth, flying out the door. "Did you?" she called, as they were driving off.

35

SUMMER AND FALL found Ruth and Grange dedicated to the earthy, good-smelling task of making wine. They could name a long list of wines they knew how to make with maximum success. There was a short list of others that always soured. During the peach season peach stones and peels were gathered and dropped into the brown churn with water and allowed to set. This would make strong peach wine by September. Or, nearing the end of summer, big Alberta clings were halved and pushed into the churn and left in water, treated occasionally, and peeked into at least once a week. Grange did the "treating"—he drank some—and at Christmas time they had brandy, with shreds of peach sticking to the sides of the glass. In summer too they made corncob wine, white and sweet and cold when they left the jars outside in the spring; and blackberry wine and muscadine and scuppernong wine and sometimes plum wine. Ruth liked wine almost as much as Grange, and once in company she got sick and threw up, and it became quite apparent to everyone that Grange wasn't the only one drunk at the gathering. By the time she was nine, even Grange was astounded by her capacity to drink wine. She would try to pretend she was unaffected by it because she liked the taste of it so much she wanted to drink it by the glassful, like milk. But he knew how, momentarily, to keep her from starting. He would move the jar from where they hid it last, and hide it somewhere else. But this precaution worked badly for him, because then he would forget where he hid it, and would have to ask her to help him find it.

He was an unembarrassed drinker, a regular heathen. Throughout the day he nursed at a half-gallon jug, wine or corn liquor, he did not seem to care which. On weekends he doubled his usual intake and would sometimes find himself unable to come home. Twice he was lying beside the highway where their own road began, unable to make it any farther. These times when they found him he went into long exhaustive monologues on the merits of freedom.

"Just leave me hyar to die like a goddam dog!" he bluffed. "A black man is better off dead and in hell!" They took him, Josie supporting him on one shoulder, and Ruth walking behind him with a switch, and carried him home. Each time he threatened to sink onto the road Ruth cut him across the back of his legs with her switch. She always felt older than Grange when he was feeling bad. When he sobered up she lectured him, wouldn't acknowledge his headache, made him get his tobacco for himself and in general ignored him so that by Monday night he was not only sober and ashamed but also a wreck, and scared stiff that he had at last pushed her too far. (After all, she was only a *little* thing, and didn't understand, and might get the wrong idee!) He thought she might at last be turned against him. He would curse himself for being the father of his son and in danger of being thought just like him by his son's daughter.

Ruth was reminded of Brownfield when Grange got drunk; it was as if the closed parts of her mind were painfully forced open, and again she saw the demon of hate and destruction in someone close to her. But she believed Grange drank because of his murderous son and because of Josie. Grange and his wife now rarely spoke to each other; the house was often miserable because of their coldness. There was always in the air something of Josie's feeling of Ruth's intrusion. Ruth also knew that Grange had had another wife, Margaret, whom he had never got over. He cried whenever he talked about her (only when he was drunk) and Ruth hated her (dead though she was and had been for many years) with all her heart.

But Grange's crimes, she believed, were never aimed at anyone but himself, and his total triumph over his life's failures was the joy in him that drew her to him. He was a sinner, which he readily admitted, but he gave of himself. (She did not then notice that what he had to give he gave only to her.) The passion he lavished on living she could never quite condemn.

When he was sober and feeling guilty and ashamed, and when Josie lambasted him prior to dressing up and "visiting" somebody else (usually Brownfield), and they were in the house alone, there was a pall hanging over the house, thickest around Grange's bowed gray head, which only lifted when she stationed herself close to him, or raised his head by shoving her own pigtails sharply, abruptly, sometimes even painfully, under his lowered chin. Then they embraced.

———

And of that other life of father and son, between the old man she loved and the younger one she feared, what could she know? And how could she judge? And what of Josie and the life of marital intimacy that was not there for Ruth to see, to understand? For all she knew her grandfather might never have been a father, her own father notwithstanding. Brownfield and Grange cursed each other, neither respecting the other's age or youth. Maybe Grange's love contained a gap. Like his life. Or where and when had the violence started? And what secrets did Josie know? How could one so young comprehend the crops of fraternity blighted, and hatred like stone, the ground between hearts scorched, and vengeance a cry in the souls of those concerned?

36

THE BEGINNING OF her life with Grange was the beginning of her initiation into a world of perplexity, and a knowledge of impersonal cruelty beyond what she had known in her own home. After her long depression and sadness had passed, except for fleeting moments when she felt tears on her cheeks for no easily discernible reason, there were casual but emphatic talks about Indians, and yellow people who lived in houses with roofs like upside-down umbrellas. Ruth learned for the first time that there was a sea and that its waters were larger than the whole of Baker County. She listened to sketches of places with foreign names, Paris, London, New York. In addition to the full and joyous days of wine-making and dancing, there were days devoted to talk about big bombs, the forced slavery of her ancestors, the rapid demise of the red man; and the natural predatory tendencies of the whites, the people who had caused many horrors.

There were days of detailed description of black history. Grange recited from memory speeches he'd heard, newscasts, lectures from street corners when he was in the North, everything he had ever heard. There was impassioned rhetoric against a vague country of wealthy mobsters called America. And, when she was old enough to carry a gun, she was taught to shoot birds and rabbits. She would rather have done almost anything else. But rabbit was good cooked with potatoes, and birds were like chicken. Still, her heart was scarcely in it.

Ruth could not understand Grange's aversion to white people. Mem had let her play with white children, and now, at her grandfather's, there were wonderful ones, she thought, down the road. Playing with them, however, was strictly forbidden. Apparently they were not, at six and seven, as completely wholesome as they looked.

"Why?" she asked, rebelling and beginning nervously to chew her nails.

"One," Grange said, "they stole you from Africa."

"*Me?*" she asked.

"Be quiet," he said. "Two. They brought you here in chains."

"Hummm?" she murmured. Looking at her slightly rusty but otherwise unmarked ankles.

"Three. They beat you every day in slavery and didn't feed you nothing but weeds. . . ."

"Like we give Dilsey?" she interrupted.

"Collards," he said. "And guts."

"Chitlins? I like them. I like collards too."

They did nasty things to women. (She was only nine then.)

"What, what!" she asked, excited.

They are evil.

They are blue-eyed devils.

They are your natural enemy.

"Stay away from them hypocrites or they will destroy you."

"They didn't do nothing to me, I think you making a mistake," she said, fingering her buttons.

"They killed your father and mother," he said.

As far as she was concerned her father still lived, although at times she wished he wouldn't.

"No, they didn't," she said, for she just couldn't see it.

37

To Grange his son was as dead as his son's murdered wife. If he had stopped long enough to consider that his son still lived, his opinion would not have been much different: he would have said he was a member of the living dead, one of the many who had lost their souls in the American wilderness. The cesspool of Brownfield's life was an approximation of nothingness. In prison now for the murder of his wife, Brownfield continued to plot evil. He spent every moment he could in the presence of vileness. His only confidante was his father's wife. Grange considered the possibility of Josie, aided by Brownfield, turning against him, trying to make him suffer for his neglect of her in favor of his granddaughter. But he did not concern himself long with such wonderings; Ruth needed him to teach her the realities of life. What plotters might do to him, his wife and son, or otherwise, was something he could confront when the time came. In the meantime, he watched Josie coming and going, he heard Brownfield's name often on her lips. He was not unmoved, but as Josie was one day to learn, he was by nature the most unjealous of men.

It disturbed Grange that Ruth appeared drawn to Brownfield at times, attracted to the same qualities that he knew repulsed and frightened her. It seemed to him that Ruth turned her father's image over and over in her mind as if he were a great conundrum. When she was thinking about him her look was confounded, as if she knew a door very well but found it lacked a key. He did not like to recall the night he had rushed to Mem's house to find Mem and her children piled in a heap in the middle of the yard. The other girls, Daphne and Ornette, were whisked away by a smooth-talking Northern preacher (Mem's father), and his wife, who were all quivering chins and amazement. The old guy was sadder than his wife, so moved by the tragedy that he wanted to take all the children, though he had not, so long ago, wanted their mother. Ruth alone could not be pried loose from her grandfather's arms. And he had wanted her so much he could not believe himself capable of such strong emotion. Not after everything. Josie had at first found his attachment to the small frightened child amusing. He'd never wanted *her* like that, she said. And it was true. His motives for marrying Josie in the first place were suspect, and she rightfully suspected them. Her weakness was that she cared for him and had waited for him a long time. She foolishly believed that having her he could do no wrong.

When he had come back from the North, knowing that even if she had not remained faithful to him she would be waiting, there was no way for her to understand the changes he felt. When he had gone through Baker County on his way North he was a baby in his knowledge of the world. Although he knew the world was hard. He had not even comprehended what he was running to. He was simply moving on to where people said it was better. Josie had had no way of knowing how revulsed he was by what he found in that world, how much he needed to bury himself out of sight of everything. She could not understand, as so many people like her (small, untraveled, thoughtless), how he loathed the thought of being dependent on a white person or persons again, how he would almost rather be blind than have to see, even occasionally, a white face. He had found that wherever he went whites were in control; they ruled New York as they did Georgia; Harlem as they did Poontang Street. If he had taken Josie with him as they had planned, perhaps she would have understood. Two things and two only he wanted when he came back to Baker County. Independence from the whites, complete and unrestricted, and obscurity from those parts of the world he chose. For this security he needed Josie's money. Josie had thought it was love for her that made him such a seeker of privacy. She thought he needed to own a secluded farm so as to enjoy her charms the better. Her vanity at all times was both provincial and great.

He had tried countless times to initiate her into the hatreds of the world, the irrepressible hatreds he contained, barely, in himself. Once he had told her of a murder (or suicide) which he had caused, and she had been horrified. As horrified that the victim was white as she would have been if she had been black. He could not make her understand there was a difference.

"One life is worth any other," she said religiously, his fat whorish wife who was raped at sixteen and never avenged.

"What about what they have done to us?"

"How could *you* do such a thing?"

"An eye for an eye—anyway, you knowed I walked out on my wife and child. They could have starved. You never made no complaints about that!"

Josie ducked her head. "That were a little different," she said.

"Why?" he asked. "Because by leaving them it meant you would end up with *both* of us?"

She began to cry. "The Lord *help* you," she blurted, her chins shaking.

"'Bout time he did," he said to her, "just about time he did!"

Now, as he sought to teach the ways of the world to his grand-daughter and she resisted him, he was reminded of his own education in foreign parts of the world. For though he hated it as much as any place else, where he was born would always be home. Georgia would be home for him, every other place foreign.

"If you don't like 'em, Grange," said his Ruth, "if you don't like 'em, seems like to me you'd a shot five or six of 'em in the head!" Her imagination beyond her warped reality was fixed by TV westerns. According to them, if you didn't like the guys on the white horse you challenged them to a draw. You always won, of course, and a child of ten is very strict at applying the rules.

"There are more of them than me."

"How many more?"

"Billions."

"Wyatt Earp one time shot five men that were gunning for him. One was on the roof over the saloon, one was in the sa-loon door, one was in the middle of the street behind a wagon, and the other one was behind him hiding behind his wife. How many is that?"

"Too many in real life."

"But you're a good man, Grange, *all things considered*, and you'd be all right."

Beside such faith his acts against injustice seemed not just puny and ineffectual and selfish but *cowardly* as well.

"I wonder if *He* don't like them too?" She looked perplexed. Always she spoke of her father as He with a capital H, as if she were speaking of God. At times like now she both hated and respected him.

"Did you know I run away from your grandmother once a long time ago?" he asked her another time.

"Was she *funny* acting, like Josie?"

"What you mean?" He was surprised to know a child so young could be so *un*blind.

"Aw, you know. I would have run away from her too. She was trashy!"

"She wasn't trashy," he said gently. "She was a pretty woman and wanted nice things like any pretty woman and when she couldn't get them, well, she wanted something exciting to keep happening to her to take her mind off them. I wanted them things too, so after a long spell of not getting no pretty things nor no excitement neither we couldn't seem to get no thrills from nothing but fighting each other." Grange looked off over his granddaughter's head.

"I worked for a old white man that would have stole the skin right off my back, if black hides'd bring a good price."

"Ah!" she said, taking a step away from him.

He knew what was wrong. "Wait 'til you're grown. You'll see. They can be hated to the very bottom of your guts, can the white folks!"

"You put it *all* on them!" she said, starting up. "You just as bad as Him! He killed . . . !" She could not go on; furious tears filled her eyes.

"Let us go look at our traps," he said, pretending not to see. He reached for his gun.

"The white folks didn't kill my mother," she said at last. "He did!"

"I won't say you're entirely wrong," said Grange, putting an arm around her shoulder. "If there's one snake that'd kill my theory it's your pa."

"Tell me something real mean that you did." Ruth was soothed somewhat by their slow walking through the woods looking at the traps.

He was afraid all their arguments would end this way, and as he could not risk losing her he could never tell her. If he could never back up his words of fighting with actual deeds done and battles won, how could he teach her the necessary hate? The hate that would mean her survival. He was ashamed of himself. It was his weakness, this certainty that she thought him good. She honestly thought him incapable of real evil, of murder, which to her would always be the unthinkable crime. She would have no sympathy for anyone who took the life of another human being. And yet, he was not innocent, he had, once he had learned it, lived his code. The resistance of his choosing was all around her. Even she was part of it. He had lost his innocence, his naïveté, all the better qualities of himself. He had discovered, as Ruth must, that innocence and naïveté are worthless assets in a wilderness, as strong teeth and claws are not.

"Well . . . ?" she began.

"There was a time—" he said, and stopped. Slowly he shook his head. All his years of violence and hardness swirled through his mind, like bits of dirty paper with dates and pictures. Alone, from the vast sea of criminal debris, there arose the memory of a night many years ago.

It was in the spring of 1926 that he had left his wife and Brownfield and the baby, Star, to go North. He had stayed with Josie for several weeks at the Dew Drop Inn until her possessive "love" and jubilation over Margaret's death began to get on his nerves. Yes, he had known about Margaret's death the day after it happened, but he had not returned home. It had hit him hard though, and he had wondered and worried about Brownfield. But he had felt he must continue North. He had his mind on living free, and that meant that even Josie, especially Josie, could not come with him.

By the middle of that summer he had worked, begged, stolen his way North, to New York. Among the frozen faces and immobile buildings he had been just another hungry nobody headed for Harlem. For some months he existed on a variety of hustles. He soon found himself doing things he'd never dreamed he'd do; he sold bootleg whiskey and drugs and stolen goods; he sold black women to white men, the only men at that time who seemed to have money for such pleasures. All of his hustles were difficult for him at first because, as his partners in crime declared, he was just a small dog from the backwoods. Luckily, his backwoodsness did not rule out the possibility of his learning new tricks. Unlike some unfortunate Southern migrants, he did not starve, though he was often close enough to it.

He had come North expecting those streets paved with that gold, which had already become a cliché to the black people who had come before him and knew better, but who still went down home every summer spreading the same old rumors. He had come expecting to be welcomed and shown his way about.

No golden streets he was soon used to. But no friendliness, no people talking to one another on the street? Never. He was, perhaps, no longer regarded as merely a "thing"; what was even more cruel to him was that to the people he met and passed daily he was not even in existence! The South had made him miserable, with nerve endings raw from continual surveillance from contemptuous eyes, but they *knew he was there.* Their very disdain proved it. The North put him in solitary confinement where he had to manufacture his own hostile stares in order to see himself. For why were they pretending he was not there? Each day he had to say his name to himself over and over again to shut out the silence.

"Grange. My name Grange. Grange Copeland is my name."

He had killed a woman with child on a day when he was in excruciating pain from hunger. He had been begging in Central Park, barely escaping arrest from mounted police. Evening was falling after a bright winter day. He crouched underneath some shrubbery, waiting for the park to empty of cyclists and walkers and the old people, who, forgotten by their children but at least well-dressed and fed, spent their days as long as there was any bit of sun in the lively park.

He had been in New York three and a half years then and was wearing the one warm suit of clothes he had managed to steal. He had become a good thief and, beyond a few beatings "on suspicion" (never for things he had done) by the police, had never been caught. There had been times when he hoped to be caught and sentenced, if only to be fed and kept bathed and warm, but his luck, like his need to run about unhampered, took him out of danger of that "safety" into another kind which suited his spirit to some degree but wreaked havoc in his mind.

Crouching in the weeds, silently kneading his fingers to keep them from becoming and staying stiff, he kept his eyes on a frail, hugely pregnant woman who was sitting on a bench by the pond. She had been sitting there a long time, obviously waiting for someone. He could discern no ring on her finger. From minute to minute she seemed to shudder, whether from cold or exhaustion he could not tell. She wore a heavy blue coat, somewhat faded, and black boots probably lined with fur. Her hair was cut very short and was blonde almost to whiteness. Her face was broad and from what he could see, very pale and drawn, though her lips, against her white face, seemed incredibly red. When he saw her closer he saw they were painted red, with the lipstick going far out over the edges of her natural lips, so that it was hard to tell where her natural mouth was, and they were bitten red, puffy and swollen, and seemingly inflamed.

He was fascinated by pregnancy, and this woman's big belly brought forth a mixture of sweet and painful recollections. The creative process was tremendous, he thought. A miracle. But when he thought of Margaret's belly, bitter grimaces forced themselves to his lips.

While he crouched tremblingly, blowing on his hands, a tall muscular soldier, also very blond, strode up to the woman and they embraced. They walked up and down the length of the pond for several minutes, with him chafing her hands and blowing against her ears. The park was nearly deserted. A park policeman rode by and smiled when he saw the lovers. Grange thought that to the policeman too they must have looked *so real*, so remindfully like somebody that might have been yourself.

Soon they sat down upon the bench by the pond. The soldier, after looking carefully all around, gingerly touched the top of the large stomach and the young woman smiled. Grange crept close beside their bench, he did not know why, except that he was drawn to this life that was starting, and drawn to the look of love on the faces of the couple. At least he thought it looked like love. He forgot his hunger for a while watching them kiss in the gathering dusk. Chaste kisses they exchanged, as befitted soon-to-be parents perhaps never-to-be-wed. But the young man, with the light from the park lamps above shining on his gold hair, took from his pocket a silver object. He held it flashing briefly in the light. The young woman sat with her face glowing, calmly, joyously, but, Grange felt, with tears, while he slipped the ring on her finger. He said a few tense words still clutching both her hands and she turned just her shortcropped head on her heavy body and stared incredulously. "Why?" she cried. And the sharp, stricken hurt sound of a woman betrayed touched his ear. He watched them arguing now, the girl trying to throw the silver ring into the pond. The young man prevented her, and finally, woodenly, she dropped the ring to the ground between their feet. They sat in silence making no move to pick it up. From what Grange had managed to hear it appeared the young man already had a wife. Soon, glancing at his watch, the soldier rose to leave and tried to brush his lips across her brow. She ducked her head.

He looked tall and brave and honorable in his uniform. Perhaps that was why the girl's face set itself in such a sneer of contempt. Grange saw the sneer when she turned her face from the young man. He saw her battered and cruel and shuttered profile. The man poked at the ring with his shoe, muttered something (perhaps concerning its value) and re-luctantly took out his wallet. (Had she said she would throw any ring of his into the pond?) Grange had never seen such money; the young man pressed a fat wad of it into the girl's lifeless hand. On the profile that was turned to Grange a tear must have fallen, for a small thin white hand quickly brushed the area near her eye, down to her chin.

And now he was turning away, and she was not looking at anything, just vacant. Her eyes turned away from the pond and back into the trees and the high hard rocks. When he was out of sight she looked in the direction he had gone, but then the dusk had made empty air of the last sliver of shadow from his strong frame. She began, silently, to cry. Then she sniffled, then the sobs came hard and fast as if she wanted and believed she could, if she tried, cry herself to death, and if not to death, to a long forgetful sleep.

Grange had watched the scene deteriorate from the peak of happiness to the bottom of despair. It was the first honestly human episode he had witnessed between white folks, when they were not putting on airs to misinform the help. His heart ached with pity for the young woman as well as for the soldier, whose face, those last seconds, had not been without its own misery. And now the perhaps normally proud woman sat crying shamelessly—but only because she thought herself alone. There she sat, naked, her big belly her own tomb. Or at least it must have seemed so to her, for from cry to cry she pressed with both hands against her stomach as if she would push it away from her and into the pond.

Grange had about made up his mind to speak to her and offer what help he could, for he feared she would harm herself with her crying and staying out so long in the freezing weather. But abruptly, when she apparently considered she had cried enough, the young woman stopped, blew her nose and wiped her eyes. Quite containedly. He could almost see the features settle into a kind of haughty rigidity that belied the past half-hour. Her face became one that refused to mark itself with suffering. He knew, even before he saw them, that her eyes would be without vital expression, and that her lips and cheeks and old once-used laugh wrinkles would have to do all her smiling from then on. He did not even feel she would regret it.

Somehow this settling into impenetrability, into a sanctuary from further pain, seemed more pathetic to him than her tears. At the same time her icy fortitude in the face of love's desertion struck him as peculiarly white American. No blues would ever come from such a saving of face. It showed a lack of self-pity (and Grange believed firmly that one's self was often in need of a little sympathetic pity) that also meant less sympathy for the basic tragedies that occurred in the human situation. She appeared to him to be the kind of woman who could raise ten sons to be killed in war, sending them off with a minimum of tears one at a time, collecting a stack of flags to prove her own bravery.

How did he expect her to act? He really didn't know. Shivering, he stepped over the low green fence and skirted the edge of the shrubbery. She was just rising to leave. The silver ring still lay in the worn dirt before the bench. The money she had let drop, carelessly, from her fingers. Bills fluttered, folded in half, in a small bright green pile. Grange had a hard time noticing anything else once he saw that the money was about to be abandoned and that it was not counterfeit. (Such tantalizingly green bills could not be!)

He had stolen so much and from so many sources in New York that stealing had become a useful and ready tool to be used at will, not unlike a second language. He knew tricks and he knew sob stories (unfortunately more true than not) to melt his victims' hearts (if caught) and he knew cunning and he knew violence. He had had few qualms about stealing before, but now, when it was simply a matter of taking, he felt a totally unprecedented hesitation.

The woman had walked some distance along the pond when he picked up both the ring and the money and counted it. His breath came in a joyful gasp of disbelief when he counted seven hundred dollars in one-hundred-dollar bills and twenties. In his excitement he dropped down upon the bench and rested his head against the back. He was light-headed from hunger and his body could barely sustain the excitement without making him black out. He struggled with dizziness and nausea, clamping his teeth hard together and gripping his left hand with his right. The money, like a heavy paper frog, seemed to jump in his inside coat pocket, but it was his heart thumping against it and drowning out everything else. He darted up briefly to look after the woman; when he was sitting down he couldn't see her, but standing he could see that she had stopped some distance away beside the deep end of the pond and that she stood, seeming to blow in the wind—perhaps his tired eyes made her waver. His first thought was to run away as fast as he could, to get out of the park as quickly as his shaking legs would carry him. Already he thought he could hear a couple of park policemen on horses patrolling nearby. But there had been something so poignant, so sad, and so infinitely pathetic about the scene he had witnessed that he found himself unable simply to disappear. Instead, in a matter of seconds, his feet turned themselves in the direction of the young woman.

All thought of his shaggy, unkempt appearance, his bushy beard and stinking underarms and breath, had ceased with his first acquaintance with starvation. He did not consider the possibility that the young woman might find cause to object to foul body odor, or to a black tramp appearing out of nowhere to solace her. He should have thought of those things, he thought later on, when the woman and her baby were dead. But he did not really then; in fact, at the time, he could think of no matterable difference between them. Misery leveled all beings, he reasoned, going after her.

Hastily he divided the money; he would give her three hundred, he would keep four hundred. She could also have the ring.

He approached her cautiously, looking over his shoulder each few steps to be sure the police were not around. He stopped four feet from her, and like her, began to stare into the pond. Gradually, for he had begun to feel unsure of what he planned to do, he moved closer, inch by studiedly nonchalant inch.

At that time of the year only the center of the pond was free from ice, the sides near the banks were white with it. It was a dismal sight; the fallen leaves had drifted down to the edge of the water and turned into a sort of patterned slime, the ice keeping them from disintegrating altogether. There was not much to look at that was not depressing. The night was grayish and cold; the park lights offered only brightness, no warmth or cheerfulness.

As she stood downwind from him she quickly sensed his presence. Putting her hand gently against the end of her nose, and looking at him with a typical New York, not-seeing look, she moved.

"Ma'am?" he said, pursuing her, holding out his hand.

She pretended not to hear him, but went to stand on a small platform that jutted out over the pond. He stood below her, watching her, holding the money and the ring in his hand.

"'Scuse me, ma'am," he said, and as if by rote his arm took his hat from his head. "I found this here back yonder by the bench and I was just wondering if . . . ?" She had turned a truly paper-white and her eyes held the cold tenseness of a prepared learned scream.

"No!" she cried shortly, holding a thin arm back and up as if to ward him off and strike him. "It's not mine." Abruptly she turned her back to him, waiting for him to leave.

"It yours all right," he said patiently, with one foot raised on the steps to the platform, the fistful of money clenched at his knee. "I seen that young solyer give it to you."

The small back stiffened. If it had not been so cold Grange would have sworn he saw, in the fleeting moment she turned to look at him, a crimson blush. He stood shivering quietly behind her.

"Give it to me!" she said sharply, turning and looking him up and down in fury. He handed it to her, along with the ring. The ring she laid on the railing, the money she counted.

"This ain't all of it," she said. "I want all of it! *You* ain't going to have any of it; before I let *you* sneak off with it I'll throw it all into the pond!" She threw one of the twenties into the pond, her painted lips smiling archly as she watched Grange go down instinctively to retrieve it from the ice. When he rose up empty-handed her mouth laughed. "Look at the big burly-head," she said, and laughed again.

Grange swallowed. He hated her entire race while she stood before him, pregnant, having learned nothing from her own pain, helpless except before someone more weak than herself, enjoying a revenge that severed all possible bonds of sympathy between them.

She stood there like a great blonde pregnant deified cow. She was not pretty, but only a copy of a standardly praised copy of prettiness. She was abandoned, but believed herself infinitely cared for and wanted. By somebody. She was without superiority, but believed herself far above him.

"Give me that money, nigger," she said, menacingly, moving toward him. His tongue would not work he was so angry.

If she put her hands on me I'm going to knock that white brat right out of her stomach! he thought grimly, watching the almost transparent white face come closer to his own. He felt, as if asleep, a sharp pain in his leg above the ankle. He had to look up into her twisted face and pitiless eyes to believe she had kicked him.

A thousand drums pounded behind his temples. His throat was dry. His eyes, bleary from hunger and fatigue, were red and wolfish as with a lunge he fell on her, bearing her to the stone floor of the platform. She began to scream as he held her by the shoulders and shook her, dragging her finally to her feet. His hunger made his rage shortlived and he could not hit her. He relived his old plantation frustrations as she stood there before him stoically calling him names. She was not afraid of him. It seemed unreal to him that she could persist in calling him nigger when he might have been challenging her to fight for her very life.

Steady on her feet again the woman tried to jump from the platform to the grass. He was standing in front of the steps and she did not "care" to order him to move. She knew his weakness before a single scream from her, and did not fear him as much as she despised him. She would get the police and they would get the money from him, teaching him a lesson in the meantime. Misjudging the distance and the weight of her heavy body, she fell through the ice into the pond. Grange had been standing mute and still, but immediately he raced down the shallow steps to try to reach her from the bank. In a split second he recalled how he had laughed when his grandfather admitted helping white "masters" and "mistresses" out of burning houses. Now he realized that to save and preserve life was an instinct, no matter whose life you were trying to save. He stretched out his arm and nearly touched her. She reached up and out with a small white hand that grabbed his hand but let go when she felt it was *his* hand. Grange drew back his dirty brown hand and looked at it. The woman struggled to climb the bank against the ice, but the ice snagged her clothes, and she stuck in the deep sucking mud near the steep shore. When she had given him back his hand and he had looked at it thoughtfully, he turned away, gathering the scattered money in a hurry. Finally she sank. She called him "nigger" with her last disgusted breath.

On his way out of the park he saw the mounted police headed in the direction of the pond.

"Git out of the park, *you*!"

"Don't you know better than to be here this time of night?"

"Yassur," said Grange, pulling an imaginary forelock. "Jest now leavin', boss."

The two men laughed scornfully.

He often thought about that woman; in fact, she and her big belly haunted him. Probably any other woman (or even pregnant bitch) he would have pulled to safety no matter how much she feared him or despised him or hated him or *whatever* that woman had felt so strongly against him. But he faced his refusal to save her squarely. Her contempt for him had been the last straw; never again would he care what happened to any of them. She was perhaps the only one of them he would ever sentence to death. He had killed a thousand, ten thousand, a whole country of them in his mind. She was the first, and would probably be the only real one.

The death of the woman was simple murder, he thought, and soul condemning; but in a strange way, a bizarre way, it liberated him. He felt in some way repaid for his own unfortunate life. It was the taking of that white woman's life—and the denying of the life of her child—the taking of her life, not the taking of her money, that forced him to want to try to live again. He believed that, against his will, he had stumbled on the necessary act that black men must commit to regain, or to manufacture their manhood, their self-respect. They must kill their oppressors.

He never ceased to believe this, adding only to this belief, in later years, that if one kills he must not shun death in his turn. And this, he had found, was the hardest part, since after freeing your suppressed manhood by killing whatever suppressed it you were then taken with the most passionate desire to live!

After leaving the park that night he had waited for an end to come to him. He was both ready and not ready. He felt alive and liberated for the first time in his life. He wanted to see a thousand tomorrows! For, perhaps because he had both killed and not killed the woman (it was her decision not to take his offered help, he reasoned), he did not know if his own life was required. But his exaltation had been part readiness to die. As a sinner, after seeing the face of God, is ready then immediately to meet him, not wanting a continuation of his sordid past to reverse his faith.

"Teach them to hate!" he shouted up and down the Harlem streets, his eyes glazed with his new religion. "Teach them to *hate*, if you wants them to survive!"

Mothers, shuffling along Lenox Avenue with dozens of black children in tow, turned to look at him with hopeless eyes. The children giggled at him as if they already understood the amusing complexity of it all.

At storefront churches he disrupted services.

"Don't teach 'em to *love them!*" he cried. "Teach them to hate 'em!"

The black, oily-voiced preachers and the beige and powdered (and elaborately wigged) sisters looked at him in horrified preeminence.

"Git that drunk sinner *out* of here, deacons!" the preachers shouted. The parasites!

The overworked deacons, with rough pious hands that beat their women to death when they couldn't feed them, would come up to him apologetically.

"You *drunk*, brother?" they asked him gently.

"Betta *sleep* it off!"

Not one of them earned enough to feed his children meat for Sunday dinner.

"*Love* thy neighbor," they whispered to him. "Do *good* to them that despitefully use you."

"We *have* loved them," Grange whispered back, his voice rising to compete with the melancholy notes of the church's organ. "We loves 'em now. And by God it *killing* us! It already done killed *you.*"

The kindly deacons walked him to the street, urging him with soothing words to see reason. Grange hated them with great frustration. Loving their white neighbors in the North as in the South got them nothing but more broken heads and contemptuous children. But did they dare to learn why they had no love for themselves and only anger for their children? No, they did not.

"Hatred for them will someday unite us," he shouted from the corner of Seventh Avenue. "It will be the only thing that can do it. Deep in our hearts we hates them anyhow. What I say is brang it out in the open and teach it to the young 'uns. If you teach it to them young, they won't have to learn it in the school of the hard knock."

"Hatred is bad for a man's mind," someone told him.

"Man don't live with his mind alone," said Grange. "He live with his mouth and with his stomach. He live with his pride and with his heart. That man's got to eat. That man's got to sleep. That man got to be able to take care of his own life. I say if love can git man all this, then go 'head and let it; but it ain't done nothin' all these years *for us*. If love can do so much good to the minds of all these here *dope* addicts an' cutthroats hangin' round this here street it mighty late startin'— on account they is so *many* dope addicts and cutthroats, and they ain't all children!

"You wants to keep on teachin' your children Christian stuff from a white-headed Christ you go right on—but *me*, an' later on *you*—is goin' to have to switch to somethin' new! And since hatred is what's got to be growin' inside of you that's exactly what has to come out, and in the right direction this time!"

He was like a tamed lion who at last tasted blood. There was no longer any reason not to rebel against people who were not gods. His aggressiveness, which he had vented only on his wife, and his child, and his closest friends, now asserted itself in the real hostile world. For weeks after the incident at the pond he fought more Italians, Poles, Jews (all white; he did not understand differences in their cultures, and if they "acted white" he punched them in the nose!), in and around Harlem than he had been aware lived there. And in this fighting too he tasted the sweet surge of blood rightfully directed in its wrath that proclaimed his freedom, his manhood. Every white face he cracked, he cracked in his sweet wife's name.

But soon he realized he could not fight all the whites he met. Nor was he interested in it any longer. Each man would have to free himself, he thought, and the best way he could. For the time being, he would withdraw completely from them, find a sanctuary, make a life that need not acknowledge them, and be always prepared, with his life, to defend it, to protect it, to keep it from whites, inviolate.

And so he had come back to Baker County, because it was home, and to Josie, because she was the only person in the world who loved him, and because he needed even more money than he had to buy the rock of his refuge.

Josie, who had lived so long in the hope of his love, was persuaded, out of her own love for him, to sell her cherished livelihood, the Dew Drop Inn. With his money and hers he bought a farm. A farm far from town, off the main road, deep behind pines and oaks. He raised his own bread, fermented his own wine, cured his own meat. At last, he was free.

But his freedom had cost him. There was Josie, learning each day that once again she had been used by a man and discarded when his satisfaction was secured. He had done her wrong, and the thought nagged at him and had finally begun to make him appreciate her for the first time. She was bighearted, generous; she could love in spite of all that had gone wrong in her life. But then there had been Ruth, breaking in on his growing love for Josie, his acceptance of her genuine goodness and adoration. Ruth, who needed him and who was completely fresh and irresistibly innocent, as alas, Josie was not. He had felt himself divided, wanting to comfort the old but feeling responsible for the new. And then there had been Brownfield, again. And though he had forgiven Josie once (true, not out of love but greed and expediency) for her attachment to his son, he did not know if he could forgive her a second time. Josie and Brownfield sought to retaliate against his indifference to them; but even for this was he not to blame?

"You are not selfish," Ruth was saying as she bent over to lift a small rabbit from a trap. "You would never steal. Even your cussing is harmless." She laughed as her grandfather took the rabbit from her, felt its smallness and let it go. "I know you don't like killing things, even things to eat."

"It ought never to be necessary to kill nobody to assert nothing," he said. "But some mens, in order to live, can't be innocent."

Ruth was still laughing. "You so tall and rough-looking with your big boots and your long gun." Impulsively she hugged his arm. "But *we* know you got a heart, don't we?"

And Grange knew he would never tell her of his past, of the pregnant woman and his lectures of hate; he would never tell her that he'd mugged old women and weak-limbed students to buy his food. He would never tell her that he was guilty of every sin, including selfishness, or that Josie's heart was purer than his had ever been. He would never tell her that the land she stood on, which would be hers someday, was bought with blood and tears. He would never tell her because she might believe him, and because with Ruth he had learned an invaluable lesson about hate; he could only teach hate by inspiring it. And how could he spoil her innocence, kill the freshness of her look, becloud the brightness of her too inquisitive eyes?

At least love was something that left a man proud that he *had* loved. Hate left a man shamed, as he was now, before the trust and faith of the young.

"The mean things I've done," he began. "Think of me, when I'm gone, as a big, rough-looking coward. Who learned to love hisself only after thirty-odd years. And then over-done it."

She was not to know until another time, that her grand-father, as she knew him, was a reborn man. She did not know fully, even after he was dead, what cruelties and blood fostered his tolerance and his strength. And his love.

Part VIII

Part VIII

38

AFTER MEM'S FUNERAL, to which he was allowed to go, though chained to a red-faced warden in dirty boots, Brownfield had thought uncomfortably but not regretfully of what he had done. But he had never been able to think himself very far. *He liked plump women.* That was the end-all of his moral debates. *Ergo,* he had murdered his wife because she had become skinny and had not, with much irritation to him, reverted, even when well-fed, to her former plumpness. He was not a fool to ask himself whether there was logic in his nerves. He knew what he liked.

The days of her plumpness haunted him as blackberry pie had done when he was a growing boy and pies of any kind were few and far between. He longed for a now over-and-done with lushness. His time of plenty, when he could provide.

Plumpness and freedom from the land, from cows and skinniness, went all together in his mind, and her face as it had been when he first knew her at the Dew Drop Inn took on for him the same one-dimensional quality as his memory of pies and a whiskey bottle. He could forget her basic reality, convert it into comparisons. She had been like good pie, or good whiskey, but there had never been a self to her because one no longer existed in him. Dead, Mem became a myth of herself, a beautiful plump girl with whom he had fallen in love, but who had changed before his eyes into an ugly hag, screeching at him and making him feel small.

If she had been able to maintain her dominance over him perhaps she would not stand now so finished, a miniature statue, in his mind, but her inherent weakness, covered over momentarily by the wretched muscular hag, had made her ashamed of her own seeming strength. And without this strength, the strength to kill his ass, to make him wallow continually in his own puke, she was lost. Her weakness was forgiveness, a stupid belief that kindness can convert the enemy. The logical next step from hitting him so magnificently over the head with the gun was for one of them to use it. That was where her staunch ten-point resolution had failed her. And he, without resolutions, but with the memory of his humiliation, could, and did, at last regain what she had stolen that Sunday morning when he lay in vomit at her feet. The punishment he had devised for her "come down" had not been enough. She had thought she could best him again by leaving him. And he had warned her, if she tried, what he would do. A man of his word, as he thought of himself, he had kept his word. His word had even become his duty.

But she was not a plump woman and he did not like them skinny. When they were like that something was wrong, and you weren't doing them right. And he did not want to know about it.

39

Josie told him that Ruth now lived, and happily, with Grange. It maddened Brownfield that his father should presume to try to raise his child. Ornette and Daphne, taken up North by Mem's father, did not concern Brownfield as much as Ruth, because when they went North he relinquished claim to them, knowing quite well he would never go North after them. In prison, condemned for ten years to cut lawns and plant trees for jailers, judges, and prominent citizens of Baker County (though he was to be paroled after seven years), he realized an extraordinary emotion. He loved the South. And he knew he loved it because he had never seriously considered leaving it. He felt he had a real understanding of it. Its ways did not mystify him in the least. It was a sweet, violent, peculiarly accommodating land. It bent itself to fit its own laws. One's life, underneath the rigidity of caste, was essentially one of invisibility and luck. One did not feel alone in one's guilt. Guilt dripped and moved all over and around and about one like the moss that clung to the trees. A man's punishment was never written up somewhere in a book before his crime was committed—it was not even the same as someone else's punishment for the same crime. The punishment was made to fit the man and not the crime. It was individual punishment. One felt unique in one's punishment if not in one's crime. This appealed to Brownfield. It meant to him that one could punish one's own enemies with a torture of one's own choosing. One could make up the punishment and no one had the right to interfere.

In the prison with Brownfield were murderers, pimps, car thieves, drunkards and innocents, and their sentences bore no set relation to their crimes. A young boy of seventeen was in for stealing hubcaps and his sentence was five years. A hatchet murderer whom Brownfield came to know quite well, who had dispatched not only his wife but his wife's mother and aunt, was paroled after three years. Before he was paroled he was a trustee. Before that he had been able to go out of the prison to attend church every Sunday and to spend a few minutes with his woman whenever the desire arose. He had played poker on weekends with the jailers. There was no order about this, which was why it appealed to Brownfield.

Brownfield brooded, while he worked—setting out dogwoods, magnolias and mimosas on spacious well-tended lawns—on his father's audacity at taking his daughter. He brooded on Grange's serenity and on his prosperity. Although he did not love Grange, he was very often depressed by the thought that his father had never really loved him.

Brownfield learned to read and write rather well while in prison. One day he was looking through the account, on the colored page, of Mem's murder, and he saw his own name. Without knowing what was happening he read the whole article and went on to read other articles. The hatchet murderer, who became his friend, told him that the same thing had happened to him. On the day he was brought to trial, he said, his woman had thrust some newspapers into his hands. Look, she had said, there's your picture! She wanted to cheer him up because she was afraid he was going to be electrocuted. The jailers had taken the papers away before he had a chance to examine them, but later, in jail, his woman brought him some more, to celebrate, she had said, his light sentence. They were both very pleased that there was a picture of him in the paper! He had sat a long time marveling at his big ugly picture in the paper, he said, and then, interested in what the paper might say about him, he began to read it. He could not recall where he learned the ABC's; when he was a child he had owned a tiny children's prayer book, from which his mother had read to him over and over. That had been his entire education, as far as he knew.

The boy who stole the hubcaps had been in high school and read well. Brownfield and the hatchet murderer took lessons from him and called him professor. One day, as Brownfield was writing his name, age and prison number on the margins of a newspaper it struck him suddenly that Mem had actually succeeded in teaching him to read and write and that somehow he had not only forgotten those days with her but had also forgotten what she'd taught him. He wondered about this, staring the while at his hands, then he burst into terrible sobs that tore his chest and brought him to the floor.

But his tears did not soften him, did not make him analyze his life or his crime. His crying was just a part of the life that produced his crime. It only made him feel lonely. Introspection came hard to Brownfield and was therefore given up before he became interested in it. The least deep thinking and he was sure he would be lost. As it was, while in prison, he wanted Josie, he wanted his father, he even wanted his mother.

He wanted Ruth. He had a great fear of being alone. He thought he could understand better than any of the other prisoners why God had created the universe when He found himself alone, and fixed it so man had two warm arms and a tongue.

"My daughter," he wrote, in crude spellbound letters. And, "I wish I had got Grange too." He did not hide these words, written on candy wrappers, newspapers and bits of paper from the trash. He left them lying around, clear marks of his existence and his plan.

Brownfield and the hatchet murderer talked sometimes about their motives in life. They watched television every Saturday evening and motives was a new word picked up from the television series, "Dragnet." The motive that got him into prison, said Brownfield, was a keen desire to see if he had any control over himself. No matter which way he wanted to go, he said, some unseen force pushed him in the opposite direction.

"I never did want to be no sharecropper, never did want to work for nobody else, never did want to have white folks where they could poke themselves right into my life and me not have nothing to do with it."

"Yeah, Lawd, and I know what you mean," said the hatchet murderer, who had been a minister before he married one of his converts and started a family. He had discovered too late that he couldn't feed his wife and her kin on what he made off the gospel. Marriage had stripped his nice black suit from him and in its place he had had to make do with overalls caked with sweat and dust he got in fields that would never be his. He knew what his friend was talking about because he had himself struggled against the unseen force. But he had decided the unseen force was God and so killed his wife and her kin. It was his way of leaving God's company.

"I felt just like these words here in the newspaper must feel, all printed up. The line already decided. No moving to the left or the right, like a mule wearing blinders. These words just run one word right behind the other to the end of the page." Brownfield looked at his friend with some small exhilaration in his eyes as he continued, stabbing at the paper with his finger. "Just think how this word here'd feel if it could move right out of this line and set itself down over here!" The two men pondered the power of the mobile, self-determined word. The hatchet murderer nodded.

"I often felt more like a shoe," he said; "a pair of farted-over brogans, just for feets to stand on. I used to put my shoes up on a shelf in the wardrobe to show how I felt. Wouldn't let my wife or her crabby snot-picking ma move 'em down on the floor."

"Yeah," said Brownfield, "you'd think more peoples would think about how they ain't got no more say about what goes on with 'em than a pair of shoes or a little black piece of writing in a newspaper that can't move no matter what it stands for. How come we the only ones that knowed we was men?"

Leaning heavily on his pencil Brownfield wrote m-e-n, then waited glumly for the word to rise and beat its chest.

"Well, that was us," he said. He looked at the hatchet murderer and smiled.

40

IT WAS NOT difficult for Brownfield to take advantage of Josie's pain. He had been surprised the first time she visited him at the jail, but had soon become able to read her like a book. Josie had given up taking her burdens to the Lord; she no longer sought to confess her sins in church; she no longer said prayers or told her troubles to fortunetellers. But all of this she could do at the jail.

She would come on Sunday afternoons when the prisoners were allowed out under the trees. She would sit on one side of a small table, Brownfield on the other. Over the months and years she poured out the anguish of her heart for Brownfield to hear. And he listened sympathetically, craftily, with a priest's show of concern.

He listened to her complaints of his father's indifference, Grange's total infatuation with the idea of preserving innocence, his blind acceptance of Ruth as something of a miracle, something of immense value to him, to his pride, to his will to live, to his soul.

"He don't even know I'm *alive*," said Josie, wringing her

hands. "All day long the two of 'em is together. I just set round, praying for a *word* from him. . . ."

Brownfield listened with a pitying expression on his face. He took one of her hands in his.

"When I get out of here I'll take her off your hands," he promised. But Josie sat up, startled.

"If you took that gal away from him it'd be the same as if you took the air. He wouldn't live out the week! I tell you he *love* her!"

"Josie," he said, "you recognize that you a *fool* for giving a shit whether he live or die?"

"Don't you say that!" she said, drawing her hand from his.

"All right, okay," he said, "don't git your back up." But he was thinking of his father's attachment to Ruth and of how perfect a revenge it would be if he could break it.

Josie was looking at him cautiously. "If you going to talk about your daddy in any mean way, I ain't coming here no more. He *love* me, your daddy do, I *know* he do. This thing with Ruth is something he can't help. But one day he coming to his senses and when he do I'm going to be right there waiting. It ain't like it was *impossible* for him to love us both!"

"'Spose he don't never come to his senses?" asked Brownfield. "*Then* where will you be?"

Josie looked bleakly out across the yard. "He got to come to me," she said. "He *got* to come."

The months went by. One day Brownfield asked about her love life. Josie, sixtyish, had always felt there would be no end to it. She began to cry.

"Which mean he don't come *near* you no more, even for that?"

Josie nodded.

"You mean to tell me," said Brownfield, "that after all you have did for him he don't show *no* kind of 'preshation?"

He began to smile. A flush came to Josie's cheeks. Before she rushed out of the room she slapped him.

After that it was easy.

"After all I done for him!" Josie began to fume when she talked with him. "He don't pay me the mind you'd pay a *dog*."

"And you sold everything you owned and worked so *hard* for to buy him his precious *farm*! Uh, uh, uh," said Brownfield. "Some peoples are just not grateful. Now, if *I* had had a woman like that to do all you done for him, I wouldn't be here today." He was elated when Josie, forgetful of everything but her anger, agreed with him. Soon he had brought her back to his original idea.

"When I gets out I can take Ruth off your hands," he said. "An' then, just think, you and Grange'll be alone just like you was before she come. Things'll be *just* the same." Josie nodded eagerly. "I won't even let them *near* one 'nother."

"But how can you 'complish that?" she asked. "Grange'd shoot to kill if you laid a hand on Ruth."

"Grange may think he above all the rest of the white folks," said Brownfield, "but he ain't above the white folks' law. Maybe the law will be on our side for a change. Anyhow, you let *me* worry 'bout that."

"So glad to!" said Josie, smiling happily. Planning as she'd done for years just how to win for good the man she loved.

Part IX

Part IX

41

"GOOD FENCES DON'T make neighbors," said Grange. "Which is why we's putting this here one up."

Ruth stood beside him holding the hammer. She was barefoot and wearing a pink dress with ruffles at the hem. As Grange stretched the top strand of barbed wire from one post to the next and secured it with a nail, she tiptoed behind him with round watchful eyes befuddled by his activity. She had never seen anyone put up a fence before.

"You finds your stakes—they marks your propity—and going by the deed, you puts your fence square on the line. Then you tightens all your wires," he said, tightening the top wire, "and you be sure all your bobs is good and sharp."

She pricked one finger on a small barb of wire, then gazed intently while the blood welled up. Quickly she stuck the drop of blood against her new dress and her eyes sobered to an expression of remembrance, horror and pain. They appeared to darken, much as the sky, which is open enough until a single cloud puts out the sun.

Grange stopped his work abruptly, not noticing the girl, one might have thought, and placed his own callused finger against a barb, pressing the wire until his finger bled.

"I never did git round to tellin' you 'bout how the Injuns got to be blood brothers with us black peoples," he said, reaching casually for her finger (at which she stared in panic), and which she gave him after first looking to see if she had wiped all the blood away. It was no longer there on her finger tip, but when her grandfather squeezed her finger the dot of blood came back. He drew her down beside him on the grass and stuck their two bleeding fingers together.

"But, Grange," she said scornfully for so young a girl, "they didn't stick *fingers* together. It was *arms*, right here"— she pointed—"they stuck this part of the *arm*." She placed her tenderer forearm next to his darker, more sinewy one.

"Of course," said Grange, "*that* was the way they become blood brothers with the white folks. But see, they didn't *mean* that. Next thing them white brothers knowed they was scalped—which give 'em some of they own medicine. Now, take with us, they was more au*then*tic. That's on account of us all gitting put in such a pass by the white folks. But with one another and with black folks they only press fingers, not arms, and not no lying wrists never!"

"Are you sure?" she asked. "Or are you lying to me?"

"Don't say words like 'lie' to me in company," Grange said pleasantly. "Folks might think you ain't being raised good."

"Well, nobody's here but me and you. Besides, I don't care what folks think. Anyhow, I don't embarrass you nearly as much 'in company' as you embarrass me with your drinking and gambling away all our money all the time."

"Um, yes," said Grange. "Like I was saying. The Injuns is

ever to be your friend. We has just performed the cere-
mony. . . ."

"But we aren't Injuns, we . . ."

"No, indeed. No matter what anybody tells you 'bout the
Injuns—I mean I don't care if it is a Injun hisself—don't you
believe nothing but that they's friendly Injuns. Even if they
don't act friendly. Them that don't act friendly just don't
know no better. You can sort of keep your gun trained on
them while you explain all this I'm telling you to 'em."

"I don't want to get scalped." She giggled.

"Just remember neither does they. Besides, this here is serious." The old man frowned. "The black man must be
friends to every other of the downtrod, especially if he's a
man of color."

"There's those poor folks down the road and you putting
up a fence to keep them away. Ain't they downtrod? They eat
dirt," she said, grimacing. "They ought to be. I don't see what
their white has to do with it."

"We has tried with them. They is the onliest group of
peoples you can't be blood brothers to. They don't want it
and we don't want it either after all these years. They is the
reason fences was invented. I mean, take before they come
here with all they Bibles, do you think the Injuns had done
hogged propity from one another and fenced it all off? No,
ma'am. They hadn't. They didn't mind letting folks use the
grass and the good earth like the Lawd intended it should be
used. Those people over there, you give 'em a chance, they try
to take our land, never mind it belong to us. They want hit,
they take hit. They been that way since hist'ry. They the cause
the fence was invented. Now. Far as we concerned they going
to have to learn to live with it . . . and I mean with the sharp
bobs turned toward them!"

Grange returned determinedly to his fencing, Ruth watching from under her long grapes. They were bleached brownish by the sun with a yellow lion-colored edge. The rest of her hair had been botchily braided and the grapes had not been worked in and caught up. She thought when she got older she would straighten her hair with combs, if Grange let her. She would convince him that grapes were too nappy to put up with. The finer points of hair care mystified her almost as much as they did her grandfather, whose only advice to her when she mentioned her hair was to wash it and grease it a little. Sometimes she even wished Josie would help her out. But just to fix her hair, not to talk and lie around the house with her titties hanging out.

"You're a mean 'un, if you ask me," she said lazily, leaning back on her elbows, turning her face to the sun. "Just a mean, mean old man. Without good home training, or somethin'," she murmured, closing her eyes.

He did not look at her, he concentrated on the fence, thrusting the post-hole diggers deeper and deeper into the hard red soil, stringing the wire tighter and tighter, raising the fence higher and higher.

Not far from where he stood there existed still, it seemed to him, at least the shadows of his first life. He was on his third or fourth and final. The first life of Grange Copeland. The glow of the sun enclosed him in a gone but never-to-be forgotten landscape with its immediate sealing-off heat. And again, as in a stifling nightmare, he saw the long rows and wide acres of cotton rising before him. He felt the sun beating down on his bent back, exploding, pounding, bursting against the back of his head through the wide straw hat. He saw Margaret (first life, first wife!) as she had been when they married, seductive and gay, a whimsical girl-lady, acting strong and stoical out of love for him. While the love lasted. He saw the change come as it had occurred in Margaret's face. Gradually the lines had come, the perplexed lines between the eyes, placed as if against and in spite of the young, smooth and carefree brow. Actually she had had a gay but somnolent face then, as if she existed in a dream. Misery had awakened her, and he had not needed to tell her she had married not into ecstasy, but into dread. Not into freedom, but into bondage; not into perpetual love, but into deepening despair. And he had not needed to tell her who was behind their misery—she knew and then he did not—for someone, *something* did stand behind his cruelty to her (he made himself believe), pushing him on to desert her, and driving her down and to the purgation of suicide for herself and murder for her bastard child.

What could he tell his granddaughter about her sadly loving, bravely raging and revengeful grandmother?

Could he tell her that the sweaty, unkind years plastered themselves across her lovely face like layers of dull paint put on every year? That sometime, in that hopelessness, when cotton production was all that mattered in their world (and not ever their cotton!), even love had stopped and that soon they had not been able even to *remember* love? Could he tell her of his own degradation, his belief in a manhood devoid of truth and honor; of the way he had kept Josie always tucked away for himself, as men tuck a bottle away against despair or snake bite? Could he tell her that Margaret had thought a marriage finished whoredom for a man; that she had thought Grange's respect for his marriage would put an end to his visits to Josie, the whore of his lusting youth? Could he tell Ruth of her grandmother's bewilderment when she learned he still saw Josie once a week, rarely missing a Saturday night? Could he tell her of how Margaret grappled with his explanation that Josie was necessary for his self-respect, necessary for his feeling of manliness? If I can never own nothing, he had told her, I will have women. I love you, he had assured her, because I trust you to bear and raise my sons; I love Josie because she can have no sons.

He could see Margaret sitting alone in the doorway of their cabin. She would watch him leave in the wagon, rolling determinedly, toward the Dew Drop Inn. Her bewilderment had changed to a feeling of inadequacy and she had tried to play her husband's game. She threw away on other men what she felt her husband did not want. And she had finally bedded down with Shipley, the man who had caused everything. This Grange had not been able to bear. His choice was either kill her or leave her. In the end he had done both.

The strangely calm eyes of the old man looked across the fence to rest on his granddaughter. He marveled that, knowing him so well, she knew nothing of that other life. Or even of the dismal birth of her own father. That gray day of retribution in sorrow when the newly born was sentenced to a familiar death.

"And what's *his* name going to be?" he had asked Margaret, feeling no elation at the birth of his son.

In her depression, carelessly she asked him, "What's the first damn thing you see?"

And he, standing before the door, saw the autumnal shades of Georgia cotton fields. "Sort of brownish colored fields," he had answered. And he had wondered, without hope, if that was what covered also the rest of the universe.

"Brownish color," she had said, pushing the sleeping baby from the warm resting at her breast. "Brownish field. Brownfield." There was not even pity in her for her child. "That'll do about as well as King Albert," she said. "It won't make a bit of difference what we name him."

Already she was giving him up to what stood ready to take his life. After only two years of marriage she knew that in her plantation world the mother was second in command, the father having no command at all.

"Grange, save me! Grange, *help* me!" she had cried the first time she had been taken by the first in command. He had plugged his ears with whiskey, telling himself as he ignored her, that he was not to blame for his wife's unforgivable sin. He had blamed Margaret and he had blamed Shipley, all the Shipleys in the world. In Josie's arms he had no longer heard Margaret's cries, no longer considered his wife's lovers who were black; his hatred of Shipley's whiteness had absolved Grange of his own guilt, and his blackness protected him from any feelings of shame that threatened within himself.

His wife had died believing what she had done was sinful and required death, and that what he had done required nothing but that she get out of his life. And now Grange thought with tears in his eyes of what a fool he had been. For, he said to himself, suppose I turned my back on that little motherless girl over there and spent my time with somebody else, some other little girl; would she understand that something *beyond* myself caused it? No, she would not. "And I could parade Shipleys before her from now till doomsday and she'd still want to know what's done happened to her granddaddy's love!" Grange mumbled to himself, his eyes moist and his hands trembling over the wires.

"Looks like some old sad story, from the way you standing there frowning. Wake up!" The child stood beside him with her hand over his arm. "You looking sort of sick from all this heat. I think you better sit down." She pulled him by the suspender strap, like pulling a horse to drink. "Too much sun is not good for old men your age."

"Shet up. What you know 'bout old age? 'Too much sun-shine ain't good for ol' men your age!'" he mimicked her, but seated himself in the shade by the fence. "By the time you git ol' enough to have mouthy grandchildren, you know what's good for you. Only by then it seem like too late to do much about it!" Quickly he rolled up his past and lay back on it, obliterating the keen spots, completely erasing the edges. "I never in my life seen such a womanish gal," he said, stretch-ing out with his back to a tree and taking out his pipe. She lit a match, held his fingers while he lit the pipe, then blew it out.

"I ain't any more sassy than you," she said smartly, push-ing him over roughly so she could also prop herself against the tree. He almost fell down.

"You ain't supposed to say ain't," he said, looking at her solemnly. ("Her eddication," he was known to declare to odd colleagues and peers, "is where I draws the line!") "And don't say you say hit because *I* say hit. I say hit 'cause I don't know no better. I mean, I *know* hit ain't correct, but I can't always remember what to replace hit with."

"A perfect score of hits!" Ruth shouted, clapping her hands. "You ain't—aren't—supposed to say 'hit' for 'it,' nei-ther. 'It' ain't got no h *in* 'hit.'" She giggled.

"I just wanted to check if you was noticing," he said, fuss-ing with his pipe. "You know the *good* part about owning a fence around propity you also owns is that you gits to shoot down any man or beast that sets foot over your boundaries. They is a law what says you can do that."

"You sure are in a bloodthirsty mood," she said tolerantly, "you *sure you* didn't get too much sun?" She lay drowsily, with her chin against her chest. Idly she thwacked him across the leg with a weed. Her new dress had grass stains on it. She inspected them with concerned attention, then turned humming, blissfully, on her stomach.

"Did I ever thank you properly for this dress?" she asked, looking up into his eyes. Reluctantly, he smiled.

"I winned that dress at the poker game last Saddity. I winned near to twenty dollars, then, dang it, I lost fifteen, and I figured I'd get that dress. I spoke to some of the womens there. I say, what size reckon do my grand girl wear?—and they say, they don't know sizes too good (they mostly steals clothes of all sizes), but they thought a twelve. So I pick that there which are a twelve, and I figured them frills round the tail made hit—it—grown up enough for you. I told the white woman what sold it to me. (She act like she didn't want me to say nothing to her, but I did.) I say, you want you one grown-up adolescent-acting, *spoiled* young 'un, you take my granddaughter. She take all my money to deck herself out. I say, she shore is spoiled all right. I say, she see this dress, and the first thing you know she done got grease on it and out setting round in the dirt in it, then she like to wind up tearing it rat down the mittle if the spirit move her to it. Yes, ma'am, I say, she *rough* stuff! I says to the woman what sold it to me." Grange laughed. "She must didn't 'preshate your fine qualities," he said. "She just stood there looking at me like she thought I'd bite, kind of holding onto her teeth like this." He clamped his lips together and made them prune up.

"You ought to call me by my name instead of 'my grand girl.' No wonder nobody knows what you talking about." She laughed nonchalantly. "Anyway, I ain't any more spoiled than you. *However*, I do thank you for this dress." She decided to use other words she'd learned at school. Grange was a glutton for them. "It is *so pleasant.*" She smiled. "It *certainly* is. You know, you have real *excellent* taste!" she deliberately spoke from the back of her mouth, so she would sound like an actress on radio. Her grandfather beamed.

Confusedly, he searched around behind some bushes on his hands and knees, and brought out a pint bottle. "I would offer you some . . ." he began.

". . . but, no thank you," Ruth added. "I'm only ten, and there are some who are concerned about their liver."

"Don't you go upsetting yourself 'bout my liver, it'll keep," the old man said, drinking his whiskey through a chuckle. When the whiskey spilled down his chin, Ruth, who had been flexing her injured finger, and thinking vaguely about Indians, swiped the droplets for her wound. "Antisepsis." She smiled loftily, licking her whole hand.

"Ruth ain't no kind of name for you! Maybe that's why I don't like to use it. . . . You rat out the Bible though, I can guarantee you that much, but it probably one of the parts I ain't read."

"God knows I ain't if you ain't," she said, collecting several whiskey droplets on her tongue.

One day they watched the people who lived on the adjoining property. There was a man who had lank, neck-length hair the color of greasy pine bark. There were half a dozen little cracker children around him. They grew in stairsteps, looked hungry and rusty, and kept straws and pine needles in their teeth. Ruth and Grange lay concealed behind some bushes on their side of the fence. It was Grange's idea that they inspect some "white people" for Ruth's further education. What Ruth noticed was that they were not exactly white, not like a refrigerator, but rather a combination of gray and yellow and pink, with the youngest ones being the pinkest.

"What they doing?" she wanted to know. The daddy of the bunch and two of the older boys lay under a tree, smoking and chewing.

"They probably plotting how to git our land," said Grange.

"Why do you think that?"

"Well, what else do you think they'd be doing, laying over there in the weeds, hiding out from they womenfolks?"

"Well, they could just be trying to get shut of the women's yapping," said Ruth.

"That's just what they'd like for you to believe," said Grange, glowering at the group.

"Do you mean to tell me that that's all they have to do— all of them, all the time—just lay around and think up ways to take this farm?"

"Yup," said Grange, momentarily peevish.

"Well, when do they talk about the weather, then, and the price of cotton and all like that?" Ruth sat upright and Grange quickly pulled her down again out of sight of the group. "I mean, what I want to know, is did anybody ever try to find out if they's real people."

"Nope," said Grange. "'Course the rumor is that they is peoples, but the funny part is why they don't act human."

"Well, when I get big I'm going to find out," Ruth said as they crawled away from the fence. "I want to see and hear them face to face; I don't see no sense in them being looked at like buzzards in a cage."

"All I seem able to teach you is that you want to know," said Grange. "I never seen such a gal as you for looking underneath revealed truth."

Later in the day he asked her, "What would you say if I told you I knows of that family we saw, and that I happens to know the womenfolks don't 'low no smoking nor chewing in they house an' parlor?"

"And that's the reason they sit ganged up in the woods?" Ruth pondered over it a minute. "Well, it makes more sense to me than the other reason did," she said simply, and her grandfather stood exasperated in his truth.

42

ONE DAY AT SCHOOL something happened that said more about white people than anything Grange had ever told her. Her day had started out, as usual, reluctantly. She hated getting up in the morning, especially when she woke up in the house: "Josie's house," she called it, instead of in the cabin, which she considered hers and Grange's, but mostly hers. She and Grange had their breakfast, oatmeal and wine for him, oatmeal and milk for her. Then they walked along the highway to the school. The school was only about half a mile from their house, even nearer through the woods, and they could walk it in a few minutes. Grange left her at the steps of the school as he always did, with the other children standing around staring, as *they* always did. It was a bright March day, warm and balmy, and the sun made light shadows on Grange's blue shirt as he disappeared around the back of the school and into the woods. Both of them loved to walk home through the woods, not only because Grange kept a still between the schoolhouse and his house, but because the woods offered the privacy and quiet they both enjoyed.

The school had three rooms. One room on the end near the well was for the first, second and third grades. The middle room was for the fourth, fifth, sixth and seventh grades, and the one on the other end was for the rest of the grades, including the twelfth. The building was raised off the ground on a foundation of cement blocks and underneath was a cellar of sorts where some of the older boys took some of the older girls. There were tall steps at each end of the building as if the schoolrooms formed a second story. Ruth climbed the steps to the platform-porch which led to the middle room with a mixture of anticipation and dread. She was in the sixth grade and her classroom contained classes four through seven. Her teacher was Mrs. Grayson. Mrs. Grayson would also be her teacher for another year until she passed into the room next door and to a teacher named Mrs. Little. Mrs. Grayson was a handsome, dark brown woman with meticulously manicured nails, and processed hair. She was in the habit of wearing everything gray, and of straightening the seams of her Red Foxx stockings with a spit-daubed finger when she thought no one was looking.

The first subject for the four classes was Health, and Mrs. Grayson walked from one group of desks to another lecturing about the care of "our clean minds and bodies." The next subject was Citizenship, and Mrs. Grayson lectured back and forth about the importance of having "forthright patriotic minds for use in service to your country." By ten o'clock, above the bored humming of the other three classes, she was talking about the importance of studying history. History, Mrs. Grayson said loudly and with great precision and straining of her vocal cords, taught you what had gone on in the world. Eli Whitney, the cotton gin, Thomas Jefferson and the Declaration of Independence, George Washington and the Minutemen. American History was more important than any other kind, she said. And why was that? she asked. Then she answered herself: "Because it is the history of you and I, the proud history of a free people! We have fought to remain free," she shouted, her shrill voice reverberating off the pasteboard walls. "Our history teaches us what has been done for us, as Negroes, and what we have done for ourselves." Pearl Harbor, she said, rhetorically, and the Civil War. History, she beamed, struggling to rise above the noise in her room and the noise from the rooms on each side of her, tells us where we are and shows us how we got there and how important history is to the total enlightenment of the world!

She had to leave from in front of their class for a few minutes because someone in the fourth grade raised his hand from the back of the room and said he couldn't hear what she had said. Ruth heard her, like a recording, ask the small boy personally, "Why is it important to study history?" The boy said sullenly, "I don't know." Then Mrs. Grayson said, clapping her hands in time to her words, "Because history lets you know what has gone on in the world!" The boy said, "Oh, yes, ma'am." And Mrs. Grayson was called across the room to someone in the fifth grade who asked wasn't it also true that George Washington was the father of our country. When last Ruth listened Mrs. Grayson was congratulating the child for having already read this from his new history book.

To Ruth, Mrs. Grayson never made sense. She mouthed all the words in the textbooks but they did not come out coherently as they appeared on the page. When she interpreted a paragraph to the class you could never tell how any of it fit together. Between the few words you were able to catch over the noise and Mrs. Grayson's own abstraction there was little that could be gleaned and put to use. However, having had

Mrs. Grayson the year before, Ruth feared her for her ability to keep track of who was shutting her out. She could pounce on an unsuspecting dreamer the minute his mind strayed. And then it was a beating or you were sent to the principal for discipline. The principal always sent you home for a week, usually without looking up from his desk or without interrupting a pupil's recitation in his classes.

As she always did when Mrs. Grayson turned her back for a minute, Ruth put on a look of concentration and fiddled intently with the books on her desk. This was her cover while she began to dream. Today she looked at the new world history book the classes had been given that morning. The new book was the main cause of Mrs. Grayson's history lecture. Before they got it from the white school they hadn't had a history book. Only a speller, a geography and a reader. Ruth had read these months before and could recite every one of them by heart because she had read them so many times. Now she looked through the new book, at the pictures, some in color but most in black and white, and at the worn brown cover which had a pretty city scene on it with blond round-eyed children crossing a street under a bridge and across from a towered clock. In small lettering to one side was written "London." But then she opened the cover, not the pages of the book, but the cover, before the pages began. On the right-hand side of the book there was another girl's name, Jacqueline Paine, and under her name was written, Baker County Elementary School, the name of the white school. All their books came from there so this did not surprise her. But then she looked down at the rest of the page and gasped. For on this page and across the entire front inside covering of the book was a huge spread drawing called at the top in big green letters, "The Tree of the Family of Man." And on this tree there were all kinds of people. At the top, in pale blue and yellow, there were the white people. Their picture showed them doing something with test tubes, the lettering on one of their jackets said "Scientist." Behind them were drawings of huge tall buildings and cars and trains and airplanes. Jacqueline Paine had written underneath their picture: *Note: Americans, Germans, People who live in the extreme Northern part of Europe.* In parentheses she had written *(England).* Below the "Americans" were people drawn in yellow, and they were wearing funny little straw hats and were driving huge water buffalo. Behind them were a lot of pretty small objects made of jade and bamboo. Under their picture Jacqueline Paine had written in her round script: *Note: The Yellow Race. Chinese, Japanese, etc., and people who live far away from us, in the Far East.* Beneath them was a drawing in red of American Indians. They were sitting placidly, one old man smoking a long feather-covered pipe. Some women were sitting next to him making beautiful rugs and pottery and baskets. Underneath their picture Jacqueline Paine had written: *Note: Our own American Indians. We saved from disease and wild primitive life. Taught them useful activities as pictured above. They have also been known to make beads.* But it was the last picture she saw on the page that made her gasp. For at the very bottom of the tree, not actually joined to it but emanating from a kind of rootless branch, there was the drawing of a man, in black, with fuzzy hair, fat grinning lips, and a bone sticking through his nose. He was wearing a grass skirt and standing over a pot of boiling water as if he expected, at any moment, a visiting missionary. Underneath his picture Jacqueline Paine, in her neat note-taking script, had written just one descriptive word. She did not even say whether he had made his own grass skirt. It leaped out at Ruth like a slap in the face. *Note: A nigger.*

When she could pull herself out of her daze, dreaming no longer, she knew something was wrong. All the children from all the classes around her were looking at her. Looking at her and snickering. Before her eyes they turned into ugly grinning savages and she gave them her most disdainful scowl. But then she looked up just in time to see the strap coming down across her shoulders. It came down again and again and the snickering was quieted by the strap's thick whistling. They knew what it felt like. Slowly, in a rage, Ruth stood up, flinging the book to the floor. Mrs. Grayson's voice sounded hysterically in her ears. "You're just like the rest of them," she shouted. "You'll never be anybody because you don't pay any attention to anything worthwhile!" Ruth walked slowly toward the front of the room. "Where do you think you're going?" yelled Mrs. Grayson, picking up the history book and dusting it off. "All people like you do is tear up other people's property! You come right back here and sit down!" But Ruth's hand was already on the door. She turned to see Mrs. Grayson advancing with the strap; over her shoulder the delicious excitement of her classmates rose so thick it could be tasted. A pure and simple lust for diversion. A pure and simple lust for blood. Her blood. "You goddam mean evil *stupid* motherfucker!" Ruth hurled at her from her huge stock of Grange-inherited words. Mrs. Grayson and the classes stopped together and took a long indignant breath. "What did you *say,* young lady?" Mrs. Grayson finally demanded, advancing more menacingly than before. "You heard me," Ruth said, trembling. "And if you touch me just one more damn time, my granddaddy and me will pull this piece of junk right down on your head and cram planks and bricks down your lying *dumb* motherfucking throat!" Quickly she pulled open the door and fled down the steps. It was not until she reached the woods that she began to cry, the tears hurting her so much she thought she'd never survive them. "Was this what Grange meant?" she asked herself over and over, wishing she were dead.

The summers offered her shelter. From May until October she was free. Free to play in the cabin they built far back in the woods, free to read comics and books Grange cunningly stole from the white library; and for confusion, she was free to read the Bible's "wherefore, hereat, thereto—lo, lo, lo!" The winters were cold and cruel, and although she loved learning she hated school. When she had lived with Mem it had not been bad at all. It had even been fun. She and Ornette and Daphne had walked to school together, laughing and gossiping, sometimes throwing sand at the white school buses that passed them. But now her mother was dead and her father was in prison. Where exactly "in the North" her sisters were remained a mystery. She could not imagine the North except as an enormous cold place full of buildings and people where birds had no place to move their bowels. This picture she got from Grange who said you could take the North and make the Southerners eat it without sauce for all he cared.

As painful as it was to her to have to admit it, she was considered a curiosity after her mother's death and though all the children at the school were poor she was considered the poorest because her father was a murderer and she had no mother. Mothers, she learned very soon, were a premium commodity among her classmates, many of whom had never known a father and if they had could no longer even remember him. She got no consideration either for living with her grandfather, who was believed to be a strange, "funny" old man. Good at cards he was, the children admitted, but too quiet to be trusted, they said. Had anybody ever heard Grange Copeland laugh at one of their fathers' jokes? they asked. Nobody had, except Ruth, and her classmates did not admire her for it. At times she was sorry she giggled in church with Grange, the community being such a pious, scorekeeping one.

Snubbed and teased she was from the month she went to live with Grange, and it became almost like a game. Children would be playing "Sally Go Round the Sunshine" or "Hey, Miss Liza Jane" and she had only to show her composed melancholy face for all merriment to cease and a harsh silence to fall. There was a rumor going around the school when she was eleven that if she ever got anybody to walk with her in the woods (she was often seen walking in the woods and talking to bushes and that was certainly odd) he would never be seen alive again. They said she had a gun that she kept hidden in the woods and that she used to shoot people's heads off so she wouldn't have to see their eyes. Eyes, they said, reminded her of her mother. Ruth knew, when she overheard this rumor, that whoever started it must have been at Mem's funeral and seen the botched up job of the undertaker. But what could she say? Her only delightful times were when new children who didn't know the story came to the school or when she discovered by accident old ones who had either missed the gossip or not been able to attend the funeral. She was not the only one gossiped about. Josie came in for heavy slander too, as did everyone in the family. By the time she was in the fourth grade Ruth had begun to walk with her head down; she brought it up gradually during the fifth grade, and by the time she reached the sixth grade it was said of her that she didn't even know she had a head, it was stuck so far up in the clouds.

As she grew older, she was even more ostracized and neglected. By the time she was thirteen everybody knew she was the daughter of a murderer (and it was not just that he was a murderer that they minded—many of their own relatives had killed—but for a father to kill a mother was a thought that shook them) and although the overt harassment had gone—nobody taunted her any more—the tension remained. Then her father was released from prison, and was seen in town. The same week he was released Josie left the house she shared with Ruth and Grange and went to live with him. A fresh wave of gossip and ridicule swept through the school. Before they had teased her and shunned her for being the daughter of a murderer, now they taunted her for being the "wife" of her grandfather, who was so different from their own palsied and placid progenitors. The day after Josie left she must have done a lot of blabbing in curious ears, for the rumor was that Grange preferred his granddaughter to his wife and so she had left the two of them to the uninterrupted enjoyment of each other. Josie made their cabin, which Grange had built only as a playhouse for Ruth, sound indecent. She just had no idea what *really* went on down there between them, Josie was heard to say. Her classmates shied away from Ruth more obviously than ever, in a derisive, suspicious way.

Rossel Pascal was the only person at school she liked, and Rossel had never spoken to her. A brooding, beautiful girl with satiny skin and dark curly hair, Rossel was the only child of an alcoholic father. He never recovered from his wife's death, people said, and, unfortunately, they also whispered, his wife had not been worth such bother. The teachers regarded Rossel with a distinct chilliness, which aroused Ruth's fury and compassion, though Rossel herself never seemed to notice.

244 · ALICE WALKER

Rossel was in the twelfth grade when Ruth learned she planned to marry Walt Terrell. Walt was the richest black man in the county. He had returned a hero from World War II, with the remains of bullets in his legs and a chest full of carefully polished medals which he wore, at the drop of a hat, on any auspicious occasion, and even to Sunday School barbecues. The school was named after him, as it stood on his property, and everybody respected him. The schoolteachers fawned on him. Still, he was old, as old as her father, Ruth thought. Why would Rossel, who was no more than sixteen, marry him?

At the graduation ceremonies Ruth watched as Rossel stood beside her future husband. Rossel's father stood close by, pale and abstracted, clearly not sober. Other people walked about and spoke, but he seemed to drift, like a chip, through the bright stream of Sunday dresses and children's voices. When his daughter's name was called his eyes brightened for a moment. Sitting beside Walt, who towered over him with his thick head and great shoulders, in that instant Rossel's father came alive. When Rossel sat down again with them she looked as if she might like to fling herself into her father's arms. Father and daughter gazed at each other with eyes like closing doors.

"Rossel," Ruth said impulsively, as they walked carefully down the high school steps, "can I talk to you?"

"Sure you can," said Rossel, deliberately careless and cool.

They walked away from the men as if disengaging themselves from a battalion of soldiers. Ruth looked behind her and saw Grange holding forth with some of the men. Whenever she walked away from him and looked at him like a stranger he seemed grotesque, his long frame gangly, his hair bushy in a style that went out with Frederick Douglass, his hands doing a wild emphatic dance in the air between him and whomever he spoke to.

"You're Mrs. Grange," Rossel said, and immediately Ruth felt an unbearable hurt, as if she had taken her cares to the Lord and he had asked if she was bringing his laundry. Rossel was smiling brightly, as if at her own drawl, which was an amusing one. Ruth herself spoke without an accent, at least she thought she spoke without one, even though she'd heard nobody talk in real life but Southerners. She did not know why she didn't sound more like them. It was true her mind tended to blot out or change to something fine and imaginative whatever Southerners said. That included everybody, except Grange, whose speech she found colorful and strong. But Rossel spoke just like a Southern white woman, with the same careless softness. And on her too the accent sounded charming and dumb. When the other children called her "Mrs. Grange," Ruth got angry, but with Rossel she felt only hurt.

"My name's Ruth," she said.

"I know," said Rossel.

They stood under some trees at the edge of the schoolyard. Behind them was the girls' outhouse, at the far side of the yard was the well. Several small children were waiting their turn for the dipper that was being passed around. A bigger boy stood by patiently, his hand holding the rope that held the big wooden bucket from which droplets of water fell and spattered on the ground.

"By the time you're old as me," said Rossel, "you won't have to drink water from that dirty old well. You all can throw away that mossy bucket and that *slith*ery communal dipper! That's gonna be progress—an' just a scant fifteen years behind the white folks."

Ruth did not know what to say. She hated drinking from the dipper too, but hadn't heard anybody say one day they wouldn't have to. Rossel's face was grim as she looked out toward the highway. Cars full of white people passed by without slowing down. There was no sign indicating that a school was near, and children who had to cross the highway did so at a run. A boy had been killed trying to get across the road, and the state of Georgia had put up a white wooden cross as a "death" marker for motorists, but had not thought to put up a warning sign.

Rossel was plainly bored; she looked questioningly at Ruth. It took all Ruth's courage to ask her what she had drawn her aside to ask.

"Why you going to marry *him*?" she managed to blurt out finally.

"Why not?" Rossel asked indifferently. "I'd rather marry the devil than get stuck with any of the stinking jobs they give you round this town."

"*Jobs?*" asked Ruth. Her idea of marriage romantically included love. But she tried to imagine Rossel as a short-order cook in a hash house. Rossel was too lovely. She tried to see her as some woman's maid. Rossel was too close to needing a maid herself. Rossel was not meant to be among the wretched of the earth, and Rossel apparently knew it.

She wanted very much to hug Rossel. But how could she hug somebody so cold, so indifferent, so unfeelingly beautiful, such a *grim* girl? Instead Ruth burst into tears, and it was Rossel who hugged her.

"Don't cry over it," Rossel said, her voice strange and thin and bleak. "Maybe someday we'll both understand why marrying him is supposed to be so much better." For a moment they clung together and then Rossel was gone, her face calm, set, resolute; the face, Ruth thought, of a doll. A face without anything but confidence in its own empty perfection.

It was a long time before she saw Rossel again, a whole year. It was at the funeral of Rossel's father, who had frozen to death in the cemetery on top of his wife's grave slab. Rossel was richly robed in black and looked like a stricken queen. She had grown older in that year, and, apparently, more devoted to her husband, for she leaned within the protection of his arms with the abandoned dependency of a child. And Walt, through his perpetually dull and military exterior, seemed to beam with pride and accomplishment.

43

ONE DAY THE question of what her future was to be loomed very large. It was the day her body decided it was ready for a future and she knew she was not. She felt tightened and compressed by panic. Grange had bought her napkins, a belt, and a lovely talc that smelled like a warm rose. He was excited and troubled over what he would say to her about such an unplanned for, though not unexpected, development. However, she was too well read to make him struggle with her enlightenment. What scared her was that she felt her woman's body made her defenseless. She felt it could now be had and made to conceive something she didn't want, against her will, and her mind could do nothing to stop it. She was deathly afraid of being, as she put it, "had," as young girls were every day, and trapped in a condition that could only worsen. She was not yet at a stage where the prospect of a man and marriage could be contemplated with equanimity.

"What *am* I going to do when I get grown?" she asked her grandfather with some alarm.

"What you mean? We got this farm. We can stay here till kingdom come."

She looked at Grange's patch of cotton that was so lovely under the moon. There was a garden and chickens and pigs. The life would be perfect for a recluse.

"I'm not going to be a hermit," she said. "I want to get away from here someday. Meaning no offense to your farm, of course. You know, I think maybe I'll go North, like you did; I want to see New York, 125th Street, all those nightclubs and people standing around cussin' in public."

"I won't let you," said Grange sternly.

"I wouldn't try to go while *you* were here," she said, as if he should be ashamed to imagine such a thing.

"I still don't want you to go up there, it's cold as a witch's titty, and nasty, and the people speak to you funny."

"You told me all that. But what would I do down here? I *could* take over Sister Madelaine's job, except she's still on it, old as she is. As a matter of fact, I suspect that's what you'd want me to do, turn myself into a fortuneteller and scare the hell out of unbelieving white ladies. But I don't think I'm cut out for digging up roots and nailing feces into trees! Ugh! Maybe I could teach down the road with Mrs. Grayson; two dumdums together. But I wouldn't have the nerve to stand in front of those children knowing they can't hear a word I'm saying. Besides, I despise Mrs. Grayson too much to subject her to the pleasure of my company."

"You smarter than her," said Grange. "You read enough stuff to know what to teach anybody."

"Being smarter than Mrs. Grayson would be my greatest liability. She'd come up behind me one day and push me in the well. Mean old bitch!"

"You don't need to get excited. She got her orders from me not to get rough with you no more. I told her I'd wring her neck till her eyes wall. Her husband's too."

Ruth sighed. "What is left!" She ran into her room and brought out the newspaper. Turning to the want ads she read: "'Wanted: Beautiful Southern Belle type with charming, winning manner for job as receptionist in law firm.'" There was only one law firm in town and it was white. "My charm probably wouldn't be up to it anyway," muttered Ruth, continuing to read: "'Wanted: WHITE LADIES—to fill vacancies in sewing plant. New plant recently revitalized and under new management needs seamstresses to make overalls. Will train.' Blah," she said. In the colored section of the want ads there was only one opening for "middle-aged colored woman to do light domestic work evenings with some light ironing and cooking. $6.00 per week." Ruth put down the paper and looked at Grange.

"You know I ain't going to be nobody's cook, don't you?"

"You ain't," he agreed.

"Well, what do you suggest I do when I'm grown? There wasn't but one Walt Terrell," she added bitterly, "and Rossel got him!"

"You won't sell yourself; don't even get that thought in your head. Maybe something'll turn up. Things change," he said, without much conviction. "Presidents change—we get some that help us sometime. Roosevelt, you don't remember him, but he once had Booker T. Washington to lunch in the White House. The rest of us was starving, but it seemed to help us some then. And today there's Eisenhower, as wishy-washy a lookin' rattler as ever was, but the court been tellin' everybody that the black schools ain't up to the white 'n they say he's back of it."

"Meantime our school is hanging together by sheer inadequacy."

"Don't interrup' me. What I know, and I reckon the *most* I know is that people change. That is the main reason not to give up on them. Why, if you had knowed me when I was a young blade, drinking and fighting and beating your grandma, you'd a give up on me. Sure, you would. You ain't long on patience. *But*, now, you didn't give up (mainly because you wa'n't born or thought of then) and here you see me tamed and fairly civilized, taking my drinks for stomach's sake, like a gentleman, toiling in the fields for just one gal, and bringing home all my money. And don't you forget, there have always been black folks fighting for better. Maybe their ranks will swell till they include everybody. I don't know how it can be done—I never *seen* such a sorry passel of niggers as in your daddy's generation—but with the right change and some kind of leader it can be.

"There was a time I didn't own my life and then there was a time I didn't care if I lost it when I had it, long as I took a dozen or so white folks with me. I'm still inclined to believe that that *was* my finest hour. But then I came back here, sick of feeling that way and seeing all the rest of our folks standing around praying. And the Lord or something dropped you in my lap. A voice said to me you stop that cuttin' up, Nig, here is a reason to get yourself together and hold on.

"When I die this farm ain't going to be nobody's but yours. I done paid for it with every trick I had. The fence we put up around it will enclose freedom you can be sure of, long as you ain't scared of holding the gun. The gun is important. For I don't know that love works on everybody. A little love, a little buckshot, that's how I'd say handle yourself.

"Anyway, you might as well know I don't care much for

nobody except you. I 'member when I was a churchgoer proper, I tried to feel something real big, something that would make me love the whole world. But I just couldn't come at that feeling no kind of way. Your grandma and me was fighting a heap then over one thing and another; and I think we scrappled so much because she *could* love all sorts of folks she didn't have no business.

"The white folks hated me and I hated myself until I started hating them in return and loving myself. Then I tried just loving me, and then you, and *ignoring* them much as I could. You're special to me because you're a part of me; a part of me I didn't even used to want. I want you to go on a long time, have a heap of children. Let them know what you made me see, that it ain't no use in seeing at all, if you don't see *straight!*"

"And all from behind a fence?" Ruth looked doubtful. "I'd be bored stiff waiting for black folks to rise up so I could join them. Since I'm already ready to rise up and they ain't, it seems to me I should rise up first and let them follow me."

"What that takes I'm afraid you ain't ready yet to give. How many black folks would you say you really know—I mean that would rise without squawking?" he asked. "And how many white?"

She counted the black ones on three fingers, only one an old warrior, the white ones not at all.

44

AFTER JOSIE LEFT, the house gradually took on the charm of the cabin, the charm of peace, of quiet and of the pursuit of interesting contentment thoroughly enjoyed. Together Grange and Ruth experimented with the beautiful in rugs, curtains, pictures and pillow covers. Ruth's room was a veritable sun of brightness and yellow and white. For her bed she made a quilt of yellow-and-white cotton and her curtains were white-dotted Swiss which she could just see through. Her desk, facing the woods, was littered with books. She liked mythology, the Brontë sisters, Thomas Hardy, any romantic writer. If she had been shipwrecked on a deserted island she would have taken *Jane Eyre*, a pocket thesaurus she had, all her books about Africa. She would have taken her maps of the continents, everything she owned by Charles Dickens, plenty of paper and a stock of pencils. She would have left on her desk her red-covered Bible, which Grange had lifted from a cart that stood outside a motel room, her big dictionary, which he got for her she knew not how, and which would have been too heavy, and her copy of Miss Vanderbilt's *Etiquette,* which she ignored as much as she could without making her grandfather feel like a fool for getting it for her. Of her clothes she would have taken her two pairs of dungarees and plaid shirts, her winter boots, her red woolen jacket and probably one dress. She would have taken her locket picture of Mem, which had been a present from Grange on her fourteenth birthday. In the picture Mem was a harried hopeful young wife with one child. She looked out of the little locket with calm, disbelieving eyes.

Grange's room was all in brown and red and blue and black. His room was a part of him and was filled with his smell, of tobacco and hay and, lightly, orange wine. When he was seated by the fire, his brown brogans rested against the brown stones of his fireplace, and his red flannel underwear, as it hung over his rocker, complemented the red among the blue in the quilt on his bed. During three-fourths of the year there were flowers in every room of the house, in the two bedrooms as well as the kitchen, and of course in the "front" room, where their few visitors were allowed to sit themselves down and partake of a sip of iris root or sassafras tea.

"What *is* this stuff?" the boldest of their guests would ask, recalling perhaps some uncharitable comment made by himself or others regarding the oddness of his hosts.

"This is the tea of survival," Ruth would say, with a wink at her grandfather, who sat silently smoking, ignoring the guest except to comment, "She give it to you, you better drink it," and seeming entirely comfortable before ill-at-ease company who invariably visited out of curiosity.

"How you know?" they sometimes asked defensively.

"I told her," would come the indifferent assertion from

Grange, with whom no one ever gathered up the nerve to argue.

The older Grange got the more serene and flatly sure of his mission he became. His one duty in the world was to prepare Ruth for some great and herculean task, some magnificent and deadly struggle, some harsh and foreboding reality. Nothing moved him to repent of his independent method of raising her. In vain did deacons of the church admonish him for teaching Ruth to avoid the caresses of pious sisters and to shun the embraces of baptizing brothers. In vain did preachers and missionaries warn him of the heathenism of her young soul. It was commonly supposed that Ruth was even taught to bite the hand that would spiritually feed her, and this supposition was correct.

"Before you let 'em baptize you in they muddy creeks an' waterholes, after I'm gone, you kick the legs out from under 'em and leave 'em drown." To that purpose he hired a poor white lad to teach her to swim.

"The shackles of the slave have one end tied to every rock and bush," he said to her. "Before you let some angel-distracted deacon put his mitts on you, you git you a good grip on his evangelical ear and you stretch it till his nose slides."

And if the various congregations believed the spirit of the devil had already entered young Ruth Copeland, her ready adoption of Grange's teachings more than proved their point. They noted with shock that her greatest delight, along with her grandfather, when they came to church, was to giggle in serious places.

Part X

Part X

45

SEVERAL TIMES after Josie began living with Brownfield, Ruth saw them loitering in the woods behind the school. Her classmates ran from her father, some of them jeered. Josie, whitely powdered and haphazardly wigged, would stand beside him supporting his drunken weight with a patient, long-suffering look that totally mystified Ruth. It was Grange's custom, particularly on overcast days, to pick her up at the school well, and if not there at the small wooden powerhouse on the edge of the playground. One day they faced a confrontation with Brownfield and Josie. On that day they had indeed strolled along the edge of the school grounds like lovers, Grange carefully tucking her scarf around her neck every few steps. They were murmuring and giggling about the black janitor at the white library in town, whom Grange managed to get drunk each time he went to the library to steal books for her. They did not see Brownfield and Josie until they almost bumped into them.

"Well, if it ain't the Gold Dust Twins," said Josie, insolently, eying their closely knit fingers. For the first time Ruth was chilled by the naked jealousy she read in her stepgrand-mother's eyes.

"Yeah," said Brownfield, who kept a proprietary hand on his stepmother's shoulder, "goddam Gold Dust Twins. Out just taking the goddam air!" He rubbed the palm of one hand boldly down the front of his pants.

Ruth was startled and became hysterically baffled, press-ing herself into her grandfather's side and trying to walk past without seeing them. For although she had glimpsed her fa-ther's profile from her classroom window she had been able to convince herself that he was not real, that he was at most a shadow from a very painful past and a shadow that could never gain flesh and speak to her. The drunken tones of his voice brought back a terror she had tried hard to forget.

"Well, well," said Grange. "My wife and my son." His eyes when Ruth looked up at him were a kind of flinty brown, almost black, and his skin seemed to have aged and become ashen and papery. It was one of the few times she thought of him as being old, one of the few times she thought it might be possible after all for him to declare he'd had enough of every-thing and die. That day he was wearing his overalls and bro-gans but with his old Sunday gabardine overcoat. It was very soft against her face, and it surprised her that her face reached all the way to his shoulder. "What do you want?" he asked the leering pair, a slight quaver in his voice.

"I want my goddam daughter!" said Brownfield. "She don't belong to you. She belong to me and I want her."

"Yes," said Josie, pushing out her still incredible bosom, "she's his child and he wants her. It ain't decent for just a old man like you to try to take care of a little girl." She turned to Brownfield for support, but he, while staring at Ruth, seemed to lapse into a trance. His daughter shivered under his dull incredulous stare. She had never considered that as a big girl she might look more than a little like her mother.

"I don't know why they give you only seven years," her grandfather said in a firm voice, drawing himself up. "They ought to have kept you in the pen."

"But she *are* his child!" said Josie, trying to laugh but seeming frantically close to tears.

"Shet up," Grange said, without looking at her. "I guess you intend to be a good mother to her?"

"Well, no," said Josie, nervously reaching out to touch her husband and then succumbing to coyness. "If she go back to her daddy I'll come back to you." This jerked Brownfield out of his trance and he gave her a dangerous smirk. Ruth thought she saw Josie wince as if preparing to move away from a blow. That tremor was too much for her and Ruth began to cry. She threw herself into her grandfather's arms, trembling uncontrollably.

"I don't want you back, you distant strumpet, let the evil that men do go before them, which is what happened in your case. I wish I never had laid eyes on you." Then he turned fiery eyes on his son.

"I took this child when you had made her an orphan. You killed her ma. Where was you all these years when she needed a daddy? Nowhere to be found! You wasn't to be found even when you lived under the same roof with her, except in a whiskey bottle. And then you was in the pen for killing the only decent thing you ever had. I don't know how you prevailed on the white folks to let you out so quick, for you ain't repented; although we know they don't give a damn *no*how as long as all we kill is another nigger! You made a bargain," he said, turning to Josie, who had begun to weep, streaking her face powder, "you stick to it. If you thought you could humble me by running off with my son you was wrong. You're two of a kind; wallow in the mud together!"

"Don't be so *hard*, Grange," wept Josie. "*Don't be so hard!*"

"He thinks I ought not have run out on him a long time ago," said Grange, ignoring Josie, "and he's right. But I tried to make up and he wouldn't let me. And *he* run out on this child. Now he won't get her back, I don't care what he do. He won't!"

"Grange, I *tried*—" Josie began, but Brownfield cut her off.

"Don't beg for nothing from him, he so damn righteous he ain't going to hear you. But *you was no daddy to me!*" he said to Grange, "and I ain't going to let you keep my child to make up for it!"

"You no-good rascal!" said Grange, pushing Ruth away from him, lifting his fists. "You say one more word—"

"You wasn't no daddy to *me!*" Brownfield shouted, but made no move to get nearer his father's fists.

"Grange," said Josie, "your son *love* you. He done told me all about how it was. You walked out on him and then look like everywhere he turn the white folks was just pushing him down in the mud. You know how it is," she pleaded. "They just made him do things when he didn't *mean* them."

For a moment Grange was too choked with disgust to speak. When he did, he turned to Ruth. "Your daddy's done taught me something I didn't know about blame and guilt," he said. "You see, I figured he could blame a good part of his life on me; I didn't offer him no directions and, he thought, no love. But when he became a man himself, with his own opportunity to righten the wrong I done him by being good to his own children, he had a chance to become a real man, a daddy in his own right. That was the time he should of just forgot about what I done to him—and to his ma. But he messed up with his children, his wife and his home, and never yet blamed hisself. And never blaming hisself done made him *weak*. He no longer have to think beyond me and the white folks to get to the root of *all* his problems. Damn, if thinking like that ain't made *noodles* out of his brains."

"Why," said Brownfield, "you old bastard!"

Josie had pulled out a handkerchief too small for her. She soon watered it through with tears. "Grange," she said, dabbing at her eyes with the small wet ball, "you know you got some blame; which, actually, you always did admit—"

"Shut up," said Brownfield.

"—and you know you used to blame the white folks too. For they *is* the cause of all the dirt we have to swallow. . . ."

"Every bit," said Brownfield.

Grange continued to speak to Ruth, his shoulder to Brownfield and Josie. He spoke rapidly, breathlessly, his hands doing their jabbing dance.

"By George, I *know* the danger of putting all the blame on somebody else for the mess you make out of your life. I fell into the trap myself! And I'm bound to believe that that's the way the white folks can corrupt you even when you done held up before. 'Cause when they got you thinking that they're to blame for *every*thing they have you thinking they's some kind of gods! You can't do nothing wrong without them being behind it. You gits just as weak as water, no feeling of doing *nothing* yourself. Then you begins to think up evil and begins to destroy everybody around you, and you blames it on the crackers. *Shit!* Nobody's as powerful as we make them out to be. We got our own *souls*, don't we?"

"For a old man what could eat ten of 'em for breakfast, from what Josie tells me, you sure done turned into a cracker lover!" said Brownfield.

"I don't love but one somebody, black *or* white," said Grange, turning briefly to his son. "An' what I'm talking about ain't love but being a man!" He turned once more to Ruth. "I mean," he said, "the crackers could make me run away from my wife, but where was the *man* in me that let me sneak off, never telling her nothing about where I was going, never telling her I forgave her, never telling her how wrong I was myself?"

"You never cared nothing for my ma!" said Brownfield.

"And the white folks could have forced me to believe fucking a hundred strumpets was a sign of my manhood," said Grange, "but where was the *man* in me that let me take Josie here for such a cheap and low-down ride, when I didn't never care whether she lived or died, long as she did what I told her and I got me my farm!"

"Ah, Grange, baby," said Josie, reaching out to him, "it not too late for us now, don't say that."

"Will you shut your slutty trap!" said Brownfield, pushing at her hand.

"And with your pa," Grange continued, "the white folks could have forced him to live in shacks; they might have even forced him to beat his wife and children like they was dogs, so he could keep on feeling something less than shit. But where was the *man* in him that let Brownfield *kill* his wife? What cracker pulled the trigger? And if a cracker did cause him to kill his wife, Brownfield should have turned the gun on himself, for he wasn't no man. He *let* the cracker hold the gun, because he was too weak to distinguish that cracker's will from his! The same was true of me. We both of us jumped our responsibility, and without facing up to at least *some* of his wrong a man loses his muscle."

Grange's eyes were misty now; he turned to face his son. "If I had my life to live over," he said, "your ma and me would maybe have starved to death in some cracker's gutter, but she would have *died* with me holding her hand! For that much I *could* have done—and I believe she would have seen the man in me."

Grange was shaking as much as his granddaughter, and this unsteadiness where he had always seen strength, emboldened Brownfield.

"You kinky-haired son of a bitch," said Brownfield, who was annoyed that his father wore his hair long, "a heap of good it would have done my ma for you to hold her hand when she was dying! When a man's starving he don't *need* none of that *hand*-holding shit."

"But my answering for everything had to be to her, don't you understand yet how it go? Nobody give a damn for me but your ma, and I messed her up trying to be a big man! After two years of never gitting nothing on the plantation I turned my back on what I did have. I just couldn't face up to never making no progress. All I'm saying, Brownfield," said Grange, his voice sinking to a whisper, "is that one day I had to look back on my life and see where *I* went wrong, and when I did look back I found out your ma'd be alive today if I hadn't just as good as shot her to death, same as you done your wife. We *guilty*, Brownfield, and neither one of us is going to move a step in the right direction until we admit it."

"I don't have to admit a damn thing to you," said Brownfield, "and I ain't about to let the crackers off the hook for what they done to my life!"

"I'm talking to *you*, Brownfield," said Grange, "and most of what I'm saying is *you got to hold tight a place in you where they can't come.* You can't take this young girl here and make her wish she was dead just to git back at some white folks that you don't even *know.* We keep killing ourselves for people that don't even mean nothing *to* us!"

"The court say I can have her back. Old man, I'll fight you on it! I wanted to give you a chance at a fair exchange, your old lady for her." He reached out to touch Ruth and she shied miserably away. "Too good for me, is you?" he wanted to know, scowling at her. Throughout this ghastly interview she had not been able to say a word. She wanted to tell Brownfield how she despised him for killing Mem and for making her suffer by being shunned and friendless, but nothing came out. She was too terrified that somehow he would make good his threat and she would be forced to leave Grange and go live with him.

"He'll never have you again," Grange said, as Josie and Brownfield stalked away. But he was holding his heart as if it hurt him, and the look he gave her was unsure.

In tears they stumbled home through the woods, where they collapsed momentarily together. They sobbed as if they knew already what was to come; and just as Ruth could finally envision a time when Grange would not be with her, she knew Grange was imagining a time when his powers of protection and love would be no more and she would be left again an orphan with a beast for a father—a beast Grange himself had created.

That night Grange pored over Ruth's Bible for hours before he went to bed. He had great admiration for the Hebrew children who fled from Egypt land. For perhaps the hundredth time he told Ruth the story of the Hebrew exodus.

"They done the right thing," he said.

THE THIRD LIFE OF GRANGE COPELAND • 267

"Did they?"

"Got out while they still had some sense and cared what happened to they spirit. Also to one 'nother. I may be wrong, but nothing ain't proved it yet." He looked thoughtfully over the book at the fire.

"What?" asked Ruth.

"We can't live here free and easy and at home. We going crazy."

"*Here?*"

"I don't mean this farm; I mean in this country, the U.S. I believe we got to leave this place if we 'spect to survive. All this struggle to keep human where for years nobody knowed what human was but you. It's killing us. They's more ways to git rid of people than with guns. We make good songs and asylum cases."

"Maybe it would be better if something happened to change everything; made everything equal; made us feel *at home*," said Ruth.

"They can't undo what they done and we can't forget it or forgive."

"Is it so hard to forgive 'em if they don't do bad things no more?"

"I honestly don't believe they *can* stop," said Grange, "not as a group anyhow." He lounged back in his chair and stuck a hand in his pocket. "Even if they could," he said slowly, "it'd be too late. I look in my heart for forgiveness and it just ain't there. The close as I can come to it is a kind of numbness where they concerned. So that I wouldn't add kindling to a fire that was roasting them, but I wouldn't hear 'em calling me neither."

Ruth chuckled.

"That ain't no feeling to be proud of," Grange said

sternly, "not if you going to call yourself a human." He leaned forward, looking sadly into the fire.

"When I was a child," he said, "I used to cry if somebody killed a ant. As I look back on it now, I *liked* feeling that way. I don't *want* to set here now *numb* to half the peoples in the world. I feel like something soft and warm an' delicate an' sort of *shy* has just been burned right out of me."

"Numbness is probably better than hate," said Ruth gently. She had never seen her grandfather so anguished.

"The trouble with numbness," said Grange, as if he'd thought over it for a long time, "is that it spreads to all your organs, mainly the heart. Pretty soon after I don't hear the white folks crying for help I don't hear the black." He looked at Ruth. "Maybe I don't even hear you."

"You'd hear me all right!" said Ruth.

"Your daddy don't, do he?" asked Grange, returning to the story of the Hebrew children.

"'If the foundations be destroyed,'" he read after a few minutes, "'what can the righteous do?'"

"Rebuild 'em?" asked Ruth.

"Too late to rebuild," said Grange, "for the righteous was there when they was destroyed." He turned to another part of the Bible and read: "'Thou hath repaid me evil for good *to the spoiling of my soul.*'" He looked up at Ruth. "The Lord knowed that you could dump shit on a fellow for just so long before he begin to stink from with*in*. It's the spoiling of the soul that make forgiveness impossible. It just ain't *in* us no more," he said with a sigh. "How can the young 'uns stay fresh here? *That's* what got *me* bothered."

"It'll be okay," said Ruth, taking the Bible from him and putting it away. "For a man who don't like church, you sure like to thumb this book."

"This is serious business, though," said Grange, looking steadily at her. "You been protected on this farm. . . . You don't know how *tired* you be after years of strugglin'. I want you to fight 'em every step of the way when they tries to abuse you. An' they *will*, 'cause you'll be a nigger to 'em. Damn! I hates they guts already for making you feel bad! But I don't want you to fight 'em until you gits completely fagged so that you turns into a black cracker yourself! For then they bondage over you is complete. I'd want you to git out before that happened to you!"

"Why didn't *you* get out?" asked Ruth.

"The world wasn't as big then as it is now. I thought the U.S. covered the whole shebang. Besides," said Grange, grimly, "I wouldn't give the mothers the satisfaction!"

"Aw," said Ruth, standing behind him and tugging playfully at his big ears, "you know you caught your soul in the nick of time, before it spoilt completely."

"I wish I *did* know that," said Grange, rising to wind the clock, "but I look at Brownfield and Josie an' I know I was *way* too slow."

In the middle of the night Ruth was awakened by a noise.

"You 'sleep?" her grandfather asked. He was standing over the bed. "I couldn't git off to sleep. I just kept thinkin' about what happened today."

Ruth sat up and turned on the light. Grange was standing in his long nightshirt, with a stocking cap on his head. "What's the matter?" she asked sleepily.

"I wanted to give you this," said Grange, handing her a small booklet.

"What is it?"

"A bankbook. I put away a few dollars for you to go to

college on. Your daddy's up to something an' I don't know how long I can keep 'im away from you."

Ruth rubbed her eyes and opened the bankbook. Her name and Grange's were on the inside. There were nine hundred dollars.

"That's just from the bootlegging," he said. He went back into his room and returned with a battered cigar box that rattled and clinked. He opened it and began to count the bills and quarters, half dollars and dimes, nickels and pennies. He counted out four hundred dollars and then took twenty dollars and some change for himself. "An' this much I winned at poker." He'd gambled almost every week since she came to live with him. Ruth took the cigar box and eased it down under her bed.

"You put it in the bank tomorrow," Grange said.

"Okay," she promised lightly, though she felt tears rising in her throat.

"I beat all my old gambling partners so bad I made 'em make over they straight life policies to you too," said Grange, holding his little bit of money in one hand and shyly holding his nightshirt away from his body with the other. "I figure if they starts to die at the rate of one a year after the next few years they money can keep you comfortable. I know a girl in college need things."

"I couldn't do that!" said Ruth. "What about their own children? They going to need things too!"

"Well, that's left up to you. If you needs the money it yours, I winned it." He was silent for a minute, looking at the floor. "You don't think I done wrong to do that, do you?" he asked. He looked down at the bills in his hand. "I s'pose it *wasn't* too *human* of me."

"I don't blame you," she said quickly. "I know you did it for me. But I won't need it with all this you already gave me! Don't be so worried about anything happening," she added, reaching out to touch his hand. "Brownfield's probably so drunk by now he can't even remember I *am* his daughter!"

"You go to the bank first thing in the morning," he said again, turning away. "I'll git up and drive you."

"You go to sleep," she ordered.

"You too," he said. But for hours the house was tense and awake, and neither of them slept.

The running of the house acquired a certain orderliness it lacked before. Bills were paid in full and Grange's bookkeeping explained to Ruth. Old acquaintances were hunted and found and made to cough up monies owed. Ruth's bank account grew in tiny bounds. Two dollars from Fred Hill, five from Manuel Stokes, sixteen from Davis Jones for that pig he ran over three years ago. The fence was inspected with care, rotting posts replaced, the wire restrung to make it more taut. Even the wine crocks were taken out of hiding and reburied under Ruth's direction. Two stills were closed down, the small remaining one, not very productive, easily destroyed. For her sixteenth birthday, when her fear of Brownfield had abated somewhat, Grange made her sole owner of their old car. He had already taught her to drive, and now it became her duty to drive into town to do the shopping, confronting for the first time, alone, the whites who owned and ran the town. Grange's plan was to teach her everything he knew. Already, he liked to boast, "Your aim's a heap better than mine!"

For all that he liked to see her self-sufficient, he was against her acting boyish. He grumbled when she spoke of cutting her hair, an unruly, rebellious cloud that weighted down her head. He insisted she trade her jeans for dresses, at least on weekends, and placed jars of Noxzema and Pond's hand cream on her dresser. He became softer than Ruth had ever known him, reflectively puffing on his pipe for hours without saying a word. He spent evenings examining maps, wondering about the places in the world he would never see, and gradually what he was groping for became almost tangible. Believing unshakably that his granddaughter's purity and open-eyedness and humor and compassion were more important than any country, people or place, he must prepare her to protect them. Assured, by his own life, that America would kill her innocence and eventually put out the two big eyes that searched for the seed of truth in everything, he must make her unhesitant to leave it.

And still, in all her living there must be joy, laughter, contentment in being a woman; someday there must be happiness in enjoying a man, and children. Each day must be spent, in a sense, apart from any other; on each day there would be sun and cheerfulness or rain and sorrow or quiet contemplation of life. Each day must be past, present and future, with dancing and wine-making and drinking and as few regrets as possible. Her future must be the day she lived in. These were the thoughts he thought, sitting before the fire, pulling on his pipe, or hunched up on his bed clipping his toenails. Survival was not everything. *He* had survived. But to survive *whole* was what he wanted for Ruth.

46

ONE DAY ON her way to school Ruth saw her father alone. He was waiting beside the road, squatting near the asphalt like a hobo over his fire, his face brightened and cleared by the clean softness of the eight-thirty sun. When Ruth saw him her heart jumped, and a nervous habit she had acquired recently, of pressing her hand against her forehead, was repeated several times before she found herself abreast of him. She quickened her pace and averted her head. She imagined herself treading cautiously around a bull in a pasture and would soon have been in a trot, but Brownfield stopped her; not by reaching out to touch her, which she could not have stood, but by simply standing alone and mute there beside the road.

Against the high green shoulder of the road he looked smaller than when she'd last seen him. She felt herself larger, because at sixteen she was no longer a child, but smaller somehow too, because she faced him alone. Brownfield was sober and that surprised her. He wore a clean shirt that fitted him loosely, as if he had lost weight or wore someone else's, and she noticed for the first time knotted coils of gray-black hair growing up from his chest to the base of his creased and dry-looking neck. As her eyes traveled up and down his face she wondered at this hair on her father's chest; she latched onto this discovery to save for a moment the shock of looking into his eyes. His eyes, which frightened her, and which she always avoided, were full of a pained sadness, which surprised her, and she felt they were trying to speak to her. Her answer was to shudder and to hug her books to her bosom with both arms. Seeing her confusion he looked down at his shoes. The air around them was filled with the sweet motey smell of hay and red dust and flowers that is Georgia's in the spring. There was the timeless sound of birds and the noise of children from the direction of the school.

"What do you want?" she asked, feeling fear and anger and hope all at once. She could not understand the hope. Surely there had never been any reason for it that her father had provided. There is something about my father that makes me pity him today, she thought, and knew a momentary wariness and more surprise. Brownfield wet his lips with his tongue. So wet with whiskey he was usually, so dry he seemed today!

"You—" he began, and faltered, "you looks just like your mama."

"Yes?" Ruth said sharply, "but what do you *want*?"

"I wants to see you, if you don't mind," he said humbly, and slowly, as if afraid of her.

In the silence, punctuated only by the birds and the distant ringing of the school bell, Brownfield kept his daughter before him and looked and looked at her. It was disconcerting and almost eerie. She felt he had never looked at her before.

"I have to go now," she said faintly, after a few minutes of his greedy staring, for if she had been an oasis in the desert he could not have gazed more longingly at her. "I'm already late for school," she murmured further, feeling hot and cold. But he said, "Wait!" and though he did not touch her or stand in her way she could not move. His close scrutiny of her continued. On the ground near his feet was a gaily wrapped package that looked as if it might be candy. She did not allow herself more than a glance at it for she wanted no part of him, but he noticed her glance and said, she thought, slyly, "A present for you. They tells me you pretty big on reading books."

Slowly Ruth recovered the indignation that came to her whenever she thought of him. After all these years of nothing he had the nerve to think he could get her to like him by offering her one lousy book!

"What is it?" she asked coolly, though a great scathing heat had started behind her eyes.

"Why, er, well, I don't recall the name, but Josie thought you might like it."

"Well, you just tell Josie I *don't* like it and I wouldn't like it as long as either of you had anything to do with it!" As she spoke she rudely kicked a film of dust over it. After she did it she became afraid but Brownfield barely noticed it. He continued to stare and almost to marvel at the size of her, the sound of her, the whole reality of her.

"Oh, shit," she muttered under her breath. What is he looking at? Is he trying to decide whether I'm worth the fuss he wants to make to get me? she wondered. And then she thought, Good God, don't let him touch me with those hands that still and always will look like weapons! Her strong indignation began to lose its heat, and she started again to tremble and to press her forehead and her cheeks. She felt all red and sweaty, as if the dust of the ground were sticking to her.

"You don't even remember your mama, do you?" Brown-field asked after a while, accusingly, his eyes full of a sudden remembrance and a fiery reclaimed jealousy.

"She . . . she *died* before I was very old," said Ruth. "But—" and she looked him in the eye—"I remember her. You don't forget your mama, or anybody that you've loved."

"But you forgets your daddy?" he asked in a gruff, argumentative tone. But then, "You don't act like you remember me. A child what's got respect for her daddy'd run up and give him a hug!" His voice, a moment ago so charged with scorn, was empty of it now. It was old and lonely and pleading. For a moment Ruth could see how much he resembled Grange. She thought of what Grange had told her about people being capable of changing, although lately he'd changed his views about that. But she did not want to hear about the change Brownfield was undergoing, for she could never believe it.

"You never cared for us," said Ruth. "You never cared for mama or Daphne or Ornette, or for me." I don't want any of your damn changes now, she thought, and hated and liked herself for this lack of charity. She glimpsed for the first time what Grange had known, the nature of unforgiveness and the finality of a misdeed done. She saw herself as one both with her father and with Grange, with Josie thrown in to boot.

Her father turned away from her for some private reflections of his own. His hands plucked nervously at a chipped button on his big shirt.

"Daphne's in—I wanted to get them back, and be their daddy—but Daphne's in a crazy house up North. And Ornette"—his mouth, usually so vile and slack with whiskey or foul words, was tight and grieving—"Ornette's a—*a lady of pleasure!*" He remembered that phrase from the letter from the old guy, the preacher, Mem's father. Brownfield had written for word of Daphne and Ornette, planning somewhere in the back of his head to entice them home again. How Josie had cackled with delight to see his sickness at what had become of his daughters! The news of their downfall, especially of Ornette's, had made her jolly throughout one entire day! Though later he had surprised her weeping into her soapsuds, squeezing his overalls and singing about feeling like a motherless child. It had unnerved him to see her so maudlin, but when he had moved to touch her, thinking they might comfort each other, she had turned away, shutting him out, forcing him back into his role of instrument and tormentor.

Brownfield's large shoulders sagged and his hands, hands Ruth had felt in fury against her own young ears, fumbled loosely with some bits of straw tugged up from the banks of the road. His mumbled, embarrassed, prudish "lady of pleasure," almost made her laugh out loud, but she was too near to bursting into tears and perhaps beating her head against the closest tree.

"You were the one who *said* Ornette would *be* a woman of pleasure, a tramp! That's all you used to call her. Just 'tramp.' 'Come here, tramp,' you used to say. *I remember that almost as well as I remember my mama.*"

The past rose up between them like a movie on a screen. The last dilapidated, freezing house which he had forced on them, the sickness of Daphne, her strange fits of which Brownfield had taken no notice, the waywardness of Ornette, whose every act was done to make someone notice her. The murder of Mem.

"You think I don't remember," said Ruth. "The trouble is I can't forget!"

"You don't remember nothing," he said. "You been *fed* on all the hatred you have for me since the time you was this high!" He turned one heavy palm down toward the ground. "You don't know what it *like* for a man to live down here. You don't know what I been through!"

A tremor of pity shot through her at his anguish, for it was real, although it changed nothing.

"I couldn't ever even *express* my *love*!" he said.

Considering the past, the word was false, a bribe, meaningless. Ruth tossed her head to dismiss it. Although it made an impression on her. She had not known he even *thought* of affection, except to make fun of it.

"Don't you *shake* your head; I loves you and you mine!"

"Yours!"

"Mine," he said, holding her with possessive eyes.

"What do you want with me *now*?" she asked. "I don't know you and you don't know me!"

"An' I know who to thank for that! Grange won't never let you forgive me. Long as you're with *him*. That sly old cooter! If he so damn good to you, why wasn't he a proper daddy to *me*?"

For all she knew it was an honest enough question. "I told you, you don't know me. If you did you'd know I'm not just a pitcher to be filled by someone else. I have a mind, I have a memory," she said.

"I loved my childrens," said Brownfield, sweating now. "I loved your mama."

These tortured words, and they did sound as if they escaped from a close dungeon in his soul, hung on the air as a kind of passionate gibberish. Ruth shook her head once more to clear it; truly she could not even understand him when he spoke of loving. It was odd, and she said nothing.

"I mean to have what's mine," her father said, much in

the way she was used to hearing him speak. He had the curt swagger and roughness of a robber.

"I'm not yours," Ruth said humbly, for she felt, momentarily, a great dam about to fly open inside her, and when and if it broke she wanted it to be soft and gentle and not hurtful to him, although whatever she said, since she could never forgive him, or even agree with him, would have to hurt some. But suddenly he reached out for the first time to touch her. And his touch was not, as some of his words had been, either pathetic or kind. He grasped the flesh of her upper arm between thumb and forefinger and began to twist it. Her defenses went up again, higher than before, and bitter tears came to her eyes. He don't know his own strength, she remembered Mem had said time after time, rubbing her own bruises.

"You belongs to me, just like my chickens or my hogs," he said. "Tell that to your precious grandpa. Tell him he can't keep you; and before I let him I'll see you both in hell!"

"You said you loved me," she said, crying. "If you love me, *leave me alone!*"

"No," he said, pushing her away. "I can't do that. I'm a *man.* And a *man's* got to have *something* of his own!"

"A *man* takes care of his own when he's got it!"

"Aw, Grange been messing with your mind. I would have took care of my own had the white folks let me!"

"*I don't like you, I don't like you, I don't like you!*" she cried, stamping her foot. Her arm felt as if a plug had been pressed out of it.

"You going to like me better when I gets you in *my* house!" he said.

"You need shooting," she said, and trembled. Making herself move very slowly she walked away from him. She held her books tightly and wondered what new thing under the sun she might learn in school that day.

When Brownfield returned to the small linoleum-and-tin-patched house he shared with Josie, he found Josie up to her elbows in soapsuds, muttering against him. Her existence with him since she left Grange, always so fraught with trials, had now reached its nadir with Brownfield's crazy desire to capture one of his family to live with him. He did not want them out of love, Josie knew; he wanted them (or at least *one* of them) because having his family with him was a man's prerogative. Josie called distrustfully on God to deliver her from evil, as she heard Brownfield walking up behind her. Two neighboring women stood by sympathetically. They took up their patent-leather pocketbooks as Brownfield came in. They never stayed in his house after he got there. Brownfield heard the thin pursy-mouthed one say to Josie that her husband didn't like her to be around so *no*torious a man, and laughed to think she imagined he could be attracted to her, a woman so thin and juiceless she made a papery rattle when she walked. As he approached her she lowered her grayish head in a vain nod of virginal piety. Her fatter, bolder friend, whom Brownfield had occasionally and casually screwed, and who was never seen without her fan, vigorously fanned herself past him as if his presence in the room had upped the temperature a hundred degrees.

"*Bye*, Baby! Bye, *Honey*! Bye, *Sweet*ness!" Brownfield said merrily as they left, switching their cheaply dressed rumps down the road, hoping he'd be interested. He knew women! A swine of a man was more interesting to them and far more intriguing than a gentleman and a prince. Pigs, he thought, liars and hypocrites!

"Say, Josie, you ever sleep with Judge Harry?"

"Naw," said Josie, with the unquestioning honesty of a woman whose self-respect has ceased to be a matter of moment to anyone, including herself.

"I thought you might have, when you was young. When me and Judge Harry was boys—actually when I were at the lounge with you and Lorene—I used to get him a little bit of pussy now and then. Guess I never ask you. 'Course I don't mean if he'd slept with you lately. Ain't nobody that hard up no more. When I was up before him and he give me ten years I spent four of the seven I did as his gardener. I didn't know nothing 'bout no damn garden, and I told him so, but he just sort of winked at me and said, 'Boy, you always did know more about gardening than anybody I ever met!' The old son of a gun, he hadn't changed a bit! And you would have thought he would, him being the judge and all. But he used to say all the time when folks came to the house and ask him why he have a prisoner hanging round, 'Brownfield and me grew up together, we understands one 'nother.' He, he, he."

Josie said nothing. Her face was puffy and sad. Her dress was ripped along the seams under the arms and her yellow flesh poked out wet and slack. She was very fat and tired.

"You know, I bet Judge Harry'd make Grange give me back my child!" said Brownfield, still chuckling.

Josie laid down her washing and looked at him. "I really would do anything to keep you from doing this dirt to my husband," she said grimly. Her smallish eyes were red-rimmed and bleak, inexpressibly hopeless and dull. All the impudence of self-determination was gone. She washed clothes for white and black to buy their bread.

"Would you kill me?" asked Brownfield recklessly, as his old lumpy woman began to cry.

Brownfield took out his pocket knife and picked up a branch and began to cut small twigs from it. He began to chuckle.

"Josie, Josie," he said, "what the matter is with you is that you so easy to take in, you so easy to feel sorry for folks; no matter if they deserves it or no. Just like, supposing you *could* sneak back into Grange's house and git back on the good side of him. And suppose he started to plot somethin' against *me*." Brownfield's chuckle was becoming a laugh. "Do you know what you'd do?" he asked. "You'd feel sorry for *me*, an' you'd probably hightail it over here to *warn* me that somethin' was afoot! You never growed up, Josie, you never learned to pick one side an' stay on it. You're a fat, stupid whore, Josie, and never learned to think with your head instead of your tail."

"What you going to do?" she asked. "You don't want Ruth back! I know you don't!"

Brownfield looked at her with a subtle half-smile. "I don't know quite yet *what* I'll do. Maybe I'll just keep the waters stirred. You told me once that the ol' man had a bad heart . . . well, maybe we ought to sorta *worry* him now 'n then, a little bit. I bet we could even bring the old sinner to God," said Brownfield, and doubled over laughing.

Josie leaned over her washing and closed her eyes. She felt she was of no use to anyone. She was reminded of a night several years before when a young sailor had come into the Dew Drop Inn and she had taken him upstairs to her room. She had been especially good to him, and when he spoke of paying she had told him to forget it; she knew he was almost broke and that he was on his way home to a wife and small children. To express his gratitude, the young sailor had wanted to take her again but she refused because she had other customers waiting. When she refused he beat her black and blue and the people downstairs had to come up and pull him off her. Thinking of the incident now, after over twenty years, Josie began to cry afresh for all the love she'd never had. She felt she was somehow the biggest curse of her life and that it was her fate to be an everlasting blunderer into misery.

"If I *do* take her back," said Brownfield, "it'll be just to make Grange sweat. But right now I like having him right where he is. We got him *scared,* Josie!"

"You can kill him, Brownfield," said Josie. "You can worry him to a heart attack and he still going to come out on top."

"How you figure that?" Brownfield asked, scowling.

"'Cause he know which side he on. And it ain't your side and it ain't even just his own. He *bigger* than us, Brownfield. We going to die and go to hell and ain't nobody going to give a damn one way or the other, 'cause we ain't made no kind of plan for what happens after we gone. But Grange thinks about the world, and Ruth's place in it. And when he dies Ruth's going to *know* he gone. I got grandchildren too, somewhere," she said forlornly, "but I don't know where."

That night he became furious with Josie when she mumbled what had become for her, the answer to everything: "the white folks is the cause of everything." Brownfield did not know why, but suddenly this thought repelled him, just as before he had found support for the failure of his life in it. He felt an indescribable worthlessness, a certain ineffectual *smallness*, a pygmy's frustration in a world of giants.

"Ah, what do *you* know?" he sneered. "Nothing. You don't know the half of what you *think* you know." He chuckled with his usual omnipotent disdain. Josie was so dumb. "Did you know, f'instance, that one of my wife's children was white? That's right, one of Mem's children was white. The one that come after Ruth. The *last* one." He laughed at the expression on Josie's face. "Naw," he said, "don't go looking sick like that and green around the gills. He wasn't a *real* white baby. She never did fool around with white men, though they tried to fool around with her and I accused her of it often enough. She was stupid enough to be faithful to me if it meant fighting her goddam head off. Naw, I mean it was one of them babies without color, *any* color, with the light eyes without color and the whitish hair without color, and everything without color. Soon's I seen it, for all that it looked jest like my daddy, I hated it. It were a white Grange though, jest the same as my daddy is a black one."

"Was it what they calls an albino?" asked Josie, beginning to tremble. "Is that what you mean by without any color?"

"Yeah, I reckon that's what you'd like to call it. Curious looking, just *all over white.* Well, you know what I did to my wife when that baby was born? I beat the hell out of her a minute after I seen that baby's peculiar-looking eyes. She was just a-laying up there moaning, she were too weak to holler, and I beat her so she fell right out the bed. I 'cused her of all *kinds* of conniving with white mens round and about, and she jest kept saying she didn't do nothing with no white mens. 'I swears to *God* I didn't!' she says. And I axed her, 'How come this baby ain't got no brown color on him?' and she says, '*Lawd knows I don't know, Brownfield,* but he yours!' and I said, 'Don't you go lying to me, woman . . . if he ain't black he ain't mine!' Well, I told her that if that child didn't darken up real soon she'd better git prepared to get 'long without him. And she cried and begged and cried and begged, and she started leaving him close to the fire and in the sun when it come out, but that baby stayed like he was, not a ounce of color nowhere on him. An' one night when that baby was 'bout three months old, and it was in January and there was ice on the ground, I takes 'im up by the arm when he was sleeping, and like putting out the cat I jest set 'im outdoors on the do'steps. Then I turned in and went to sleep. 'Fore I dropped off, Mem set up and said she thought she heard the baby but I told her I had done looked at him and for her to go back to sleep. I kept her so wore out them days that she couldn't even argue; she was so tired she didn't fall asleep like folks—she just fell into a coma.

"I never slept so soundly before in my life—and when I woke up it was because of her moaning and carrying on in front of the fire. She was jest rubbing that baby what wasn't no more then than a block of ice. Dark as he'd *ever* been though, sorta *blue* looking.

"Now, 'cording to you I done that 'cause I thought that baby was by a white man. But I knowed the whole time that he wasn't. For one thing, although it were white, it looked jest like me—or rather like my daddy, as it had a right to since it was a grandson. It looked like the two of us. Ugly. For another thing, I had talked to old Dr. Taylor in town about it, and he said these things happen. Then, when the baby's hair begin to grow it was stone nappy. I knowed he was my child all right. Mem knowed I would have broke her neck if she so much as let a white man *look* at her. If some white man had knocked her in the head and raped her she still would have caught hell from me! She knowed the score. You should have seen her when she was young and pretty and turning heads, putting on veils and acting like a cripple or something when white mens was around. They used to ax me how come I was to marry something so ugly, but they jest didn't know what all your sister's child *had* under all them veils!"

Oddly, it was the first time Josie felt genuine pity for Mem. She stared at Brownfield with horror, seeing for the first time that he was, as a human being, completely destroyed. She was shocked that what he was telling her went beyond the meanness to which, by now, she was thoroughly accustomed, into insanity, the merest hint of which always unnerved her.

"I know what you think," he said to Josie. "You sitting there saying to yourself, he crazy! That's why all this is. But I *ain't* crazy, no more'n anybody else. All it was was that I jest didn't *feel* like trying to like nobody else. I jest didn't *feel* like going on over my own baby, who didn't have a chance in the world whether I went on over him or no. It too *much* to ask a man to lie and say he love what he don't want. I had got sick of keeping up the strain."

"If you had kept up the strain," said Josie, with a rare combination of logic and courage, "you'd a had a son now."

"Little white bastard!" said Brownfield, waving her away.

Oh, no. He wouldn't repent. None of what he had done mattered any more. It was over. What had to happen happened: the beautiful faded, the pretty became ugly, the sweetness soured. He had never believed it could turn out any other way. But what had *she* thought, his quiet wife, when he proved to be more cruel to her than any white man, or twenty? She was not a fighter, and rage had horrified her. Her one act of violence against him, which she must have considered an act of survival, brought her lower than before. Instead of rage she had had an inner sovereignty, a core of self, a rock, which, alas, her husband had not had. She had possessed an embedded strength that Brownfield could not match. He had been, at the best times, scornful of it, and at the worst, jealous.

"It's done, *done!*" he muttered to himself as he drifted near sleep. But now Ruth's face floated before him and her eyes glared accusingly at him. *Ruth,* with her thin legs and startled eyes, always running from him, her mind behind the eyes always in flight. She still ran *toward* something. This annoyed Brownfield. What did she see in the world that made her even wish to grow up? he wondered. He had to make her see that there was nothing, *nothing,* no matter what Grange promised her. He had seen the nothingness himself. And if she hated him more than ever, what did it matter? That was what the real world was all about.

But what about *love*? he asked himself, and a great hollow emptiness answered.

"It's a lie!" he cried into the dark, causing Josie to jump in her sleep. For Brownfield felt he *had* loved. But, as he lay thrashing about, knowing the rigidity of his belief in misery, knowing he could never renew or change himself, for this changelessness was now all he had, he could not clarify what was the duty of love; whether to prepare for the best of life, or for the worst. Instinctively, with his own life as example, he had denied the possibility of a better life for his children. He had enslaved his own family, given them weakness when they needed strength, made them powerless before any enemy that stood beyond him. Now when they thought of "the enemy," their own father would straddle their vision.

Brownfield ground his teeth under the pressure of his error, though too much thought about it would make it impossible to sleep. It occurred to him, as an irrelevancy, that Ruth might never believe "conditions" caused his indifference to her. He wished, momentarily, that he *could* call out to someone, perhaps to Mem, and say he was sorry. But what could he give as proof of his regret? He must continue hard, as he had begun. He would take his daughter from her grandfather, not because he wanted her, but because he didn't want Grange to have her. He gave no thought whatsoever of how he might attempt, once he had Ruth under his roof, to treat her kindly.

Part XI

Part XI

47

THE MONTHS THEY waited to see what Brownfield planned to do, the world moved in on Ruth. She found it not nearly so lovely as she had occasionally dreamed, nor quite as unbearable as she had been prepared to accept. She found it a deeply fascinating study, a subject for enthusiasm, a moving school. It all happened with the news and the Huntley-Brinkley Report.

It was her last year in school and each afternoon she hurried home to watch the news on television. She became almost fond of Chet Huntley and David Brinkley, especially David Brinkley, who was younger than Chet and whose mouth curved up in a pleasingly sardonic way. The only black faces she saw on TV were those in the news. Every day Chet and David discussed the Civil Rights movement and talked of integration in schools, restaurants and picture shows. Integration appealed to Ruth in a shivery, fearful kind of way. Her grandfather thought it negligible. Ruth often wondered if she would have liked the newscasters as much were they not discussing black people. She thought not; for though she had listened to them before, only now did they become real to her;

she could look at David's smirk-smile and often cheer the bit of news that caused it. Each day there were pictures of students marching, singing, praying, led by each other and by Dr. Martin Luther King. She accepted the students and the doctor as her heroes, and each night she and Grange discussed them.

"Do you think he's got something going?" she asked Grange one night, pointing to Dr. King's haggard, oriental eyes which looked out impassively and without depth from the TV screen.

"I'd feel better about 'im if I thought he could be the President some day," Grange said. "Knowing he ain't never *going* to be somehow take the *sweet* out of watching him. He a *man*, though," he said. "'Course," he had continued, "I believe I would handle myself different, if I was him. Then again, I ain't handling myself at all, setting here on my dusty, so I ain't the one to talk. The thing about him that stands in my mind is that even with them crackers spitting all over him, he gentle with his wife and childrens."

"Why do they have to *sing* like that?" she asked one night, moved to tears without realizing it.

"For the same reason folks whistle in a graveyard," Grange answered.

"They don't believe what you do," she said another evening, seeing black hands clasp white hands, marching solemnly down an Atlanta street. "They think they can change those crackers' hearts."

"I'm glad," said Grange. "On the other hand, they might be trying to learn in two weeks what it took me twenty years; that singing and praying won't do it. If that is the case I'm still glad. No need for them to stay all murked up in fog the way I was an' the way your daddy is yit." He leaned closer to the TV, his face contorted. "Look at them ugly cracker faces," he said. "What kind of 'heart' is anybody going to rouse from behind them faces? The thing done gone on too *long;* them folks you see right there before you now, chasing that nigger down the street, they is wearing what heart they *got* on they sleeves. Naw, better than that. They is wearing they *tiny* hearts on they *faces*. Which is why they faces is so ugly. If any amount of singing and praying can git the meanness out of them eyes you let me know 'bout it. Crackers been singing and praying for years, they been hearing darkies singing and praying for years, an' it ain't helped 'em. They set round grinning at theyselves, floodin' the market with electric can openers! Ugh!"

"I think I believe like the students," Ruth declared. "Ain't nothing wrong with *trying* to change crackers."

"What I want is somebody to change folks like your daddy, and somebody to thaw the numbness in *me*." He looked at his granddaughter and smiled. "Course," he said, "you done thawed me some."

One evening, as she was watching the Huntley-Brinkley Report, Grange came home looking sick.

"What's the matter with you?" Ruth asked, looking up. She thought their time had come, that Brownfield had done his worst.

Grange didn't answer. He turned his chair from the TV and toward the fireplace. He took out his pipe and knife and scraped out the pipe bowl. Then he filled the pipe with fresh tobacco. Ruth turned off the television and sat beside him. Soon the two of them were engulfed in thick, aromatic smoke.

"You 'member my old gambling buddy, Fred Hill?" Grange spat into the fireplace. "They found 'im yestiddy face down in a ditch."

"Too drunk to move?" asked Ruth.

"Naw, not no *more* drunk, he wasn't. Half his head was blowed off."

"What?"

"From here to here," said Grange, running his finger from ear to chin.

"Well, who done it?"

"Them as has the last word say he done it hisself."

Ruth was stunned.

"'Course, wasn't no gun nowhere *near* the ditch," said Grange.

"How did he manage to shoot half his head off without a gun?" she asked.

"A neat nigger trick," said Grange.

He stared into the fireplace for ten minutes without speaking. "I once seed a woman," he said, "had been strung up, slit open and burned just about up." He thought for five more minutes, Ruth waiting impatiently for him to speak. "They said she was one of them people *bent* on suicide. Kill herself three ways." He smoked, pulling on his pipe as if to jerk it from between his teeth. "Do you know, they writ it up in the paper just that way. Said she was *one* nigger with determination!"

Ruth sat thinking about Fred Hill. She'd heard about the "suicide" case before. Fred Hill was a short, pudgy, tan-skinned man with boyish bowlegs; when he walked he seemed to be swinging. His head was very round and he had had no neck. She had watched him play poker with Grange around the kitchen table. He had taught her how to shoot marbles when she was nine. Now he was dead.

"What was you watching on TV?" asked Grange.

"News."

"Fred Hill's grandson is making news. Tried to get into one of them cracker schools."

"And did he make it?"

Grange leaned his head back and looked at the ceiling, his chair tilted back on two legs. "Naw," he said, "he didn't make it. How you going to study in a cracker school with half your granddaddy's head missin'?"

"Well," said Ruth, attempting to see a bright side, "you don't need your granddaddy's head to study. You just need your own."

"Everything going to prove you wrong, girl," he said, getting up and walking heavily out into the dark.

And then it was spring and school was over and the student marchers were in Baker County. Ruth saw a long line of them parading up and down the streets when she went into town. Their signs were strange and striking. I AM AN AMERICAN TOO! said one. THIS IS MY COUNTRY TOO! said another. I WANT FREEDOM TOO! said still another. Although she had seen marchers before on television she was amazed to see real blacks and whites marching together in her home town! There were trim white girls in jeans and sneakers with clean flowered blouses marching next to intense black girls in high heels and somber Sunday dresses. There were dozens of young black and white male marchers; it looked peculiar to Ruth to see them whispering confidences to one another, curious that she could detect no sign of mutual disgust. "Are they for real?" she wondered. She watched wide-eyed, her glances moving from the marchers to the residents of Baker County. Baker County had been so surprised by the students' arrival it had not done anything yet. Even the sheriff stood on a street corner and stared with his mouth slightly open. His deputies hung around him, so closely it looked as if they needed protection, or at best, minute instructions on how to handle the demonstrators. Local blacks and whites stood under the trees on the court-house lawn and gawked at the white girls. Some of the men sneered and called them dirty names. Of all the people marching the white girls got the most abuse. One of them carried a sign that said BLACK AND WHITE TOGETHER and each time she passed a group of whites they spat at her and hissed "I'll *bet!*" One of them added, aiming a Coke bottle at her, "You nigger-fuckin' whore!" Ruth passed close beside this girl and noticed her right ear, the one next to the bystanders, was bleeding, and that she marched with stiff wooden steps as if to a chilling inner music. Tears slipped quietly and endlessly down her pale cheeks and the sign in her hand had begun to waver.

As Ruth was leaving town someone pushed a piece of paper into her hands. At the top of the page she saw a white man and woman chained to a rock. The rock was called "racism"; underneath was written "You Will Not Be Free Until We Are Free." She looked back to see who had given it to her and saw a tall, thin young man in overalls like her grandfather's. He was trying to hand the leaflet to whites who passed, but none took it. She looked back a couple of times and one of the times he was watching her. She felt her heart give a kind of bump against her ribs, such as she'd never felt before. The young man continued handing out leaflets, though only black people took them. The sun on his skin made him all aglow in different shadings of brown, like autumn leaves late falling from the tree.

On her way home she drove the car with her left hand and with her right she touched the paper, then her face and hair, then the paper again, and its message meant less to her than the young man who'd given it to her. Drawing close to their white neighbor's mailbox, she stuffed the leaflet in, then drove pensively onto her grandfather's farm.

Three days later Ruth and Grange were sitting on the front porch. They had just learned that Brownfield, in order to get Ruth, had decided to take them to court. To calm their rather severe case of jitters, Ruth was eating watermelon compulsively and reading *Bulfinch's Mythology*, and Grange was just as compulsively polishing shoes. When they saw the dust in the distance Grange went inside and got his shotgun and leaned it against the banister in front of him, then sat down and continued polishing shoes. The car turned into the yard, made a half-circle around the trees and came to a stop. It was a dark blue car, covered with layers of red dust, as if it had traveled hundreds of miles over Georgia's back roads. The thin young man from town got out on the driver's side. A white girl and boy were in the back seat and a black girl got out of the front seat on the side of the car near the porch. Ruth looked the black girl up and down almost hostilely. It surprised her that she felt a small tug of jealousy. After all, she knew nothing about the young man who'd given her the leaflet and who now stood before her—not even his name.

"So this is where you live!" the young man said, looking up at her from the yard. He was beginning to grow a beard and it made his shapely lips very rosy and well-defined.

Grange looked over at Ruth. She was standing at the edge of the porch with one arm around a roof support. Her eyes were shining! He could almost feel the hot current that flowed through her, making her soft young body taut and electric with waiting. He would not have admitted that he was slightly shocked, but he was.

"This is where I live," Ruth answered the young man. "Anybody could have told you!" She was laughing a shy but bubbly delighted laugh; forgotten completely was the fact that nobody ever visited the farm without her grandfather's permission.

"Where you know him from?" asked Grange, who at that moment decided he didn't like young men with beards.

The young man made long strides up the steps and across the porch to Grange. "How do you do, Mr. Copeland," he said, smiling. He was thinking how much Grange reminded him of Bayard Rustin, except Grange was more leggy and stuck his thumb in his belt like a cowboy. He held out his hand for Grange to shake. Grange scowled up at his smile and looked at his granddaughter, whose eyes had never left the young man, and whose eyes also roamed up and down the young man's body. She was a Copeland, he thought. Sighing and putting down his polishing cloth he shook hands with the young man. His handshake was warm and firm and he was taller than Grange. Grange felt old and gray and as if his hand couldn't squeeze hard.

"How you?" he mumbled. Something about the young man seemed familiar to him. He looked up at him quickly. "Say, don't I know you from somewhere?" he asked, cocking his head to one side. The young man's smile turned into a chuckle.

"I was the little joker used to trail along behind Sister Madelaine," he said. He had spent much of his childhood ashamed that his mother was a fortuneteller, but by the time he left Morehouse and joined the Movement he was as proud of how she earned her living as his best friend was that his father was a surgeon. His mother had faced life with a certain *inventiveness*, he thought, and for this he greatly respected her.

"Yass . . ." said Grange, thawing, "I can see the resemblance." He had no remembrance of the young man as a child, but he had known and admired his mother for years. He hadn't ever believed in her magic powers much though.

The black girl had come and stood beside the young man. The two whites had not come closer than the steps.

"My name is Quincy," the young man said, "and this is my wife, Helen."

Grange shook the young woman's hand, then looked over her head at Ruth. Ruth's arms had dropped to her sides and the corners of her mouth sagged. Not only was Helen the young man's wife, but she was pregnant. Ruth saw her grandfather's look and shrugged her shoulders. She pushed a chair behind Helen and mumbled for her to sit down. Quincy had settled himself on the banister.

"Who them?" asked Grange, pointing with his chin. "Is they white, or do they just *look* white?" His whisper could be heard for yards.

"This is Bill and this is Carol," said Helen. "They're working with us." Bill and Carol nodded, but made no move to climb the steps. Bill was dark and muscular with brown eyes. Carol was small with freckles like a second skin.

"They've heard, as have we all, about how you feel about white folks. We had planned to leave them outside the gate near the highway, but we were being followed," said Helen. She sat solidly in the chair, her hands on top of her rounded stomach. She laughed suddenly, looking down at Bill. "He's already been shot at once."

Grange looked down at the young man who looked back at him with nothing in particular in his eyes. Bill took Carol's arm and they walked slowly back to the car. Grange wanted to invite them up to the porch but the urge lasted only a moment.

He could not bring himself to admit a white woman under his roof. He said nothing, however, to Ruth, who traipsed out to them with cool water, and he watched her chatting with them for a minute or two.

"Mr. Copeland," said Quincy, "do you vote?" Ruth had given him water too and he sipped it, looking very relaxed on the banister, with one leg dangling over the side.

"Vote for what?" asked Grange.

"For sheriff and governor and police chief and county commissioner."

"Nope," said Grange.

"Why not?" asked Helen. She had finished half her glass of water and now rubbed the bottom of the glass over the top of her belly as if to cool it.

"'Cause every one of 'em is crackers," said Grange, "an' there ain't a teaspoon of difference between one cracker and another."

Quincy laughed. Helen laughed too, but then said firmly, "That's not what we found out in Green County."

Grange snorted. "I used to live there," he said with authority, "an' I don't know what you found, but it wasn't that crackers'd let niggers vote. Last hanging they had was some nigger trying to cast his vote for the cracker of his choice."

"Well," said Quincy, "they voting for the cracker of they choice *now.*"

"They voting now?" asked Grange.

"Yep!" said Quincy. "We worked there last summer. They're voting in droves."

"Ain't a cracker in Green County worth the bother," said Grange.

"What about black folks?" asked Helen.

"The black folks wasn't shit neither when I was there," said Grange. "Everyone that wanted to try somethin' to help his people got knifed in the back by 'em." He took out his pipe and began pulling on it, chewing the stem. "You don't mean to tell me that some fool of *ours* is trying to run for office in Green County, do you?" he asked.

"Not *this* year," said Helen.

"Where you *from*, girl?" Grange asked sharply.

"Green County," she answered sweetly, laughing at him.

"Well, I be damned," said Grange. He felt he had been caught sleeping, and that his nap had lasted twenty or forty years.

"Who your peoples?" he asked, thinking that perhaps she was lying.

"My mother's name is Katie Brown. My father's name was Henry. They lived on old man Thomas's place."

Grange remembered the Thomases, but not the Browns. "You say your pa's name *was* Henry?" he asked.

"He was killed in '55," she said. "Shot down right in front of the voting booth."

"Where's your ma at?" he asked.

"She couldn't be dragged away from Green County."

"She ain't still on the white man's place?"

Helen laughed. She laughed a lot. She seemed as carefree as a bird. "She was until we got there last summer," she said. "We moved in with her. All of us. Me and Quincy and Bill and Carol. But that was too much for the Thomases. They had said how sorry they were that old Henry was shot down thataway and had helped me when I went away to college, but when they saw me with Bill and Carol they kicked Ma off the place."

"And then?" asked Grange, leaning forward in his chair. He wanted to reach out and touch Helen, she was so calm. He felt her calmness *meant* something, and he wanted desperately to know what.

"And *den*," Helen said, chuckling, "*den*, Ma hauled off and cussed old man Thomas out and his ancestors back through the Civil War and spit on his wife and they had her locked up."

"She got out," said Quincy. "We had some smart lawyers come down from New York. When she got out she moved to a little house just down the road from the Thomases. She browbeat the preacher who owned it into letting her set up a center for us. It was full of all kinds of people all summer long. She's there still."

"That woman's plainly done lost her mind," said Grange. "You all ought to go get her."

"She loves it there," said Helen, shrugging her shoulders. "If anything she wants us to come 'home' and settle down beside her."

"And one day we might," said Quincy.

"Quincy's going to run for Mayor," said Helen. "I'm going to be first lady of Green County."

"You're all crazy," said Grange. "You best be spending your energy in getting yourselves out of here. How long you think you going to be able to laugh like you do?" he asked Helen.

"I ain't going to let *them* make me stop!" she said.

And Grange thought, You may keep being able to laugh when other peoples is around, but when you and your husband and the baby is all alone dodging bullets and jumping out of your skin at every noise, will you be able to laugh *then*? He imagined Helen in ten years, her young husband maybe

buried in some swampy unmarked grave, her child hounded
by grownups and children who hated niggers. He saw her at
the mercy of some white town whose every gesture would
mean she was worthless, an intruder, an American on good
behavior. Suppose she couldn't ever become "first lady" of
anything. Then where would her laughter be?

"We want you to register," said Quincy. "I even got my
mother to register, though she swears she's been hexing the
bad crackers all along!"

"I can't promise you," said Grange. He felt a deep tender-
ness for the young couple. He felt about them as he felt about
Dr. King; that if they'd just stay with him on his farm he'd
shoot the first cracker that tried to bother them. He wanted to
protect them, from themselves and from their dreams, as
much as from the crackers. He would not let anybody hurt
them, but at the same time he didn't believe in what they were
doing. Not because it wasn't worthy and noble and inspiring
and good, but because it was impossible.

"What I'm scared of, children, is the bitterness; the taste
of bile thrown up by the liver when you finds out the fight
can't be won."

Quincy put his arm around his wife, his hand moving up
and down her side. He held her loosely yet completely, as if
she meant everything to him, and the glow in her eyes was
pure worship when she looked up at him. Grange was
touched almost to tears by the simplicity and directness of
their love and he shuddered with fear for them.

"If you fight," she said, placing soft black fingers on
Grange's arm, "if you fight with all you got, you don't have to
be bitter."

Grange walked out to the car with them and opened the
door for Helen. "Wait a minute," he said. He turned and went

into the house and pulled a watermelon from under the bed. It was cool and green and heavy. He took it out to the car and handed it into the back seat. Helen was laughing again and all of them thanked him profusely. Grange still couldn't quite look at the white girl but he gave a short nod to the boy. And when he waved good-bye he waved to all of them.

He turned, smiling, and saw Ruth sitting dejectedly on the steps.

"I bet *all* the *good* ones have got taken!" she moaned, frowning at him.

"You really got a kick out of him, didn't you, girl?" asked Grange. "One day another one'll come and he won't have a wife and you can grab him before he starts looking for one."

"I don't expect a whole stream of 'em to come passing by *here*," she said with dismay. "I think I'm going to have to go out an' *find* the one I want."

"What about this farm?" Grange asked.

"Oh, good grief!" she said, and stormed into her room, slamming the door and throwing herself across her bed.

48

ON THE MORNING they were to confront Brownfield in court, Grange helped Ruth tidy up the house with a reserved concentration. Both found it difficult to speak. Grange's hair, as white as any snow but more silvery and of course crinkled and bristly electric, was combed in the fashion Ruth so loved, brushed straight back on the top and sides, neat but bold. Combed back this way, flatly, his hair would rise again slowly, crinkle by crinkle, so that soon, with the sun making it shine, he would look like Ruth's idea of God. He was wearing his best and only dark suit with vest to match and his coat flared over his hips, emphasizing the leanness of his long legs and the tense long strides that somehow reminded Ruth of Randolph Scott.

They had an old 1947 Packard, black, chromeless, which they parked on the street near the courthouse. The courthouse was in the center of the square in the middle of town. It was red brick, made something like a big dusty box. Its corners were decorated with concrete cornices full of ornate scrolls; the steps were tall and wide, though hopelessly unimpressive. They were beginning to crack.

Because it was a Saturday morning few people were in town. The cotton farmers and dairymen would come in later. On the top of the steps Ruth turned for a last look at the town.

"I wish they'd move their damn stone soldier," she said, glaring at the Southern soldier facing his old and by now indifferent enemy of the North. "I can't see what time it is." There was a new electric clock the size of a stop sign across the street in the window of the drugstore, but the stone soldier's meager hips were enough to cover it.

"But I got my watch," Grange said with some surprise, drawing out a heavy gold watch on a chain. Then he took her elbow firmly, too firmly for her to pull away. "Don't you worry," he said, shaking her gently. "I wouldn't be worth nothing if I couldn't take care of my own. And I want you to always remember—you is my own." Grange kissed her on the top of her hair, lightly, and they walked together into the house of justice.

The judge was a kindly eyed, sallow-faced condescending water sportsman. A picture of him holding a fat glistening string of fish was the "in color" photograph that graced the front of the Baker County *Messenger* the week before. His face was the alert, watchful and yet benign face of a man who had started out in life with nothing and who had added positions as he added weight until he came to rest with heavy jowls and a judgeship in the same county where he was born penniless fifty years before. Behind his benign look was a door, never publicly opened, which led back into a soul so empty of charity and so full of dusty conceits that his townspeople could hardly have stood the sight. Not that their own souls' doors were securely fastened enough to allow them to wonder about someone else's. Even that of their judge. All in all, however, he was not a bad man, as bad men in the South go. He had never personally trafficked in violence; he had not even strenuously condoned it. He had, however, meted out unjust sentences and had been the beneficiary of much yard labor and housework which the city paid for and which he was able to secure from his position on the bench. In short, he was a petty person, with all the smallness of mind that went with being so. He was capable of stealing the labor of innocent people, almost always black, sometimes poor white, but was not capable of stealing large sums of money. Because of this honesty his townspeople respected him and made him a deacon in the First Presbyterian Church. Among the black boys for whom he felt responsible he was affectionately known as "Judge Harry." His relationship with the "nigras" was generally good.

It was over so quickly! The judge showed them to his colored chambers. He and Brownfield exchanged jovialities. Grange stared beyond them, his face pale.

"How old are you, Ruth?" the judge asked.

"Sixteen."

"You won't be a grown woman in the state of Georgia till you're two years older," the judge said.

The room was quiet, except for Josie's breathing. She wheezed.

"You want to be with your *real* daddy, don't you, Ruth?" the judge asked kindly, looking at her with eyes that neither asked questions nor cared about answers.

"No, sir," she said firmly.

Grange started to speak of his son's criminal record, of his neglect of his children, of his threats.

"This man killed his wife, your Honor!" said Grange, out of order.

"Now, I didn't ask you nothing yet," the judge said pleasantly, hurt. "You don't have no right to go making unsolicited speeches in my chambers." He looked at Brownfield solemnly and winked. Ruth knew it was over for her and Grange; she held tightly to her grandfather's hand. She could not look up into his face for she could feel the tremors running through his body and knew he was crying.

"Hush," she whispered under her breath, "hush, old baby." His breath caught in a sob; she knew it was from helplessness. Ruth was so angry she couldn't cry.

What the judge and Brownfield and Josie were doing was not important to Ruth. Not while she leaned her soul toward Grange and encouraged him to share her resignation. When she looked at the judge again he was taking a pair of tall slick boots from a closet near his desk.

"But no rough stuff now, Brown, you hear me?" He was smiling in that way Southern white men smile when they control everything—birth, life and death. Ruth hated him forever. She had been given in all speedy "justice" to a father who'd never wanted her by a man who knew and cared nothing about them. Any of them. Just a man who was allowed to play God. Ruth felt something hot standing in front of her. It was Josie, flushed and vermillion.

"You got to go with your daddy now," she said, relieved, and Ruth was annoyed to see a pitying tear in Josie's eyes.

"But don't worry," Josie continued, venturing to sit on the bench next to Grange, "I'll take care of him."

Brownfield came toward them grinning. "Got you this time," he said, gloating.

Grange slowly raised his head and slowly stood. He looked down coldly at his son. One thumb strayed to and fro under his belt.

"Touch her and I lay you out," he said; with one long arm he pushed Ruth behind him. Brownfield looked around for Judge Harry, who was just going toward the door.

"Judge Harry!" Brownfield called confidently. Judge Harry glanced back, took in the situation and walked purposefully to the door. Grange's next words were like a cold blast against his back.

"Halt, *Justice!*" said Grange. The contempt in his voice was as tangible as the floor on which the judge stood.

Brownfield made a lunge for Ruth and managed to catch her arm for half a second. Then he felt himself thrown back as if by a great gush of wind. He saw lightning and thought he smelled a bitter smoke. He sank limply to the floor and did not manage to get a word out before he died. Underneath his flared tail coat Grange had carried his blue steel Colt .45. With it he had shot down his son.

"You can't do this in a court of law," the judge began to babble; he was still holding his fishing boots. His eyes bulged when he saw Brownfield's blood spreading along the floor.

"Shet up, *Justice,*" said Grange, "or you sure 'nough going to be deaf, dumb and blind." He grabbed Ruth by the arm, stepped around Josie, who was sobbing over Brownfield, and headed for the door.

"We'll catch you, Copeland," said the judge. "You can't run away."

"I ain't running away," said Grange, briefly, "I'm going *home*, and the first one of you crackers that visit me is going to get the rest of what I got in this gun."

"We don't have a chance," said Ruth, as they raced home, sirens already sounding behind them.

"I ain't," said Grange, "but you do." He ran his hand over his eyes. "A man what'd do what I just did don't deserve to live. When you do something like that you give up your claim." He slumped on the seat. "And what about that judge?" he asked bitterly. "Who will take care of him?"

Out of the car and into the house they ran. Police cars were racing down the dirt road to the house. Grange combed the house for guns and took off in a trot through the woods toward the cabin. Immediately cars circled the house; Ruth waited quietly on the bed. Grange had not even left her gun, knowing as she knew that she would live longer without it, at least in this battle. Ruth heard the men begin the sweep toward the house and then she heard a shot from far back in the woods. Grange leading the police away from her. Suddenly the air rang with the rush of bullets and a few minutes later, just as suddenly, everything was still.

To a person peeking it would have seemed that Grange prayed, sitting there dying outside the cabin that had been Ruth's "house," with the sun across his knees, and his back against a tree. But if it was a prayer, how strange it was; for it was all about himself, and his deliverance to and from, and his belief in and out. Actually it was a curse.

It is true he opened his mouth wide in a determined attempt to pray. So near the end of the journey it seemed appropriate, as a drink is an appropriate end to a long dry poker game. But it was not, in fact, to be the case with Grange. He could not pray, therefore he did not.

He had been shot and felt the blood spreading under his shirt. He did not want Ruth to see. Other than that he was not afraid. He did not even hear the rustle of footsteps creeping nearer.

"Oh, you poor thing, you poor thing," he murmured finally, desolate, but also for the sound of a human voice, bending over to the ground and then rearing back, rocking himself in his own arms to a final sleep.

Afterword
BY ALICE WALKER

I BEGAN WRITING *The Third Life of Grange Copeland* during the winter of 1966. I had an apartment on St. Mark's Place in New York, in the East Village, dank, poorly lighted, with a large intimidating colony of resident roaches; and so I spent most of my time in the room of a young law student at NYU whom I had met in Mississippi while working in the Civil Rights Movement the summer before. His room was small, but a large double window opened out just above the treetops of Washington Square. He brought a metal folding table from his mother's house in Brooklyn and we covered it with a madras bedspread; we made sure that a brown earthenware vase a former classmate gave me, when I graduated from Sarah Lawrence a few weeks before, was always full of white daisies or, in spring, pink peonies. The table was placed beneath the window, the trees and grass of the park were in front of me, the flowers always to my right, my notebook and typewriter at my fingertips. Still, it was not the country, and the people in the novel complained.

Shortly before I married the young law student, I applied to and was accepted as a fellow [sic] by the McDowell Colony in rural New Hampshire. There I labored through a month and a half of snowy winter, the silence of my fir tree–encircled cabin broken only by the tapping of my typewriter, and the singing of Clara Ward and Mahalia Jackson, which mingled with the crackle of the fire. On weekends the law student drove up to visit, his tiny red Volkswagen stuffed to the windows with flowers, grapefruit and oranges.

I wrote several chapters of the novel while at McDowell, but I left in March to be married. My husband and I moved to Mississippi that summer, where he continued his legal activities in behalf of human and civil rights while I wrote textbook materials for the fledgling Headstart schools that were being set up all over the state, taught at two local colleges, and did other, more expressly political, work. I also continued to carry the novel forward. It was completed in November of 1969, three days before my only child, a daughter, was born. I was twenty-five.

It was an incredibly difficult novel to write, for I had to look at, and name, and speak up about violence among black people in the black community at the same time that all black people (and some whites)—including me and my family—were enduring massive psychological and physical violence from white supremacists in the southern states, particularly Mississippi. I will always be grateful that the people involved in the liberation of black people in the South almost never spoke of expediency, but always of justice, of telling the truth, of standing up and being counted, of fighting for one's rights, of not letting nobody turn you round. "Two wrongs don't make a right," they said. "Everybody's got a right to the tree of life," they said. "We want our freedom and we want it now," they said. Black women and children did not merely echo these expressions, they, along with black men, formulated them.

But even so, given the amount of pain involved in the thinking about, and in telling, why write such a novel?

The simplest answer is, perhaps, that I could not help it. A more complicated one is that I am a woman of African heritage and so naturally I insist on all the freedoms. Why not?

The most disturbing incident in the novel, the brutal murder of a woman and mother by her husband and the father of her children, is unfortunately based on a real case. In my small hometown of Eatonton, Georgia, there was when I was growing up, and there still is now, an incredible amount of violence. "Eatonton is a violent little town," is what is said by the locals when all other attempts to explain some recent disaster have proved useless. The black people there, as in so many parts of the world, are an oppressed colony, and as one of our great African-American writers has said (and I paraphrase), in their frustration and rage they *of course* kill each other. But what, I wondered, would happen if you could show the people in the oppressed colony the futility of this? In any case, perhaps the violence of my hometown was impressed upon me even more than upon many others because I visited the local black funeral home several times a week. I had a job as babysitter right next door, and my sister worked in the funeral home itself, as beautician and cosmetologist. On one side of the hall she shampooed, pressed and curled the hair of the living, on the other side she did the same for countless cadavers; she also made up their faces and sometimes bodies, covering bruises, cuts, gunshot wounds, scratches and tears as best she could with her magic tricks arsenal of assorted powders and paints.

But even she was unable to do much for the victim around whose demise this story is built. Needing to share her frustration and, I assumed, outrage (we never discussed how she felt), she invited me into the room where Mrs. Walker (same last name as ours) lay stretched on a white enamel table with her head on an iron pillow. I describe her in the novel exactly as she appeared to me then. Writing about it years later was the only way I could be free of such a powerful and despairing image. Still, I see it; not so much the shattered face—time has helped to erase the vividness of that sight—but always and always the one calloused foot, the worn, run-over shoe with a ragged hole, covered with newspaper, in its bottom.

Another irony: Mrs. Walker's daughter was one of my classmates. Her name was Kate. Was this not the name of my own grandmother, also shot to death by a "lover"? And who, in whispered family conversations, was somehow blamed for this? I think I must have spent the rest of the school year staring at Kate as at an apparition. When I offered my sympathy (a Southern expression, so sweet, if ineffectual, "to offer one's sympathy") she barely responded. The weight of caring for the household and for numerous siblings now rested on her. She was, like me, thirteen years old. She wondered aloud if they, the white prison authorities, the only kind there were and probably still are, in Eatonton, would let her father out of prison soon. He was the only means of support the family had. By now her father's violence haunted my dreams; I never wanted him to be let out.

In my immediate family too there was violence. Its roots seemed always to be embedded in my father's need to dominate my mother and their children and in her resistance (and ours), verbal and physical, to any such domination. Discussing this with my husband, who came from a different culture entirely (or so I thought) from mine, I discovered there had also been precisely the same kind of violence in *his* family. Seeing the dead body of Mrs. Walker there on the enamel table, I realized that indeed, she might have been my own mother and that perhaps in relation to men she was also symbolic of all women, not only including my husband's grandmother and mother, who were as different from my own, I had thought, as possible, but also of me. That is why she is named Mem, in the novel, after the French *la même*, meaning "the same."

How can a family, a community, a race, a nation, a world, be healthy and strong if one half dominates the other half through threats, intimidation and actual acts of violence? Living as I was in Mississippi it was easy to see how racist violence sapped the strength and creativity of the entire population. Mississippi was the poorest state in the nation not because of the federal government's meddling in its affairs, beginning with the Civil War, as white apologists for the state's poverty at the drop of a hat exclaimed, but because every tiny surplus of energy not used in immediate living day-to-day was put into maintaining a hypocritical, artificial and basically untenable separation of the races, with domination of black people attained through violence. Beatings, castrations, lynchings, arrests or imprisonments were daily events, as they are now in a similarly doomed racist society in South Africa. It is almost bitterly comic today, as we see our exploited, poisoned, depleted planet wobbling underneath our collective weight, to think that white supremacists have actually thought, and in places still think, that they can acquire peace and security for themselves in the world by dispossessing people of color.

Mrs. Walker was half of her world, as people of color are more than half of the people on the planet. Could I make the reader realize this fact, and see the connection between her oppression as a woman (and the oppression of her children) and ours as a people? Could I make the reader care? Is grief alone to be our profit from experiencing tragedies that few people wish to see? And what of the writer's duty to those who fall, pitiful, poor, ill-used, under an embarrassed pall of silence?

"We own our own souls, don't we?" the beautiful old man, Grange Copeland, demands of his son, Brownfield, who unfortunately cannot answer this question in the affirmative any more than our current legion of community drug users and dealers can. Their self-hatred and sense of futility is the same as Brownfield's, as is their violence against others, though now stretching beyond mere family members and menacing entire peoples, entire worlds.

In a society in which everything seems expendable, what is to be cherished, protected at all costs, defended with one's life? I am inclined to believe, sadly, that there was a greater appreciation of the value of one's soul among black people in the past than there is in the present; we have become more like our oppressors than many of us can bear to admit. The expression "to have soul," so frequently spoken by our ancestors to describe a person of stature, used to mean something. To have money, to have power, to have fame, even to have "freedom," is not at all the same. An inevitable daughter of the people who raised and guided me, in whom I perceived the best as well as the worst, I believe wholeheartedly in the necessity of keeping inviolate the one interior space that is given to all. I believe in the soul. Furthermore, I believe it is prompt accountability for one's choices, a willing acceptance of responsibility for one's thoughts, behavior and actions, that makes it powerful. The white man's oppression of me will never excuse my oppression of you, whether you are man, woman, child, animal or tree, because the self that I prize refuses to be owned by him. Or by anyone.

There are some people who could never be slaves; many of our enslaved ancestors were among them. That is part of the mystery and gift passed on to us that has kept us, generation after generation, going. This is the understanding that is encoded in the lives of the "soul survivors" of this novel, Grange Copeland and his granddaughter, Ruth. It is an understanding about the possibility of resistance to domination that all people can share.

—ALICE WALKER
Wild Trees
Mendocino County
California
October 1987

Printed in the USA
CPSIA information can be obtained
at www.ICGtesting.com
CBHW021718150424
6958CB00015B/87